LAST WORDS

LAST WORDS

a novel

LORRAINE TAYLOR

Covenant Communications, Inc.

Covenant.

Printed in Canada
First Printing: June 2003

10 09 08 07 06 05 04 03   10 9 8 7 6 5 4 3 2 1

ISBN 1-59156-207-4

Library of Congress Cataloging-in-Publication Data

Taylor, Lorraine, 1958-
    Last Words : a novel/Lorraine Taylor.
       p. cm.
    ISBN 1-59156-207-4 (alk. paper)
    1. Mormons-Fiction. 2. Parent and child--Fiction. 3. Children--Death--Fiction. I. Title
PS3620.A958L375 2003
813'.6 dc21
                                   20030043464

*Mom and Dad, your legacy of faith and courage continue
to inspire me each day. Thank you.
This is your story.
I love you so very much!*

"Ask, and it shall be given you . . ."

PROLOGUE

March 1975
Hailey, Idaho

"How I hate you!"

The whispered words, a final blasphemous prayer coming from the frail, dying woman, penetrated the heart of the sorrowing man standing at her bedside, burning like painful, fiery darts. His brown eyes mirrored his pain as the embittered old woman died. He was her son, her firstborn. His face, save the anguished eyes, reflected none of the hurt and betrayal caused by his mother's rejection. Her denouncement of him, stated so plainly with her dying words, came as no surprise to him.

She had rejected him as a child, leaving him with the man who had fathered him, a man she hated and despised with a passion as strong and as powerful as her onetime love for him had been. Her son had spent his entire life trying to find some means of gaining acceptance, some way to establish the bond of mother and son. At times he had felt success, but his wounded heart recognized the finality of her last words to him: "How I hate you!"

The brutal words would haunt him for the rest of his life, a whispered reminder of his failure to capture his mother's love. His face, lined and gray from the tiring hours of vigilance spent at her bedside, was a face shaped by character and a lifetime of experiences. Cap Martin was forty-eight years old, but he suddenly felt like an orphaned babe. Tears glimmered in his eyes, but he held them in check. His years in the United States Navy had reinforced what he had learned as a child—to hold on to his emotions, to hide the pain, the hurt, and the fear.

To the woman standing by his side holding fast to his strong, brown hand, his pain and anguish were tangible. She wasn't as adept at hiding her emotions, and tears of anger streamed down her softly lined face. Her bright blue eyes darkened with resentment toward the woman who had just died. She had watched her husband over the years struggling to come to terms with his mother's continued rejection.

Lara Martin was a petite woman. The top of her head barely reached Cap's shoulder, but their twenty-six years of marriage had melded them together so that she fit perfectly by his side, curving into the protective shield of his arm. She was small in stature, yet strong enough to support him and to stand by his side as his equal.

Cap wasn't tall, but his stocky, muscular stature gave others the illusion of bigness. His face was weathered and worn by years of hard labor. He was an outdoorsman, both by career and hobby. His dark hair was lightly streaked with gray strands, and his skin had the texture of fine, tanned leather. His hands were short and broad with blunt fingers. They were strong hands, surprisingly soft for a man who worked as long and as hard as he did in the outdoors. And they were gentle hands, capable of soothing and caressing and communicating love through his touch. His face was square and angular, reflecting his Native American heritage in the high cheekbones and strongly planed surfaces. His eyes were light brown with a touch of mahogany adding warmth to their depths. His lips were firm and narrow, often set in grim lines that hid his true emotions. His smiles were rare, but, when present, were wonderful, creasing his cheeks with deep grooves of humor.

Lara was a pretty woman, her figure softly rounded from mother-hood, her face lined from the years of worry. Her hair, prematurely gray, framed her lovely face with a soft halo of silver. Her bright blue eyes still retained the sparkle and warmth of her youth, and she smiled often, lending a beauty to her features that came from her inner spirit. Her complexion was good and her skin retained the warm glow of a permanent, golden tan. Her hands were quick and sure, capable of accomplishing any task, and always quick to soothe and comfort. She was a charming woman, shy and quiet around strangers, but always willing to reach out with a helping hand to those in need. She wasn't loud or flamboyant, but she touched the lives of many with her loving smile and gentle ways.

They looked good together. They were a couple, and the years of toil and survival and love had forged a strong, unbreakable bond. Not that the years had been free of struggle or strife between them. There had been moments when Lara had felt like walking away from it all, and Cap had experienced his share of disillusionment. But they had stayed committed to their marriage and to their love. They had been willing to fight the battles in order to gain the victories. And they were winners. Lara knew that Cap would make it through this bitter experience.

As they left the hospital, Cap and Lara were both silent, lost in their reflections of the past and their contemplation of the future. Lara knew that the coming days would be difficult for Cap, and Lara hoped that she herself would be able to set aside her feelings of animosity toward her mother-in-law. She would do it. She had to. For Cap.

Cap was aware of Lara's quiet support, and he reached for her hand, holding it quietly in his own as they drove toward the house that had been his mother's home for the past thirty years. He was quiet, lost in a world of remembrances. Her death wasn't real to him yet. All he felt was the devastating sting of her parting words. It was a pain that he had lived with for most of his life, but he had learned to temper that throbbing ache by telling himself that the devastation of his mother's rejection didn't matter. But he knew that it did. It had always mattered, and it probably always would.

CHAPTER 1

June 1932
Hailey, Idaho

The spring rains had brought new life to the valley and the nearby surrounding foothills. An emerald carpet of lush, green grass filled the rolling vista with color and provided a vibrant backdrop for the small, white church nestled in the bosom of the Idaho mountains. The faint strains of the "Wedding March" wafted through the air, blending with the musical cadences of nature. The song of a meadowlark and the gentle humming of honeybees lent magic to the crystal purity of Pearl Olsen's wedding.

The small church was only partially filled, its front pews scattered with the few friends and family members in attendance. They had been summoned with hastily placed phone calls to witness the union of Pearl Olsen and Jake Martin.

Luckily, the church and the minister had been available, making the arrangements for the ceremony surprisingly uncomplicated. The bride had donned an unpretentious dress of white linen, embellished by a lacy handkerchief tucked into the small, embroidered breast pocket. A tiny hat, complete with a small patch of white lace, shadowed Pearl's eyes, and her fingers clutched a small bouquet of mountain wildflowers.

The groom was dressed in his best suit, well-worn but neatly pressed. His head was bare, the thick, black hair slicked back from his broad forehead. His dark eyes were inscrutable and held an air of mystery as he gazed down at his bride.

Pearl returned his look, her face demure and set in peaceful lines. Only her eyes reflected the excitement and the heat of her love. Jake Martin had entered her life barely a month before, and he had swept her off her feet, overwhelming her with his magnetism and his charm. His deep voice, excited and eager, had shared his plans for the future. He was a gold miner, and he had staked a claim situated in a small dell named Simm's Canyon. His confidence inspired Pearl, and she had found herself caught up in the excitement of his dreams. His life was an adventure and his words filled her with a longing to share his quest.

Just as his words sparked her own dreams, his kisses and his touch sparked a passionate nature that was new and electrifying to her. She had fought to control her desires, angering Jake when she pulled back, using his desire to accomplish her goal. And in the end she had won. He had proposed, and she had been ecstatic.

So she married him that bright spring morning, giving no thought to the gossip or to the tall, silent man who stood hidden in the shadows of the church cloakroom. William Aldrich was a man in mourning. His young, handsome face was lined with grief, and his broad shoulders slumped in defeat as he watched the girl he so desperately loved marry another.

He shook his head as thoughts of what should have been filled his mind with haunting clarity. He should have been the man standing at her side, pledging his life and his love. They had talked about a fall wedding, and Pearl had shown him the fabric she had purchased for her wedding dress. His entire countenance darkened as he watched her slim figure turn toward Jake. She looked so lovely, and her smile was bright and full of hope. His heart broke as he turned away, unable to watch as she became another man's wife.

He walked slowly out of the church, feeling the anguish of the truth he had seen etched in the pure lines of her lovely profile. She loved Jake Martin. And her love for Jake was the passionate, all-consuming love that William had for Pearl. The kind of love she had never shown for him.

He walked away from the church knowing that he couldn't stop the inevitable. He had lost her. His sore heart ached, and his broad shoulders trembled from the weight of his loss. And as he walked out of her life, his gentle gray eyes reflected his continued devotion to her.

He prayed for her happiness with a generosity and a sincerity that few would have understood.

It was a singular moment in time—William's last farewell to Pearl, the murmured words "I do," and the ceasing of the meadowlark's song. As well-wishers gathered around the smiling newlyweds and the lone figure of a young man disappeared from view, a single dark cloud drifted in front of the sun, shadowing the valley in gloom.

CHAPTER 2

December 1932
Simm's Canyon, Idaho

It was Christmas Eve, and the honeymoon had ended months earlier. Pearl sat on a stool in front of the old potbellied stove, trying to gain some comfort from its feeble warmth. Outside, the bitter wind shrieked down the barren corridor of the mining encampment. A knitted sweater hung around her bony shoulders, and her eyes were red from weeping. Her small hands, once smooth and white, were now rough and reddened from exposure to the harsh elements.

The realities of Jake's dreams had been a cruel surprise to Pearl. Her idealistic imaginings had given way to despair after the first month. Simm's Canyon was a primitive, isolated hole of pure misery. The small encampment consisted of a dozen dilapidated shanties, the majority of which were the shared quarters of the miners. They were rough, crude men, and Pearl despised them. Her husband was just like them.

Jimmy Slade, proprietor of Slade's Saloon, owned one of the shacks. He was a short, brawny man with hard features, and he knew the needs of the miners. He had appeared soon after gold was discovered in Simm's Canyon, and he knew that he had found his own mother lode.

Pearl had spent the first few months of their marriage lonely and miserable under the scorching summer sun, waiting for Jake to return home in the evenings. The only other women in the small community were the girls who worked for Slade, and Pearl avoided them. Then the winter had come, and she found her boredom and misery compounded by the days spent huddled by the fire, lonely, miserable, and cold.

This Christmas Eve meant nothing to Pearl. She looked around the interior of the shanty in despair. They had nothing. Their furniture consisted of a rickety table with two dilapidated wooden chairs, a rusty iron bed with a lumpy mattress and two thin blankets, a small dresser, and the potbellied stove. There were no decorations to herald the Christmas season, but Pearl didn't care. She was depressed. She was lonely. And she was angry.

Her eyes began to glitter with her anger, and it felt good to have the darts of resentment and fury warming her blood. And as her cheeks became stained with the unnatural red of her ire, Pearl wondered where her love had gone. She no longer had any feelings of tenderness for Jake. He no longer sparked her passion, and her rage deepened as she fingered the dark bruises covering her arms, chest, and legs.

Pearl's throat constricted as she realized that what they shared had nothing to do with love. It was based on violence, anger, and domination. Her blood boiled in response to the way he made her feel. And she hated him for the power he held over her. He was crushing her spirit, and she despised herself for allowing him to do so.

Pearl questioned her own sanity. Why did she stay? It would be a simple matter to just slip away. Jake was gone for long hours at a time, hidden deep in the bowels of the mountain searching for the yellow god that he worshiped. But she stayed, and she knew that she wouldn't leave him. She had no place to go, no one to run to. She heard his staggering steps on the shanty stoop. The door was flung open, and Pearl looked Jake right in the eyes as he moved toward her.

CHAPTER 3

September 12, 1934
Simm's Canyon, Idaho

The wind howled menacingly down the narrow gulch, rattling the weathered timbers of the small shack in what seemed like a deliberate attempt to bring it to the ground. Inside the dimly lit one-room shanty, the air was thick with smoke from the oil lamp. The only sound besides the raging wind was the muttered curse of the grizzled and weary doctor. The woman lying upon the bed was beyond sound. Her pale face, streaked with sweat and tears, showed the agony of pain, a torment almost beyond human endurance.

Her breathing was shallow and ragged, her pulse weak and thready. Doc Barlow was working feverishly to save her life. Pearl was having a baby that was too big for her small frame. Doc Barlow had been fetched from the small town of Emmett, located twenty miles north of Simm's Canyon. The man who came for him was barely coherent, but Doc Barlow was able to understand enough of his drunken rambling to know that he was desperately needed. He knew of the shantytown, and he ignored the distaste that rose in his throat at the thought of treating one of the slovenly miners, or worse, one of the diseased girls who worked for Slade's Saloon.

He had driven as fast as his old Ford truck would allow, and he had been waved to one of the rickety shacks by a man stumbling down the street waving an empty whiskey bottle in the air. Doc Barlow was surprised when he entered the cabin. Rather than a bruised and broken miner nursing his wounds from a drunken brawl or a spent and wasted harlot, his patient was a young woman who still retained the blush of youth and the beauty of easier years.

His heart softened with pity as he watched her bloated, writhing figure on the bare, bloodstained mattress. Her cries of agony were weakening, and he knew that he would have to work fast. Barely acknowledging the nearby figure of Macy Calhoon, one of Slade's girls, Doc Barlow quickly went to work.

"What's her name?" he asked the woman standing behind him.

"Pearl. Pearl Martin," replied Macy. Macy watched the doctor with a look of utter relief on her face. Jake Martin had fetched her when Pearl had started into labor, and as the hours had passed, Macy knew that Pearl was in trouble. She had tried to get Jake to send for the doctor hours ago, but he had slapped her hard, wrenching her arm as he threw her back through the door of the cabin. Macy had finally eluded him, running to beg Slade to send someone for the doctor. Slade had recognized the urgency and the fear in Macy's voice, and he had driven into Emmett himself to fetch Doc Barlow.

The doctor softly issued curt commands for hot water, clean towels, and blankets. Macy rushed to do his bidding and cringed inwardly when she handed over the inadequate wad of rough, stained towels that were all she could find. Doc Barlow gritted his teeth as he set to work, knowing that he didn't have much time if Pearl were to survive the birth of her baby. The contractions were racking her slender frame with great waves of pain, and her voice was hoarse from hours of endless screaming. Her hands lay limply by her side, clutching feebly at the sheet beneath her. Her hair lay in tangled, sweaty curls around her face, and her eyes were dim with pain and hysteria.

As the doctor worked desperately, Pearl's body gave one final, convulsive squeeze. Her body went rigid, and her back arched involuntarily. The doctor grappled for the shoulders of the baby that had suddenly appeared, and as he quickly withdrew him from the birth canal, Pearl's body went totally limp.

The birth of the baby had cost her all she had. With one last gasp, her eyes closed and her heart stilled. With a loud, explosive curse, the doctor tied and severed the umbilical cord and all but threw the small, limp baby boy onto the bare dresser standing beside the bed.

All of his attention was on Pearl as he moved to her side and began trying to resuscitate her. He was determined that this poor little girl would not die in the middle of the squalor and loneliness of the wretched cabin. He thought to himself as he worked over Pearl about his own children and how he had waited anxiously for the announced birth of each one, his wife hidden from his view by the sterile white curtains of the hospital ward. He thought angrily about the missing husband, wondering where he was and why Pearl was having to go through this alone. He had no idea that the stumbling fool he had encountered on his arrival, the drunk waving him on with the whiskey bottle, was the missing father.

And he had no idea of the anger and fear that had driven Jake Martin to the bottle that night. Jake had viewed the pending birth of his child with mixed feelings. He had felt the pride of ownership and power as he had watched Pearl's burgeoning figure. Her condition was due to him. He had impregnated her with his seed. Yet his pride was not the noble pride of fatherhood. Rather, it was the misguided pride that stemmed from his power and control over Pearl. But that evening when the labor pains had started, he had been unable to face the responsibility of staying by Pearl's side.

While the doctor, summoned without Jake's assistance, labored over Jake's dying wife, Jake passed out behind the flimsy protection of an old, rotting shed behind Slade's tavern, the empty bottle lying on the ground next to him forgotten, and his mind oblivious to the drama taking place in his home.

When Doc Barlow literally tossed the infant boy behind him, Macy, standing in the doorway, watched the small, limp body in terror. His tiny, wrinkled body was blue, and his eyes were closed with no sign of the first breath of life. She hesitated as her gaze shot back to the doctor. Surely he didn't intend to let the little boy die. Her heart lurched and softened as she turned her eyes back to the baby, his peril unobserved by the frantic physician who focused all of his energy and efforts on the woman lying so still on the soiled bed.

Feeling as though a will other than her own was guiding her, Macy found herself moving forward, her arms reaching for the silent baby. Her rough, worn hands picked up the tiny body. She shivered as she felt his cold skin. Coming out of the stupor caused by the tragic events, she grabbed at one of the few dry towels remaining and began to rub it over the baby's body, shaking him gently as she worked.

With a determined look on her face, she talked to the little boy. "Come on, honey. You didn't fight to come into this world just to have it all end like this. Your mama's gonna need you." Tears blurred her vision as she whispered, "Come on, honey. Oh, dear Lord, help me."

Her whispered plea was a prayer in her heart. She wasn't a religious woman. She lived a life of sin and she knew it. But she wasn't praying for herself. God probably didn't have any use for her or her kind, yet she knew that He loved this tiny little boy, and she found the faith to pray for the baby. She felt a sense of calm as she lowered him to the top of the old, rickety dresser. She bent over him, placing her mouth over his nose and mouth, blowing gently as her hands continued to massage his limp body.

She continued to breathe for him, working the towel up and down his still chest. Tears mingled with her breath as she continued, her heart drawn out in prayer for this little boy who deserved the chance to live.

"You're gonna make it!"

As she paused in her ministrations, she noticed a difference in the baby's countenance. He no longer looked so blue, and as she raised her head to look at him, she saw a minuscule movement in his chest. Biting her lip and gasping for breath, she felt her own chest tighten as she saw another small movement. He was breathing on his own. She felt a flutter under her hand resting on his chest, and she knew he was going to live. Using the towel as a blanket, she picked up the featherlight body. Wrapping him as warmly as possible in the towel, she cradled him in her arms, a smile breaking through her tears as she heard and felt him take a deep breath. She laughed out loud as she heard the feeble yet very real cry that accompanied his exhaling.

She stood there holding the baby and laughing out loud as his feeble cries turned into lusty wails. She rocked him back and forth, her wizened face and world-weary spirit reflecting a renewed hope in life as the baby cried and breathed and greeted life.

"Bring the baby here."

The doctor's voice penetrated Macy's happy haze, and she started as she realized that she was being watched by two sets of weary eyes.

The doctor looked tired, but relieved. He had given his all to Pearl, and he breathed a sigh of relief as he had watched her responding to his ministrations. He had been vaguely aware of Macy and the baby, a part of his heart hurting for the baby that he had so callously tossed aside. He'd had to make a choice: save the baby or save the mother. He had chosen the mother, and thus had concentrated on saving her life as he had quashed the pain of knowing that the newborn was probably going to die.

Pearl's open eyes, glazed with fatigue and despair, also watched as Macy stepped forward with the tiny bundle in her arms. Pearl was beyond responding, beyond caring, beyond pain. Even though the doctor had saved her from physical death, nothing could save her from the emotional and spiritual death that had started during the first two years of her marriage to Jake. That death had found its completion during the birth of the baby. She watched Macy approach, holding the baby out to her. Pearl turned her head away, refusing to look at the small person she had helped create.

Macy placed the boy on her chest, and Pearl's arms reflexively closed around him. His greedy, hungry mouth instinctively searched her for a source of nourishment, and she felt the cold of her heart turn to ice. Distaste for the act of nursing turned to distaste for the baby, and solidified the hatred in her heart for the man who had caused her spirit to die.

CHAPTER 4

September 1942
Adak, Alaska

"Hey, Will, I got some mail for ya."

William turned and reached eagerly for the bundle of mail being handed to him by his buddy Sal.

"Thanks, bud."

He turned away and thumbed through the small stack of letters. There were a couple of letters from his brothers and one from Natalie, a girl he had met while in boot camp. He smiled as he thought of her cheerful, homely face, and he decided that he would save her letter for last as he shoved it and the two letters from his brothers into his pocket. She always made him feel better, helping to ease the ever-present pain of losing Pearl, and he was grateful for her warm friendship.

His smile of anticipation faded, however, as he looked down at the last envelope in his hand. He recognized Pearl's spidery handwriting and immediately forgot his other mail. He slowly tore open the envelope. It had been years since he had seen her, and this was the first time she had written him. Just looking at her sprawling handwriting brought back all the pain he had hidden in the depths of his lonely heart. A rushing wave of agony swept over William, and he hunched his shoulders against the driving rain.

He hurriedly walked across the military compound toward his hut, anxious to get out of the elements. As he neared his hut, he became impervious to the harsh mountains rising behind him in volcanic splendor, his thoughts now focused entirely on the letter in his hands and the woman who had written it.

He entered the small hut, grateful for its feeble protection, and he sighed in relief when he noted the absence of his bunkmates. He had only been on Adak for a few weeks, but it seemed like years. The island was a tiny speck set in the chain of Aleutian Islands curving outward from the mainland of Alaska, reaching for the far shores of the Soviet Union. The miserable weather and the primitive living conditions belied the rugged beauty of the island. He hated the prospect that he might be stationed for several more months on the isolated military installment. His task, along with that of his entire battalion, was the construction of an airfield, barracks, warehouses, and other essential buildings for the fledgling settlement. He sank to the edge of his metal cot, barely feeling the relief of its thin mattress, and cursed the fates that had sent him to this primitive, cold, and eternally wet island.

His discomfort faded, however, as he toyed with the opening of the ripped envelope, hesitant to pull out the single sheet of paper enclosed. Finally he pulled out the folded parchment, dropping the envelope while his trembling fingers opened the letter. The paper sheath drifted to the floor as he began to read, his heart beating in sudden anticipation.

> *Dear William,*
>
> *I can't stand the thought of you being so far away from me. I got your address from your brother Harold. He told me you were in the navy and that you were in Alaska. I know that it has been a long time since we last spoke, but I always drew such comfort just knowing that you were nearby. I can't understand what made you join the navy. Don't you know that I need you?*

William paused, his mouth tightening with frustration at Pearl's implied criticism. *She* had left *him* when he needed her. Emotion swelled in his throat, choking his already-labored breathing as he continued to read.

I hate my life. Marrying Jake was the biggest mistake I ever made. I fear that I shall suffer for my foolishness for the rest of my life. We have three kids now: two boys and a girl. I feel so trapped. I would leave tomorrow if only I had someplace to go. If you were home, things would be different. I wouldn't feel so alone.

William, dear, I must go. The kids are screaming for attention. Jake will be home soon, and he will probably be drunk. I almost prefer it when he's drunk. At least it seems like he has an excuse for being so cruel. Pray for me, William, and remember how much I need you.

The letter closed with her bare signature. There were no words of concern for his welfare, no apology for her defection so many years ago. William's gentle heart forgave the selfishness. His love for her was unconditional, and he sat with his head down, cradled in the palms of his large hands. His shoulders were slumped with fatigue and concern. She sounded so unhappy. If only he could go to her, he would take her and the children away to a safe place.

Carefully he folded the letter and placed it in his left breast pocket. He would carry it close to his heart, close to the warmth of his love. He was already formulating his reply, and he murmured a quiet, sincere prayer for her safety. He lifted his head, his gaze focused on an unseen horizon. His gray eyes gleamed with purpose and determination. However long it took him, he would return to Idaho, to Pearl and her children.

He would be out of the military in six months. He had planned on reenlisting, had thought to become a career man. But he now had a greater purpose in life, and his heart swelled at the thought of sharing his life with Pearl and her children. The years of loneliness were carried away by the wave of love sweeping through his heart. *Six months, honey, then I'll come. We'll be a family. You and me and the kids.*

Quickly grabbing a pencil and a pad of paper, William scrawled out a reply to Pearl. As he sealed the letter and addressed the envelope, William paused and gently fingered the rectangle of paper. His thoughts were already spanning the distance to the time when he and Pearl could be together. A smile of pure happiness creased his handsome face as he whispered, "Soon, Pearl. I'll be home soon."

CHAPTER 5

May 1943
Simm's Canyon, Idaho

"William!" Pearl's voice resounded with gratitude as she threw herself into the arms of the tall man standing on the stoop of the weathered shanty. The building was even more gray and dilapidated than it had been the day Pearl moved in, and even then it had looked as if the slightest wind would knock it down.

"Pearl." William's voice was husky with emotion as he held her close. "Pearl." All he could do was whisper her name as he embraced the knowledge that the woman he loved so desperately was finally in his arms. Years before when he had walked away from Pearl's wedding to Jake Martin, William had felt his heart shatter. He had known that he would never love another, and it seemed like a miracle that he should actually be standing here holding her in his arms.

"I'm ready to go, William. We've got to go now!" The edge in Pearl's voice sparked an answering sense of urgency in William's mind, and he reluctantly released Pearl as she turned and picked up a battered suitcase. For the first time he took a look at her and her surroundings.

Pearl was as pale as a wraith, her hair matted and held close to her head in a tangled ponytail. Her face, while still young, had lost the bloom of youth. Her eyes reflected no emotion as she pushed at him to take the bag. Her mouth was set in a line of grim determination, and her hands trembled as she pushed William back down the shallow steps of the stoop.

"Go, William! Hurry! We have to leave now."

"But, Pearl, what about the children?" William's heart constricted with sorrow as he realized that Pearl had only one suitcase. He inadvertently stepped backward at her insistence, but not before he saw the three small faces peering at them from the gloomy interior of the cabin. He caught an image of dirt and grime and unkempt hair. But what burned an everlasting image into his mind was the depth of sorrow emanating from the three pairs of watchful eyes.

"They're staying here." Pearl's voice was cold and invited no argument as she ran past William, her features pale and fervent as she made her escape.

William stood for a moment, torn. How could she do this to them? "Pearl, wait!"

As Pearl turned toward him, her face anxious and her body language communicating her fear of the delay, William begged, his voice hoarse from the depth of his feelings, "We can't leave the children!"

Pearl stared at him, her anger shooting invisible daggers at him, and William felt the force of her ire. He shuddered from the vehement animosity he heard in her voice as she answered, "They are not coming!"

Pearl turned and ran toward the truck. William watched her with sorrow darkening the gray depths of his eyes. She was giving him no choice. If he were to ignore her command by gathering the children into his arms and bundling them into the cab of the truck, he would lose her. And he couldn't go through that loss again. He had just found her after a decade of separation.

With one last, hungering glance at the small, shadowy faces hiding in the dark, William made the decision to follow her. Sadly he watched the flimsy door of the shanty swing shut, blocking from view the heart-wrenching picture of the three lost children. As he climbed into the driver's side of the vehicle, William knew that the image of sadness shut behind that door would remain in his memory for a long time to come.

William and Pearl drove away, impervious to the soft sounds of the children sobbing in the dark as they huddled together and waited for their angry father to return home. Cap Martin, eight years old, cried as he held tightly to his little brother and sister. And as their mother abandoned them, the children lost another piece of their childhood.

CHAPTER 6

July 1950
Boise, Idaho

The night was dark and peaceful, the velvet sky studded with bright pinpoints of starlight and the heavily wooded land filled with the dancing shadows of midnight. The shabby clapboard house was palely illuminated by the sliver of moon floating in the sky among the diamond-bright stars. The croaking of a bullfrog, hidden in the foliage surrounding a nearby pond, emphasized the sense of isolation encompassing the house.

Jake Martin sat sprawled in his easy chair. He was drunk, and he sat in a stupor, numb from the effects of the alcohol, the main staple of his diet. Suddenly the creaking of the front screen door broke the quiet of the night. It slammed shut, and Sandy Martin's cheerful humming alerted Jake to her presence.

He lurched to his feet as she came through the door, her thirteen-year-old face aglow with excitement. Her pockets jingled with the metallic clang of the generous tips she had earned that evening at the café. Her excitement made her careless, and she froze midstride, the chipper song catching in her throat as she came face-to-face with her father.

She didn't have time to escape the dangers of Jake's drunken violence, and she cried out, "No! Please, Pa, don't! I'm sorry." Her impassioned cries of apology went unheeded as his large fists found their target.

Cap Martin and his younger brother, John, huddled together beside their bed, hands clasped over their ears, eyes squeezed shut as they tried to shut out the sounds of what was taking place in the other room. Cap would soon be sixteen, but he and fourteen-year-old John felt like small children as they listened to the cries of their younger sister.

Jake Martin was a mean man. And he was a meaner drunk.

Once the sounds of violence faded, leaving a silence heavy with fear, Cap went to Sandy and found her huddled and bleeding in the corner of the dank bathroom. He swallowed back his emotions as he bathed her bruises, quietly cursing their existence, hating the brutality.

Cap picked Sandy up and carried her into the bedroom, where he gently laid her down on the narrow cot that served as her bed. Tucking a thin quilt around her slight frame, Cap turned and slumped onto the lumpy mattress of the bed he shared with John.

He looked around the cramped, dirty room, lost in thought. A few minutes later he became aware of two sets of eyes watching him. John was sitting on the floor, his back resting against Sandy's bed. Sandy had awakened, her battered body curled into a fetal position, her bruised and swollen eyes fixed on his face. He saw his own emotions mirrored in their sad eyes. Their lives revolved around a cycle of abuse and violence. They lived with hopelessness, victims of Jake's meanness.

Their mother had left them in the spring of 1943, and the beatings had started that day, four months before Cap turned nine. John had been six, Sandy five. Memories of that day were locked far in the recesses of Cap's heart. He couldn't bear to relive the sadness and desolation he had felt as he had watched his mother leave.

He felt his heart twist with a mixture of anger, pain, and frustration. He felt the tension building in his gut, an acrid burning causing him to clench his teeth in physical pain. He knew that he couldn't stay in the house another minute.

Cap jumped up from the bed, its rusty frame creaking from the force of his movements. It was time to take control; they had allowed themselves to be at the mercy of their father's cruel attention long enough. "Mercy?" Cap muttered to himself, the irony of his thoughts striking him suddenly. There was no mercy from their father. His actions were those of a man beyond reason.

Cap knew that he himself was near the breaking point. His hatred towards his father was building to a feverish pitch. He hated the smell of alcohol, hated the way it affected his father, emphasizing the small meanness of his heart. And he felt the anger and the hatred mingling with the resentment, the loneliness, and the longing for his mother.

She was such an unknown entity.

With a shrug of his strong, broad shoulders, Cap turned to face his brother and sister, his brown eyes gleaming with the sudden determination to escape from his father's house.

"I'm gettin' outta here, guys."

John looked at Cap, his eyes reflecting the same burning anger. "I ain't stayin' here either. I'm goin' with you."

Sandy sat up in bed, her young face swollen and purple with the angry marks of her father's abuse. "I'm not staying here alone with him." She crawled out of bed, ignoring the painful throbbing of her aching body. John stood and joined Sandy by the bed.

Cap had to resist the sudden surge of emotion. His handsome, young features softened as he looked into the earnest and trusting faces of his brother and sister. His smile broke the tension in the air, and he turned from them, hastily gathering a few personal belongings and shoving them into a rucksack that he pulled down from the top shelf of the closet.

"Okay then, let's get cracking!"

It only took them a few minutes to collect their effects, including a couple of thin, ragged quilts. As they crept through the kitchen, Cap snitched a bag of cookies and some crackers, shoving them into a small paper sack, which he handed to Sandy.

As Cap led the way through the dimly lit house, the deepening shadows emphasized his stealth. As they crept by the crowded, messy front room, they saw Jake sprawled across the couch, passed out in a drunken stupor.

Cap paused, listening intently, his vigilant wariness well-founded.

They continued to move with care, knowing that if they woke him they would not be able to escape his attention. When the screen door squeaked loudly, they all paused, frightened until Cap's confident nod signaled that it was safe for them to continue their exodus.

As they left the hot, stuffy house, they breathed in the cool freshness of the night. To Cap, it was the sweet perfume of freedom, and he breathed deeply to rid his nostrils of the alcoholic stench that permeated the house.

Cap led the way, having no definite destination in mind. Their only goal that night was to escape the viciousness of life with their father. Cap shuddered as he recalled Sandy's cries for help, and he knew that he needed to purge his mind of the echo of those helpless pleas. The darkness hid the image of her broken, bruised face, but couldn't dispel the memories of all that had transpired earlier that evening.

His thoughts were deep and troubled as they walked, and as he reveled in the sense of freedom and peace that he found in the darkness of the night, he knew that the time had come for him to leave Boise. There was nothing here for him, nothing but bad memories and fear.

With sudden determination, he turned and faced John and Sandy, his hands thrust deep into his pockets, his shoulders hunched as he shared with them his deepest desire, his voice a whisper in the night. "I'm gonna go find Ma."

Equal in their fervor, John and Sandy bombarded Cap with their eager cries to come along. Cap knew that he couldn't leave them behind. Once Jake learned of Cap's defection, there would be no escaping his wrath. Sober or drunk, Jake hated his former wife for her desertion, and he had made his children pay for that hatred. And if only one of them were to leave, those left behind would face Jake's revenge. The thought of that was unbearable.

"Okay, you can come with me. I have a little money saved." Cap tapped his back pocket where he had his wallet. "It should be enough to get us to Hailey. I'll call William tomorrow." Cap didn't tell John and Sandy, but he always carried with him the first letter William had sent the year after he took Pearl away. It expressed their stepfather's regret that they couldn't join him and Pearl in Hailey. But William had included their phone number with the encouragement to call if they ever needed anything. Cap had never called, but he remembered William's promise of help. He resolved that tomorrow he would call.

His quietly spoken words registered with John and Sandy, and they threw their arms around him, entangling them all in a fierce hug. Sandy was the first to break away, and as she did so, she took Cap's hand in hers. John, standing on the other side of her, took her free hand, and they resumed their escape down the road, their joined hands binding them together even as their excitement and their desire to escape their father's harsh company bound their souls together.

Time passed unheeded, each of the Martin children lost in their separate thoughts. Ten minutes later, Cap stepped off the road and led his siblings into the woods that lined the street. They had put a considerable distance between themselves and their inebriated father, so Cap felt safe in stopping for the night. He found a small clearing that was carpeted with fallen pine needles and scrubby grass. "Let's rest here."

John and Sandy wearily nodded their assent. It was late, and they were emotionally whipped. John spread the quilts on the ground, and they all sank to their knees, exhaustion overtaking them as they gave in to the weariness. Before collapsing back on the blankets, they dined on the crackers and cookies that they had pilfered from the kitchen.

John and Sandy drifted to sleep while Cap relaxed on his quilt, fatigue falling over him like a shroud. He felt numb from the perpetual storm of emotions that encompassed his existence. As John and Sandy slept, Cap studied their faces by the softened light of the moon. They were both pale and looked so terribly young. He clenched his teeth as he fought to hold back the tears threatening to engulf him.

He knew that the coming days would bring many changes. They would follow through with their plans to find their mother. But he was filled with the fear of rejection. He tried valiantly to push those fears aside and finally managed to conquer the tears as he, too, gave in to the weariness. Cap's last conscious thoughts were of his father, and he vowed that he would never again subject himself to the familiar and devastating pattern of abuse.

Soon the moon drifted across the night sky, its path traced by flickering starlight, and even though the ground was hard, Cap, John, and Sandy slept soundly, the protection offered by the canopy of the midnight sky more real than the elusive net of safety they had found under their father's roof.

CHAPTER 7

Shivering, Cap groped in his sleep for his blanket. The only thing his fingers touched, however, was the cool, dew-damp grass. His eyes slowly opened as he attempted to orient himself to the strangeness of his surroundings. A slow smile warmed his face as he looked over at John and Sandy as they lay sleeping by his side. He could tell by the color in the sky that it was still early. He jumped to his feet, suddenly awake and energetic. He was filled with enthusiasm and eagerness spurred on by his hopes for the future.

Reaching down, he gently shook John's shoulder. John rolled over and groaned as he, too, came awake, stiff and cramped from sleeping the night on the ground. As he sat up, John nudged Sandy and told her, "Come on, sleepyhead. Wake up."

Sandy opened her eyes and peered up into the smiling faces of her brothers. She smiled back as she remembered the plans they had made the night before. Her face looked fragile and tired, the dark bruises on her cheek and around her eyes emphasizing the delicate bone structure. She ignored the pain and stiffness that screamed at her as she reached toward Cap. He grasped her hand and pulled her to her feet.

It was late morning by the time they arrived at the bus depot. After purchasing their tickets, they found a public rest room to wash their hands and faces. Sandy pulled on a clean blouse and spent a few minutes combing water through her hair before she tied it back in a loose ponytail. She grimaced at the signs of battle darkening her face, but she knew it could have been worse. "At least he didn't break anything this time," she murmured as she stroked the two slightly crooked fingers of her right hand, permanent reminders of a previous run-in with Jake.

After brushing her teeth, Sandy rejoined her brothers. She smiled slightly, her eyes sad but hopeful as she saw that they, too, had donned clean shirts and had carefully brushed their hair.

Cap called William from the bus depot, grateful for the few letters William had written to them over the years, and even more thankful the letters hadn't been intercepted by Jake. Cap explained to William the events of the previous day and told him they were coming. He then hung up before the man could say no. His fear of rejection was still strong, and Cap didn't want to give William any opportunity to refute their plans.

Before long it was time for them to leave, and with a tremendous sense of relief, they boarded the bus that would transport them to a new life. The journey to Hailey passed quickly, and after the bus pulled up in front of the depot, Cap, John, and Sandy eagerly scanned the sparse crowd standing in front of the bus stop. Cap felt his heart constrict as he skimmed the unfamiliar faces.

John quietly said, "I guess she must be busy. I mean, that's probably why she isn't here."

Sandy's face mirrored her sadness while her knowing eyes silently agreed with the resigned look reflected on Cap's face. Seeing the adult acceptance in her youthful face, Cap quickly quelled his own disappointment as he forced a cheerful note into his voice. "Never mind, I know there's a good explanation."

John and Sandy smiled, their mouths curved in gentle expressions of gratitude for Cap's attempt at relieving their disappointment. They gathered up their meager belongings and stepped out into the blinding sunshine. Heat radiated from the concrete sidewalk, and Cap felt the sweat begin to trickle down the middle of his back. He licked his upper lip, tasting the salty beads of perspiration.

Cap forgot the discomfort of the heat as he gazed at the brilliant blue sky and searched the horizon, jagged and magnificent from the grandeur of the surrounding mountains. The air smelled clean and fresh, and he smiled as he studied the lovely setting of the small community.

John and Sandy, walking by his side, soaked up the spirit of hope that seemed to emanate from the serene, peaceful valley. They listened while

Cap asked a friendly passerby for directions. The woman's instructions were clear and easy to follow. As they headed for their mother's home, they forgave her for her nonappearance at the bus depot and immersed themselves in contemplation about what the future might hold.

Fifteen minutes later they arrived, flushed and excited, at the tree-lined drive of the rustic log house that was their mother's home. It looked warm and inviting nestled in a grove of cottonwood and evergreen trees. Flowers bloomed in window boxes, and a sweet scent of freshly mown grass mingled with the pungent scent of pine and the gentle essence of the flowers.

Despite the welcoming appearance of the yard, Cap slowed his approach to the front door as a sense of isolation and desertion encroached on his spirit of excitement. When he reached the front door, he took a deep breath, raised his hand, and gave two sharp raps on the pine door. Exhaling as he lowered his arm, Cap, with John and Sandy, waited.

They waited in vain. No one answered their summons, and the three finally looked at each other, wondering what they should do. Cap took it upon himself to try the door. The knob turned easily under his touch, and the door swung silently open. Without speaking, Cap looked quickly at John and Sandy before he stepped across the threshold.

"Ma? William? It's me, Cap. John and Sandy too." Stepping farther into the house, Cap's head turned slowly from side to side, taking in the unfamiliar sights of a home he had never known.

The small living room was clean and tidy, furnished with well-worn but carefully maintained furniture. The wooden surfaces of the tables and chairs gleamed, and dainty, hand-crocheted doilies adorned many surfaces. The sofa and matching chair were faded, but the worn chintz of the overstuffed cushions looked comfortable. Colorful, braided rugs were scattered over the wood floor, emphasizing the patina of the worn but highly polished surface. White lace curtains fluttered at the windows, and the scent of lemon oil mingled with the pungent blend of nature wafting through the open windows.

The room was peaceful and quiet. And empty.

As they wandered through the house, they discovered the same peaceful, empty charm in each room. The kitchen was clean and gleaming, but devoid of life. The two bedrooms held neatly made twin beds, but the simple wooden dressers were empty.

Cap's features froze with disbelief as he walked to the shuttered closets and pulled them open. They, too, were empty. William and Pearl were gone.

The charming little house, furnished so warmly and invitingly, was empty and deserted, lacking the welcome of its human inhabitants. Cap felt his heart beating in his chest and echoing against the hollowness of the empty rooms.

She had done it again. She had deserted them, and Cap blamed himself for the hurt and the sorrow he saw in John's and Sandy's faces. His early morning phone call had alerted her to their coming, and it had given her the time to leave, to escape once again the responsibility of her children. Anger surged in his heart, and he fought to gain control of his emotions, forcing his features into a mask of immobile indifference as he turned to face John and Sandy. He saw his own emotions mirrored in their young faces, and his anger died away as they shared the moment of intense, mutual pain.

Sandy walked away, heading toward the kitchen, as John and Cap stood immobile in the bedroom. Suddenly Sandy's voice, high-pitched with excitement, broke the heavy silence. Cap averted his gaze from John's face, but as he walked past, he laid a comforting hand on his brother's shoulder. John silently followed him into the kitchen, where Sandy greeted them, her face wreathed in a smile.

"She left us a note, Cap."

As she handed it to him, Sandy continued, "She apologizes for not being here. William has a temporary job in Wendell, and he had to be there today. She said that you hung up before William could tell you about it. They were packed and just about to walk out the door when you called."

Wendell was a small farming town about ninety miles south of Hailey. William occasionally took temporary jobs to help fill in the gaps that occurred in the construction business. This job in Wendell entailed working on a dairy farm for the next several months. The pay was good, and he felt it worth his while to relocate for those months, especially considering that the job came with a temporary home.

Pearl's note explained all of this, and as Sandy turned the note over to Cap, she pointed to the line she had read last. With a smile, Cap took the note from Sandy and continued reading.

"We would be happy to have you join us down here." Cap's grin widened as Sandy and John whooped in delight. He shushed them and continued, "Unfortunately, we are living in a small trailer and there won't be enough room for all of you."

Cap frowned as Sandy and John fell silent. Cap swallowed hard, a premonition of what was to come making his stomach churn. "In the envelope are two bus tickets to Wendell. Cap, please see that your younger brother and sister get on the bus to come down here. The tickets are for tomorrow morning, and the bus leaves at 8:00."

Sandy's wail of grief cut through Cap's words as she flung herself into his arms. "How could she? Oh, Cap, I won't go without you."

"Neither will I," stormed John. "She can't do this!" Pausing to gather control of his anger, John continued, "Come with us. Surely she won't turn you out if you come with us!"

Cap smiled grimly at John's naive suggestion. He knew that she could and would turn him away. He stood silently, his face stony and unreadable as he fought the waves of pain coursing through his body. He wasn't surprised. She had been rejecting him all his life, and this latest incident came as no shock.

"Shut up, you two." Cap's voice was quiet but authoritative. John and Sandy quickly heeded his command, their eyes fastened on his inscrutable face. Cap's expressive brown eyes were serious as he spoke. "You two will be on that bus in the morning. She wants you to join her."

Ignoring Sandy's muffled cry, Cap continued, "She says that I can stay here if I want. The lease is paid up through the spring, and she says that I shouldn't have any trouble finding work to pay for my keep. She even says that I should get back into school, seeing how this is my senior year."

Cap's lips curved into a sardonic smile as he contemplated the ironic cruelty of her motherly advice. Stay in school, get a job, stay in my house. But do it alone. Hiding his hurt, Cap repeated his admonition for Sandy and John to follow their mother's instructions. His heart ached at the thought of sending them off while he stayed behind. The future months stretched before him, lonely and empty, but he wouldn't deny his siblings the chance to build a relationship with their mother. He wasn't wanted, but at least she was willing to give John and Sandy a chance. And he refused to get in their way by placating his own grief and sadness. If he just said the word, he knew that they would stay with him. And he knew that they could make it on their own. But Sandy and John needed their mother.

So did he, but it was too late for him. They had finally escaped the fierce grasp of their father, and though Pearl had turned him away, he refused to even contemplate the possibility of returning to Boise. He would stay here in his mother's empty house. He recognized the wisdom of her misplaced concern that he finish his schooling. He would follow her suggestion, and he would survive.

That evening dragged by, and Cap passed the long night sleeplessly, contemplating his future. The next morning he held back tears of heartache as he saw John and Sandy safely placed on the bus. He watched it disappear from view, and he couldn't help but envy the chance they were being given to be with their mother. Overwhelmed by loneliness, he turned and slowly made his way back to the silent, empty house that would be his home for the next few months. Cap's shoulders were rounded and bowed with the burden of his emotions, his face devoid of all expression. He felt numb and alone.

As he walked up the winding path, pine needles crunched under his feet, and he heard the call of a lone mountain blue jay, its woeful cry finding a silent echo in his own heart. He approached the door, stopped, and turned to look at the mountains rising majestically around him. He listened to the wind rustling through the towering trees and heard the musical cadence of the nearby Wood River rushing through the mountain valley. He breathed deeply, inhaling the clean, pure air, and suddenly, he felt a lift to his spirits that eased his loneliness.

Cap marveled at the unexpected release from the sadness that had gripped him so fiercely just seconds before. As a light breeze tickled his brow, the whisper of a childhood memory began to fill his mind.

* * *

Jake Martin had closed his mine at Simm's Canyon when Cap was eleven years old and had moved with his children to Boise. Cap remembered feeling hopeful that the move might also bring a change in Jake's behavior, but his hopes had been in vain. In fact, Jake's anger, drinking, and subsequent abuse of his children had escalated. Cap remembered escaping from the house one hot summer afternoon, his face bearing the marks of pounding fists.

The sun had shone hot and searing as he ran through the woods, the rush of the breeze caused by his flight drying the tears on his cheeks. He hurt. The force of his dad's punches and kicks had been so fierce. The beatings made Cap feel so small and so weak. He hurt.

He hated his dad. He hated the hitting and the screaming and the kicking. But in his heart he knew that he didn't want to hate. He yearned for his dad to love him, to want him. But Jake didn't love him, and he didn't want him. As Cap ran, the aching soreness of his body had faded into a dull throb. With a cry of utter desolation, Cap dropped to the ground, unaware of his surroundings.

He pulled his knees up under his chin and wrapped his arms around his legs, his forehead resting against his knees. He was oblivious to the light traffic that traveled through the intersection near where he sat.

Cap was also unaware of the middle-aged woman standing at the window of the small corner grocery store across the street. She had seen the small body careening out of the wooded acre across the street. She had seen his tears glistening in the sunlight, and now she watched as he collapsed on the side of the road, oblivious to the world around him.

Reaching behind her and taking off the blue gingham apron tied around her thickening waist, she laid it on the counter near the cash register as she hurried over to a cooler that stood next to the front door. Opening the lid, she reached in and drew out two frosty bottles of root beer and flicked off the bottle caps.

Catherine Jones called to her husband, the proprietor of the small store, "Jerry, I'm gonna take me a little walk. I'll be back in a bit."

His muffled reply went unnoticed as Catherine strolled out into the sunshine, her dark blonde hair lightly streaked with gray shining in the afternoon light. She smoothed a stray wisp of hair back, tucking it behind her ear. She squinted up at the sun, the movement causing the fine-lined crow's feet at the corners of her eyes to deepen. She firmed her usually smiling lips with determination as she looked both ways before crossing the street.

Cap was unmindful of her approach, but as she dropped to the ground beside him, smoothing her flowered cotton skirt over her legs, he started in surprise.

"Hi there." Catherine's friendly greeting was met with silence as Cap shyly looked away from her probing blue eyes.

"I saw you over here and thought you looked like you could use a cold drink."

Cap looked at her in surprise as she handed him the bottle of icy cold liquid, the condensation beading on the smooth surface as the heat of the day tickled the chilled glass. Cap reached for the bottle and quickly gulped several mouthfuls of the foaming soda. He grinned sheepishly as the carbonation made him hiccup and burp at the same time. "Excuse me."

Catherine laughed and took a sip from her own bottle.

"Thanks, ma'am. I sure appreciate this."

"It's my pleasure." Catherine studied the handsome face gazing so thoughtfully back at her. The face was youthful, but the ugly bruises and swelling around the eyes emphasized the painful aging reflected in the depths of his eyes, signs of a childhood gone awry.

Cap looked away, the kindness he saw in Catherine's face inexplicably hurting him. A moment of silence passed between them before Catherine reached over and laid a gentle hand on Cap's arm. "You look like you need a friend. Can I help you in any way?"

Cap felt the rush of tears well in his eyes, and the clogging of emotion in his throat prevented him from speaking. He couldn't remember anyone ever speaking to him in such a kind, gentle manner. Shaking his head from side to side, the muscles in his throat working to dispel the lump choking his words, Cap set aside his bottle of root beer and used his hand to brush the tears from his eyes.

Catherine watched him as he fought for control. "Did someone hurt you?"

Cap tried to answer her, his voice thick with emotion. Finally he released the words in a torrent. "I don't know why he does it. I don't know why my dad hates me so much."

The hurt and bewilderment in Cap's voice caused Catherine to reach over and squeeze his fingers in sympathy. Her gesture encouraged him to continue. "We try so hard to be good. But it never helps. He hits us anyway."

"Who is 'us'?" Catherine asked.

"Me and John and Sandy."

"Your brother and sister?"

"Yeah."

A moment passed as Cap and Catherine sat on the street corner, their silence heightened by the background noise of the passing traffic.

"I just couldn't take it anymore." Looking over at Catherine for the first time, Cap gazed at her, his sad eyes steady as he said, "I just ran. I wanted to keep on running. I just didn't know where to go." Cap dropped his head into his hands. "Sometimes I feel so alone."

"I know what you mean. You can feel alone even when you're with a whole bunch of people."

"I wouldn't know about that. The only people I ever see are my dad and John and Sandy."

"What about your mother?"

"She left a long time ago. I haven't seen her since I was a little kid."

Catherine felt her heart constrict at the loneliness she heard in the boy's voice. It was as tangible as the hard ground upon which they sat.

"I want you to know something, son. Even when you feel the most alone, even when you are hurting from the bruises," Catherine traced a gentle finger along the curve of Cap's swollen, discolored cheek, "even when you are hurting from the yelling and the name-calling," Catherine tapped her finger against his left breast, "you are never really alone."

Her words captured his attention, and Cap looked up at her, his eyes questioning and brightening with the light of dawning hope. There was something about her words that spoke to his spirit.

"There is someone who is always watching over you. Do you know who that might be?"

Cap shook his head, puzzlement creasing his forehead. Catherine smiled gently as she turned her gaze to the bright blue sky. Her eyes widened, and she whispered, "Do you believe in God?"

Cap shrugged his shoulders. "I dunno. I've never really given it much thought."

Catherine's lips curved upward, her grin widening. "God is real. Just look around at all the beautiful things He's made for you and me."

Cap allowed his eyes to sweep across the beautiful surroundings. The bright sunshine felt warm on his face, and the filtered light glowed among the leafy, green trees. But he frowned as he asked, "Then where is He?"

"He's right here." Catherine tapped over her own heart. "And He's right here." She again tapped Cap on the chest. Cap looked confused, so Catherine continued, "His Spirit is inside each one of us." Catherine looked at Cap out of the corner of her eye, wanting to gauge the impact of her next words. "His Spirit is even inside your dad."

Cap's whole face frowned, and he felt a hardening of his heart as he said, "If that's the case, then I don't want anything to do with Him."

"I can understand how you might feel that way, but try to understand something. Even though all of God's children have His Spirit in them, some of us make choices that prevent us from coming to know Him. It sounds like your dad is like that."

Cap's face softened slightly as the truth of her words registered, and his eyes widened in surprise and understanding. "Yeah. He drinks an awful lot, and he's awful angry all the time. I guess with all the booze and stuff, if that spirit is there, it's probably pretty hard for him to feel."

Catherine graced Cap with another one of her loving smiles. Cap suddenly looked at her, a question in his eyes. "What did you mean when you called us 'God's children'?"

"We are His children, every one of us. Just like you are your mom and dad's son here on earth, we are all God's spirit children. He is your Father in Heaven." Cap looked interested as Catherine continued, "Luckily, unlike your mom and dad who have hurt you, your Heavenly Father will never hurt you or desert you. He'll always be there for you."

"Really?"

"Uh-huh!"

"Wow!"

Catherine sighed as she looked across the street and saw her husband waving at her from the open doorway of the store. "Try to remember that, okay? If you listen real hard, and can find a real quiet spot in your mind, you'll sense His presence. And if you watch real careful, you just might find angels sent from Him, angels who'll protect and comfort you. Will you remember that?"

"Yeah, I'll try."

"Good. Well, I better go. My husband is wanting me to get back to work." Catherine smiled as she stood up and reached down to take Cap's empty pop bottle.

Cap had watched her cross back to the other side of the street, his heart a little bit lighter and the hurt from his injuries fading. Her words had brought him a measure of comfort. For a while he had remembered her counsel, and it had helped. But after a time, the feelings he had experienced while she talked to him had faded away.

* * *

As Cap stood in the deserted yard of his mother's empty house, the pungent, pine-scented air caressed his senses and the soft touch of the breeze cooled his face. He had never learned the woman's name, nor had he ever seen her again. But her words and the way he had felt that day came back to him as he anticipated the coming year. He also remembered what she had said about angels, and he knew without a doubt that *she* had been an angel sent to help him that day long ago.

He looked up into the summer sky and suddenly knew that whatever the coming year held for him, at least he would be safe, and somehow he knew that he wasn't really alone.

He had always loved being out-of-doors. He realized that not only could he survive in this small mountain town, he could also find a degree of happiness. The inner core of strength that had seen him through the trauma and the despair of his abused childhood took hold, and he felt the emptiness of his heart filling with a small seed of hope and determination. Unconsciously, he straightened his shoulders as he strode forward and entered the deserted house.

CHAPTER 8

May 1951
Hailey, Idaho

Cap felt a stirring of excitement as he locked the door of the cabin and turned away from its lonely facade. His winter of isolation was past. It was springtime, and just as the earth was beginning to awaken from its winter rest, he felt alive and excited for the new life that awaited him.

He had filled the long months with work and study. He felt the pride of his accomplishments as he remembered the recent ceremony signifying his graduation from high school. No one had been in the audience to cheer for him when he accepted his diploma, but he was proud of himself for surviving the loneliness and completing his education.

And now it was time to step into the future. He thought of his plans and stopped for a minute to clutch the small card that epitomized his dreams. The day after graduation he had visited with the navy recruiter who had come to the high school promoting military service as an alternative to college. Cap had no desire to stay in school. He was ready to see the world, to find a niche for himself.

Cap decided to join the Seabees. He was to report to the naval training camp in San Diego, California, by the end of June. He was going to travel and he was going to build for the navy. He loved working with wood and constructing things with his hands. When the recruiter had mentioned the Seabees, Cap had known immediately that was what he wanted to do.

First, though, he was going to visit his brother and sister in Wendell. He had written to them over the winter, and their letters in return had been filled with news of their activities. William had written to Cap also, and the boy had come to welcome the wise words of counsel his stepfather shared. William had related stories about his own time spent in the military as a Seabee, and those stories had encouraged Cap to follow in his footsteps.

As he headed for the bus depot, Cap began to trot. He was anxious to see his brother and sister. He missed them terribly.

And he felt the exhilaration of the freedom awaiting him. Life stretched before him, beckoning to him like an exciting new friend, and he was determined to break away from the memories of his childhood.

Two hours later, the bus pulled into the small, dusty town of Wendell. Cap grimaced as he looked out the bus window and studied the sleepy-looking town. The buildings were shabby and dusty, reflecting the tired, work-worn appearance of the farmers and merchants milling around Main Street. He made a face when he realized that Wendell was even smaller than Hailey. And though it had a certain country charm, it was missing the sweet clarity of the mountains, and he suddenly felt grateful that he hadn't had to spend the long winter here.

A wide smile cracked the youthful maturity of Cap's face when he caught sight of Sandy and John, and he could almost feel their excitement as they waved and smiled at him. He waved back before turning from the window and grabbing his rucksack from the bus's overhead rack.

Bounding down the steps of the bus, Cap met John and Sandy as they threw themselves at him. They were all laughing and talking at once, and Cap felt happier than he had in months. As his brother and sister stepped away from him, Cap quickly perused the small crowd standing outside the bus depot, but the absence of his mother's face came as no surprise.

"She had to work today, Cap. She has a part-time job at Millie's Café," John said quietly.

Cap looked at John out of the corner of his eye as he fought to dampen down the familiar surge of disappointment. "That's okay, buddy. I came to see the two of you. You're here and that's what's important."

"William should be home by the time we get there, Cap." Sandy's soft voice was quiet with understanding. "He wanted to come with us, but just as we were leaving his boss called and said that he needed William to help him repair one of the fences."

"You should have heard him, Cap." Sandy giggled as she remembered the look of disgust on William's face. "He's so tired of this job."

John laughed out loud as he, too, remembered William's words. "He said that he's tired of 'cow-towing' to a bunch of ignorant heifers."

Cap smiled. "How much longer does he have before this job ends?"

"He'll be done at the end of the month. The foreman he's replacing will be back in a couple of weeks."

Cap watched Sandy as she explained, "William said that if it hadn't been for the good wages, he'd have left this job last winter. I think he hates those cows!"

"Does he still drink milk?" Cap asked, humor lighting his expression.

"Not much," John answered. "He still likes some of that fresh cream in his coffee, though."

Cap and his siblings had been slowly making their way towards the dairy farm while they were talking. As they covered the last few feet of the dusty driveway, Cap looked up and saw his stepfather standing outside a small trailer house.

William's gentle face was lined, and his soft gray eyes reflected the warmth of his welcome as he held his hand out and grasped Cap's in greeting.

Watching Cap, William could almost understand Pearl's strong aversion to her oldest son. He was a younger mirror image of Jake. Cap had his father's strongly defined features, a remnant of the man's Native American heritage, and he had grown into a muscular, handsome young man. William grimaced at the thought of Pearl's reaction when she saw him.

While Cap resembled his father physically, the resemblance ended there. Cap had a gentler nature that was evident in his bright, eager gaze. However, William knew that Pearl would be unable to see the difference.

"Welcome to Wendell, Cap."

"Thanks. It's good to be here."

"Come on in the house, son, and put your things down." William turned and led the way into the small, dark trailer. "Your ma isn't home right now. She works two or three days at the café. She was supposed to be off today, but they called her in this morning."

William's gentle explanation helped soothe the ache in Cap's heart. Cap suddenly realized that William understood his feelings. William knew the kind of love that kept the hope alive in Cap's heart. He had fallen under Pearl's spell years ago, and he still loved her despite the bitterness and the anger that had turned her into a petty, selfish shadow of her former self. William knew that Pearl's weaknesses would eventually destroy her. They were making her an old woman before her time, and at times he wondered how much longer he could stand the meanness and the harsh words, but then she would look at him and he would see the pain and the sorrow in her eyes. He would catch a glimpse of the soft, lovely young woman who had first captured his love, and he knew that he could never leave her. She needed him, and to him, that need made up for the lack of real love on her part. He had enough love for the both of them, and he knew that she would die if he ever left. So he stayed.

William grinned at Sandy and John, his face softened by the love he felt for them. He loved them as if they were his son and daughter, and he felt his heart swell as he welcomed another son into his home. William deeply regretted the lost years, but the past was gone. However, as Cap's, John's, and Sandy's laughter filled the small confines of the trailer, William cherished thoughts of the future.

Cap looked around the cramped living area of the small trailer and realized with sudden insight that he would have been miserable if he had come with John and Sandy to live here. He was grateful for the freedom and space he had enjoyed in Hailey, and despite the long, lonely hours, he wouldn't have changed the way he had spent the winter.

Catching William's gaze, Cap smiled and suddenly realized that he had grown up. And he realized that part of his search had ended. He felt William's love enveloping him, and for the first time in his life, Cap experienced the warmth of a parent's love.

CHAPTER 9

May 1951
Wendell, Idaho

"Hi, Ma," Sandy greeted Pearl as she came through the narrow door of the trailer.

Pearl smiled a wan greeting as she noted Sandy's bright smile and sparkling eyes. "Where is everyone?" Pearl asked. The house was quiet and warm with the late afternoon calm of a spring day.

"John and Cap are helping Dad with his afternoon milking."

"He's here?"

Sandy glanced at Pearl, the terse query dampening the joy she felt over having Cap with them.

"Yeah. He got in a couple hours ago."

Pearl walked across the small room and paused for a second before she headed for her bedroom. "I'm tired."

Pearl Martin Aldrich, a woman who had lived and died a thousand times with the hurt, anger, and betrayal of her life with Jake, turned her back on her daughter. Sandy's words filled her with dread.

Pearl was tired and she wanted to hide. She wanted to hide from the pressures of her children's expectations, to hide from William's pity. She knew he loved her, but she also knew that his love was tempered by the pity he felt, and though she was a broken, bitter woman, she still had her pride. That pride could not face the pity that she saw in William's eyes, heard in his voice, and felt in his embrace.

Without a word, Pearl walked to the back of the small, cramped trailer, closing the thin door to her bedroom behind her.

Ten minutes later, just as Sandy was pulling a roast from the oven, filling the room with its mouthwatering aroma, the front door once again scraped open. William, followed by Cap and John, came into the house, their deep voices resonating in the silence.

"Hey, sis, something smells wonderful!"

Sandy smiled at John. "Hope you're all hungry. I've got a feast fit for a king!" Sandy loved cooking, and she had spent the day in the kitchen preparing a sumptuous meal, happy to honor Cap's homecoming with her efforts.

Cap walked up behind her and kissed her cheek. "Looks like you've been cooking all day."

"I have, but you're worth it." Sandy turned, put her arms around him, and hugged him fiercely, her slender arms powerful with emotion. Her hug wasn't only a gesture of welcome. She wanted to shield him from the pain that she knew he would feel once reunited with his mother. Sandy knew that nothing had changed. Pearl's cold query and subsequent ignoring of Sandy's response had reinforced that fact.

The soft creaking of an opening door heralded the moment of confrontation. Time seemed to suspend itself as Pearl stepped out into the hallway and slowly walked towards her family.

Cap swallowed, his throat constricted with a sudden paralyzing dread as he watched his mother coming toward him. She hadn't changed much over the years. And he almost cried within as he realized that it had been years since he had seen her. He had been a boy when she had left. Now he was a man.

"Hello, Mama," he said softly, his voice husky with emotion.

He didn't know what he had expected. She barely acknowledged his greeting as she stood staring into his face. He couldn't know the terror that was coursing through her veins as she was swept back in time to another place, to another man who had stood before her, his handsome face smiling and his voice full of promised love. That love had never found fulfillment. That handsome face and loving smile had hidden a heart consumed with greed, selfishness, and an unquenchable thirst for violence.

As mother and son stood facing each other, both were lost in their own pain while the silence that had followed Cap's greeting remained unbroken. It was only a moment in time, but it seemed an eternity that

Cap looked into the eyes of his mother, searching for something. He searched desperately for even just one tiny hint of acceptance. He had given up hoping for love. All he wanted from her now was acceptance, as her son, as an individual separate from his father.

What he saw in her eyes, in her face, was the emptiness of a heart broken and shattered by the cruelty of the life she had experienced with a man named Jake Martin.

And suddenly, Cap felt a glimmer of understanding. He felt a bond with his mother like no other he had ever before experienced. And suddenly he knew. And he understood. And he felt as if he could almost begin to forgive. In a split second, the face before him gave way to a thousand ugly images as the years he had spent living with his father flashed across his memory. He heard the voice shouting out obscene and brutal threats. He saw the face distorted by anger and rage. He smelled the nauseating odor of stale liquor and unwashed human flesh. He felt the unmerciful pain of pounding fists.

He knew. And he understood.

He looked deep into the flat, lifeless eyes looking up at him, then reached out with a gentle hand and touched the surprisingly smooth cheek of his mother. He flinched only slightly as she turned from his touch, but just for an instant before she turned her back on him, he thought he saw a glimmer of a tear momentarily softening the emptiness of her eyes.

"Supper's ready." Sandy's soft voice broke the quiet. John, Cap, and William all sighed as they watched Pearl turn and walk back into the bedroom, the flimsy door erecting a barricade that could not be broken.

CHAPTER 10

May 1951
Wendell, Idaho

The evening air was soft with the lavender sky of dusk as the lonely street lamps lit up the narrow, two-lane street that ran the length of the small country town. The main road was bisected by an even narrower lane that ran, paved, for three city blocks before turning into a dusty, rutted road.

Two miles outside of town, Lara Straddler sat on a straight-back chair, leaning forward toward the chipped mirror hanging just above her dresser. Her room, though cramped and badly in need of new paint, reflected the quietness of the girl who slept there. She had covered the narrow bed with a quilt, her first sewing project made two years earlier under the watchful eye of her Grandma Straddler. A lacy doily made of delicate white cotton thread held the place of honor in the middle of the scarred dresser top.

The same gentle, hard-working hands that had tied the quilt and spun the lacy cotton thread into a beautiful dresser scarf were deftly applying a minute amount of makeup to a slightly smiling, girlish face. Lara Straddler was going dancing.

Lara was a quiet girl who was comfortable with her self-perception as a plain, uninteresting person. She felt that the only importance she had for her family was in her role as housemaid and cook for her father and her brothers. Her mother directed her activities with the hand of perfection, and she expected Lara to set aside her own wants and needs in order to cater to those of her father and her brothers.

Lily Straddler had spent the past twenty years doing just that for her husband, and she had spent the previous years of her girlhood doing the same for her father. She had been raised to serve the men in her life, and she saw no reason to raise her daughter any differently.

Lara didn't mind the demands on her time. She had learned to quash the girlish dreams of love and romance and adventure. Lara's eyes softened as she thought of her father. Sam Straddler was a good man. Quiet and introspective like his daughter, he understood the faraway look that he would often see in Lara's eyes. He, too, was a dreamer.

And like Lara, he had learned to lay aside his dreams in the face of the reality of his life, a life of hard work, simple pleasures, and a quiet pride in the accomplishments of his family. He felt himself lucky to have four strong sons and a lovely daughter to brighten their home.

Lara knew that her father loved her. Though he was not a demonstrative man, Lara knew that he appreciated all that she did for him. And she knew that he loved and appreciated her mother.

She sometimes wondered why. Her mother, hardworking and dedicated to her family, was also reserved and of the mind that affection did not need to be demonstrated. And sometimes Lara wondered about her mother's love. She quietly accepted the fact that her mother cared about her without really knowing for sure if it was true.

Like her dreams, however, Lara had learned to push aside those questions in the face of the hard work that kept her busy from sunup to sundown. Lara yawned at herself in the mirror as she remembered how the dawn had just barely started to break that morning when she had called her brothers to the breakfast table. And that had just been the beginning of her day.

As Lara prepared herself for the dance that night, she thought back on the rows of onions that she had topped that morning. She gently rubbed some soothing lotion across the sunburned bridge of her small, slightly upturned nose. The backs of her legs were also sunburned, and she wondered briefly if she would be able to dance. Pouting at herself in the mirror, she refused to entertain such a disappointing outcome.

Like her father, Lara took great pleasure in the simple things of life. And the grange dance was one of those rare pleasures. She had been waiting for this dance for months, saving all the spare pennies and nickels that she could find until she had enough money to buy a length of flowered poplin to make a new skirt.

Lara was handy with a needle, and she had spent many hours late at night fashioning her skirt. As she finished applying her lipstick, Lara turned from the mirror and stood up. Lying across the quilted bed in front of her was the new skirt.

She buttoned up the simple white peasant blouse and smoothed a cotton slip over her slim hips. Lara smiled as she looked at the results of her sacrificed hours of sleep. The skirt was cornflower blue with a sprinkling of tiny white flowers. The blue deepened and reflected the blue of her large eyes. With no trace of vanity, she admired the depth of color reflected in her eyes as she held the fabric against her cheek.

It was just a simple piece of clothing, but as she stepped into it and fastened the waistband, she couldn't help but feel pretty and feminine. She spent her days in the company of men, working alongside them in her cutoff jeans and baggy T-shirt. Her brothers teased her unmercifully, and her oldest brother Tom often made fun of her looks.

She believed Tom when he called her ugly. She believed him when he said that her arms and legs were as skinny as sticks and that she had hands and feet like a lumberjack. She believed him when he said that she was the ugly duckling in the family and that they must have found her in the duck pond.

And when she looked at her brothers, she wondered why they were so handsome when she was so plain. All four boys, from Tom, the eldest at nineteen, down to young Matthew age six, were tall and well built, with dark wavy hair, strong chins, and finely sculpted cheekbones. And they had been blessed with the Straddler eyes—large eyes framed with long, curling lashes. Their eyes were so blue that they looked as if a piece of the sky had been stolen to paint them with a bright splash of color.

Usually Lara felt plain and homely, but not tonight, not while she was wearing her new skirt. She finished buttoning the band around her waist and twirled, making the flared skirt swing around her slender calves. Tonight Lara felt pretty.

Looking in the mirror, she saw a slender girl with a delicately curved figure enhanced by the softness of her skirt and blouse. She saw the shiny fall of brown hair the color of autumn leaves lying in soft curls around her face. She saw a delicate chin and a pretty, well-shaped mouth curved into a timid smile. And lastly she saw her eyes, the Straddler eyes, eyes that were large and expressive and as blue as the summer sky, and for tonight, eyes that were sparkling with excitement and anticipation. Slipping on her clean, white canvas shoes, Lara didn't mind that they were a size eight. She looked at her hands that had been cleaned and smoothed with lotion and for once was relieved that they didn't seem so large and out of place.

And with that she turned from the mirror and bounded out the door down the hall. Her mother looked up from her sewing basket as Lara stepped into the front parlor. For a moment, her mother's eyes softened and a hint of a smile touched the corners of her lips as she gazed at her daughter.

Lara saw the look, and in that instant she knew that her mother loved her. The moment passed as Lily turned back to her sewing and said, "The boys are already outside. They're waiting for you." As Lara turned away, her mother said, "Keep an eye on Matthew. He'll be wanting to run around with his friends, and who knows what kind of mischief he may find."

For a moment Lara wondered why she had to be responsible for Matthew. Why couldn't Tom or Luke or Paul keep an eye on him? But as she assured her mother that she would, Lara accepted her role of baby-sitter for young Matthew. It was her job as his sister to watch him. It was an accepted fact in the family that the Straddler men were taken care of by the Straddler women. And for a moment Lara wondered how she and her mother had been stuck with those care-taking roles. She realized, however, that it was probably her mother, Lily, who had established the role in the first place. With a shrug, Lara tossed aside her musings. There was too much to look forward to this evening to waste any time worrying about something that she didn't have the power to change anyway.

The boisterous, teasing voices of her brothers greeted Lara as she ran to join them. Usually she was shy around the boys, especially her oldest brother, Tom. He had a way of making her feel self-conscious and inferior. But tonight his words didn't bother her and she happily climbed into the car, eager for the night's activities to begin.

It only took a few minutes before they reached the large white building on the outskirts of town. The old grange had been built in

1924 and had served the small community well. It was the site for monthly town meetings, and when the old schoolhouse had burned down in 1937, it had served as a classroom for the children of Wendell until the new school could be built. It had housed wedding receptions for some of the more prosperous inhabitants of Wendell, and in 1945 it had been the site of a grand reception welcoming home the remaining contingent of Wendell's contribution to the armed forces. Twelve boys from Lara's hometown had been called to serve their country during World War II. Eight returned for the celebration. A very different homecoming had awaited the four who were buried in Wendell's small cemetery east of town.

And the grange was the most popular choice for the annual dances. The parking lot was already overflowing with cars and pickups, while laughing, chattering groups of men, women, and children crowded into the confines of the grange hall. Many of the men were lounging around outside, smoking and talking, sipping from bottles of cold beer stashed in a cooler behind the building. The young men Lara's age were casually hanging around the main entrance, gawking at the arriving girls. Lara felt self-conscious as she followed her brothers into the building. She kept her eyes downcast as she walked by the boys, trying to ignore their whispered comments followed by loud laughter. She felt herself blushing, unsure of why they were laughing but somehow convinced that she was the object of their mirth.

With a sigh of relief, Lara walked past the last of the boys and quickly called out to Matthew to stay close and inside the grange. She watched as he joined a group of his friends, then turned away with a sigh. Her brothers were getting too old to want to dance with her, and she began to doubt the wisdom of coming tonight. She was shy and reserved. She hadn't dated much during high school, and even though she had grown up with brothers, she was still self-conscious around boys.

The music was wonderful, though, and she felt her toes begin to tap in time to the lively tune. Her heart raced at the anticipation of being swept around the dance floor. She loved to dance, a product of her family who also loved music and dancing. Their family gatherings often included aunts, uncles, and cousins who played fiddles, guitars, and banjos. And she had grown up learning to dance from the time she could walk. As the music swept over her, she became impatient with her desire to move in time with it.

Lara looked around the room, trying to identify a friendly face, wondering if she would be able to work up the courage to ask someone to dance with her. It was almost unheard of for a girl to ask a boy to dance, but Lara's urge to swing and move to the music was almost overwhelming. The dance floor was crowded with laughing couples engrossed in the music and in each other. Lara's gaze then swept the sidelines, where other girls stood hopefully scanning the crowds. Loud, rambunctious laughter caught her attention, and as she followed the sound with her eyes she gulped, knowing that she would never be able to approach the groups of men and boys loitering in the corners and near the doors of the large hall.

Disappointed, Lara felt her spirits begin to plummet as she once again turned back toward the crowded dance floor. As she did so, her eyes caught on the lone figure of a slim, strongly built young man. His dark hair and complexion made him stand out in the room. He looked out of place, and yet there was something that drew her toward him.

He was young, probably only a year older than Lara, but there was an air of maturity about him. Even from across the room, Lara could sense a level of wisdom that usually only came after a lifetime of trials and experience. She felt her heart begin to beat more rapidly, and her breathing quickened as she realized that he was watching her. She suddenly felt shy and awkward under the warm scrutiny of the unknown young man. Lara felt warmth flood her cheeks as she tore her gaze away from his and lowered her eyes.

A feeling of inevitability forced Lara to raise her eyes, to meet the steady gaze of the strange young man. She found herself sending a shy smile in the direction of the boy. Her face glowed with wonder and excitement as he smiled back at her, his lips curving into a devastating grin, creasing his cheeks with deep dimples. Lara felt compelled to move forward and had to resist the impulse, instead willing herself to remain standing still. She suddenly felt unsure and frightened as she saw him push himself away from the wall. Lara then realized that he was moving. He was walking forward, and he was headed in her direction.

CHAPTER 11

Cap noticed Lara the moment she walked into the grange. Her shining chestnut hair gleamed in the dim lighting, and the delicacy of her features attracted him immediately. He could tell that she was shy when she waved to her brothers as they moved off. He could tell they were her brothers, for they shared the same rich brown hair, the same fine-boned facial structure, and the same eyes.

Her eyes. Cap could tell from across the room that they were large and expressive. He watched her as she slowly turned, scoping out the room, and he recognized the bashful awkwardness that she felt from finding herself alone in the large crowd of dancing couples. The sway of her body told him that she was listening and responding to the lively music. She had the body and the grace of a dancer, and he wondered to himself how it would feel to hold her in his arms.

Cap found it impossible to tear his gaze away from her lovely face. He wanted to meet her, and yet he didn't want to interrupt this time he had to quietly observe her. She was so beautiful. He just wanted to take a few more minutes to memorize her face and the graceful moves of her body.

With a start Cap realized that she was returning his gaze. He felt his own cheeks flush with embarrassment. He had been caught staring at her, and he felt the warmth of mutual awareness staining his face crimson. Cap took a deep, stabilizing breath, trying to quell the sudden pounding of his heart. He smiled to himself as he saw the confused blush slowly spread across the smooth curves of her cheeks. Her eyes were blue, an unbelievably deep blue, fringed with long, thick lashes. Cap was intrigued as she timidly lowered her lashes, confusion and self-consciousness evident in the suddenly awkward shifting of her slight shoulders.

Cap watched, captivated, as she slowly raised her eyes and once again met his gaze across the room. A sense of coming home descended on Cap as a slow smile warmed her features and brightened the look in her eyes. He felt his own lips curve into an answering smile, and Cap knew that the time had come.

Using his arms to push himself away from the wall, Cap moved determinedly across the dance floor, dodging the dancers who clogged his path. Not once did he look away from the waiting girl. Time seemed endless before he reached her.

And as he looked into Lara's eyes, Cap felt like he was facing a miracle. He felt the dark, empty void of loneliness filling as he faced this lovely young stranger. And he didn't even know her name.

Smiling, his handsome face reflecting the warmth of his feelings, Cap reached out with his right hand and said, "Cap Martin."

"Lara Straddler," she replied, placing her hand in Cap's warm, firm grasp.

Cap and Lara stood with their hands linked for several seconds, gazing into each other's eyes, and Lara felt the same sense of wonder that had filled Cap's soul the moment he had seen her enter the dance hall. They both knew that they had found something wondrous that night, and as they stood together, a bond began to form, and Lara's smile grew bright, no longer shy and retiring.

Cap said, "Let's dance." He reached for her and turned her into his arms, marveling at how delicate she felt. No words were spoken as they began to sway in time to the music. The previous toe-tapping jig had ended, and in its place the strains of a lilting waltz floated to the rafters of the open-beamed dance hall. Cap puzzled over what he was feeling. Holding Lara in his arms felt so right.

He didn't know this girl dancing in his arms.

And yet he felt he had known her forever.

They remained silent as they swayed in time to the music, their feet barely moving. It was a magical moment, and neither wanted to break the spell that held them firmly. When the song ended, they came to a stop, surrounded by the other dancers, yet isolated in a world that belonged only to the two of them. Cap kept his arms around Lara, her right hand nestled in his, resting against his left shoulder.

Lara stirred in his arms, and he felt her take a deep breath before she pulled away. Her step back was slow and hesitant, as if she, too, had found a haven, a safe place that bid her welcome home. A place she was reluctant to leave.

Cap's hands fell slowly to his side as she stepped away, and he drew a deep breath, missing the warmth and the completeness he had felt holding her in his arms.

"Would you like to take a walk outside, Lara?"

Cap's question was a welcome invitation. Lara smiled broadly and nodded. Taking her hand in his, Cap led her through the crowd and out into the night.

As they walked, Cap asked Lara questions about herself, his voice warm and inviting. She found herself telling him things that even her family didn't know. They talked about her dreams and her goals for the future. Lara felt as if she had found her best friend, and as they walked under the starry night sky, she opened her heart to Cap.

They found an old fence with broken timbers that fell into a crisscrossing pile, forming a wooden bench. Cap tested it with his weight and, finding it sturdy, offered Lara a seat. She smoothed her skirt as she sat down, scooting over to make room for Cap. The bench was narrow, but allowed them to sit closely and comfortably. Lara's trust in Cap allowed her the freedom of leaning in to him, safe in the knowledge that he wouldn't hurt her or take advantage of her vulnerability.

And she was vulnerable. Never in her life had she felt this sense of connection to another human being. And it had happened so quickly. And had come so unexpectedly.

Cap felt Lara's sensitivity, and he sensed the trust she seemed to place in him so unquestioningly. He vowed that he would do nothing to violate that trust or to hurt her. If he were honest with himself, he would acknowledge that he, too, was vulnerable as he gave Lara his heart.

And as Lara began to ask him questions and encouraged him to talk about himself, Cap found it easier than he had thought to open himself up to her, to tell her about his family and the loneliness he had felt over the years. He told her of his plans for the future and the career he hoped to find in the military.

The hours passed, but the young couple was unaware of time. They sat together on the old broken plank, their hearts and souls communicating in a way they never had before.

Lara became chilled and shivered slightly. Cap, sitting so closely beside her, felt the shiver and put his arms around her. "We should be heading back in. I don't know what time it is."

"I don't know either, but I don't want to go in. At least not yet."

"But you're cold."

"I'll be okay, Cap." Lara snuggled in closer against his side, and Cap tightened his hold on her. "I just don't want this night to end."

"Neither do I, Lara. Won't your family be wondering where you are?"

Lara thought for a moment about the charge that she had been given to watch over Matthew. She grimaced and silently hoped that he had behaved himself. Looking across the dark expanse of the field that separated them from the grange, Lara noticed that the lights were still burning brightly even though the parking lot was emptying of the cars that had jammed its boundaries earlier that evening.

"It looks like the dance is ending."

"Will your brothers be waiting for you?"

"Probably." Lara grinned naughtily. "I don't really care, though. They can wait."

Cap chuckled as he turned Lara toward him. "You know what?"

Lara looked into his eyes, answering his question with a smile.

"I came down here to see my family, to tell them good-bye, never expecting to meet someone like you." Cap suddenly became serious. "I don't want to go now."

"I don't want you to go, either." Lara's eyes filled with tears. "How long do you have?"

"I have to report to basic training in three weeks." As Lara's tears trickled down her cheeks, Cap whispered, "Oh, honey, don't cry. We'll make the most of the next three weeks. You just see if we don't."

Lara smiled and nodded behind her tears, unable to find her voice to answer him.

"Oh, babe." Cap could control himself no longer. He crushed Lara against his chest, wrapping his arms around her, caressing her back as he held her close. His face rested warmly against Lara's cheek and with a shy gasp, she turned her face to meet Cap's searching lips.

The stars overhead twinkled and smiled down on the young lovers as their kiss deepened, symbolizing the love they had discovered so suddenly. Lara returned Cap's kiss, and Cap sighed as he slowly pulled away. Cupping her face with both his hands, Cap caressed her cheeks with gentle fingers.

Lara's eyes glowed as she gazed at him, her heart drinking in the sight of his handsome face and the love she saw reflected there.

"We gotta go, babe."

"Oh no, Cap. Not yet."

"Now." Without another word, Cap arose and grasped Lara's hand. He pulled her to her feet, and together they strolled through the moonlit night. A few moments later, they reached the edge of the darkened parking lot. It was almost empty, but Lara recognized her folks' car among the few remaining.

"Cap?" Pulling on his hand, Lara stopped. "I don't want my brothers to know that we've been together."

Cap looked puzzled and slightly hurt. Lara continued, "Please try to understand. I want them to meet you, just not tonight. They'll tease me and give me a hard time. And I don't want that. I want to remember tonight just as it is. I don't want to have to put up with their comments, especially from Tom, my oldest brother. He can be kind of crude and I don't want him to spoil everything that has happened tonight."

Cap smiled understandingly, and with a gentle touch reached up and pushed a tendril of hair off her face. "I understand. Can I come by tomorrow?"

"Oh yes, please!" Lara's smile lit her face. Tenderly she reached up and touched Cap's cheek. With gentle pressure she urged his face downward. Their final kiss lasted only a moment, but filled them both with the promise of eternity.

"I'll see you tomorrow."

"G'night, babe."

"G'night, Cap."

Lara left Cap standing in the darkened shadow of one of the outbuildings. Circling around, she entered the parking lot from the street side, a lone streetlamp lighting her approach.

Luke, who had been posted outside to watch for her, saw her coming. "Where've you been, sis? We've been looking all over for you."

"I'm sorry, Luke. I got hot and went for a walk. Is it late?"

"Not too bad, but everyone's just about gone. Tom's inside with Matthew. He's crashed. He fell asleep about twenty minutes ago."

"We'd better get him home then."

As Lara and her brothers loaded into the family car, she was silent, her head filled with the delightful memories of that night. Her brothers were oblivious to the blush on her cheeks and the sparkle in her eyes. They were never interested in her activities, though, so it didn't surprise her that they didn't try to question her or probe her for information about her evening.

The next day, Cap stopped by to visit and to meet Lily and Sam. And two weeks later, having spent every spare moment they could with each other, Cap and Lara stood before the justice of the peace, families gathered close as they exchanged wedding vows and became husband and wife.

Gazing into his new wife's upturned face and kissing her sweet lips, Cap was able to lay aside the ache in his heart caused by the sight of William standing alone beside Sandy and John. The absence of his mother no longer seemed to matter. All that mattered was the love he felt for the woman standing by his side. For the first time in his life, Cap felt complete. He knew that he had found something very precious, and as he made Lara his wife, he knew that whatever hurt he felt from his mother's continuing rejection would not be able to touch him in quite the same way or to such a devastating degree. He knew that with Lara by his side, he would be able to face whatever the future held.

CHAPTER 12

"Seek and ye shall find . . ."

February 1954
Guam, U.S. Territory

The sand felt warm on her bare toes as Lara Martin walked along
the curving crest of beach. She smiled as the foaming waves washed
over her feet, deliciously cool and refreshing. The hot, tropical air at
times left her feeling limp and washed out. And she felt so very tired.

But she didn't mind any of it. After almost two years of continual
separation from her husband, she was happy to be where she was—far
from her girlhood home in Idaho but only five minutes away from
the small apartment she shared with Cap. The housing provided for
the enlisted men and their families on the military base was small and
shabby, but the love Lara and Cap shared made it a home.

After their wedding, they'd had one week of glorious togetherness
before Cap had left to embark on his career in the United States
Navy. He had joined the Seabees, and for the first eighteen months of
their marriage, he and Lara had only been together for a week or two
at a time. The sporadic visits were joyful, full of loving and laughter
and warmth. For both of them, though, the leaving was tearful and
painful, and the absences long and lonely.

But those distressful, lonely times were gone, at least for the
present. When Cap had received his current orders, he had called Lara
on the phone, his news exciting and full of promise. By the time he
finished, they were both laughing because they knew that for the next

year they would be together. Cap was being stationed on Guam, a small island in the South Pacific, and Lara was going to accompany him.

And after hearing Cap's good news, Lara knew the time was right to share her own piece of good news.

"A baby!" Cap had whispered, his voice cracking with emotion. "Oh, honey!"

Lara had smiled, and with a lump of pure joy lodging in her throat, needed no other confirmation of Cap's feelings. He was as excited as she was about having a baby.

That had been six months ago. And now Lara walked along the beach, letting the warm Pacific water soothe her aching feet as she gently cradled her swollen stomach, savoring the feeling of the baby moving inside of her. She was excited at the prospect of motherhood, and she felt a natural affinity for the baby being nurtured in her womb.

Part of Lara was afraid of the responsibility of raising a child. Lara's fear, however, was offset by the deeply embedded trust she had for Cap and his love for her. She knew that his love was great enough to encompass this baby and any other children with which they might be blessed. They had talked about having many children, and both felt an overwhelming desire to share their home and their hearts with the offspring of their love.

As the sun slowly sank behind the backdrop of the horizon, covering the ocean's expanse with the soft cloak of evening, Lara felt the tiny child nestle in her womb, and she sighed in content.

CHAPTER 13

April 1954
Guam, U.S. Territory

"A baby girl?" Cap whispered, his voice hoarse with emotion. "Lara? How is she? And the baby . . .?"

"They're both fine, Mr. Martin," the smiling nurse responded. "Mrs. Martin is tired, but she's fine."

"When can I see them?"

"You can go in now if you'd like."

Cap followed the nurse down the white, sterile halls of the military hospital, oblivious to the sights, sounds, and smells of the busy corridor. The nurse paused before a closed door, gently tapping on it. After a moment she pushed the door open and motioned for Cap to precede her.

As the door swung shut behind him, Cap quietly approached the single bed by the window. Lara lay very still, her face pale with fatigue. Cap stopped at the side of her bed and looked down at her. He felt his heart swell with love. She looked so small and so young, and so utterly beautiful. With a gentle hand, he reached out and pushed a stray lock of soft, chestnut-brown hair out of her face.

Lara felt his loving touch and opened her eyes. Without a word, she smiled at him, and he knelt beside the bed and took her in his arms, cradling her with all of the love and tenderness that filled his heart. She was such a gift to him. She had brought warmth and love and acceptance into his life, and she had given him a child. He vowed to himself that he would never subject his own child to the loneliness and heartache and fear that he himself had known.

Lara, her voice tired but reflecting the love she had for her husband, asked, "Have you seen her yet?"

"No, I wanted to see you first."

"Oh, Cap, she's beautiful. You should see all of the dark hair, and she's so tiny." Lara's voice shook with the joy and the wonder of having just become a new mother. Tears cascaded down her pale cheeks as she smiled up at her husband, the love of her life, the father of her daughter.

Cap leaned forward and kissed her tears away, following their path across her soft cheeks until he came to the corner of her smiling lips. He looked deep into her eyes, his love and devotion shining in the warm depths of his gaze as he whispered, "I love you so very much!" With tenderness, he kissed her sweet mouth.

He stood and his smile grew as the middle-aged nurse came through the door, cradling a small, pink bundle in her arms. Cap felt his hands tremble as the nurse stopped beside the bed and gently placed the bundle in Lara's outstretched arms.

Lara and Cap were oblivious to the nurse as she left. They had eyes only for the tiny baby girl who lay quietly in Lara's embrace. Cap reached down and pushed aside the edge of the blanket and, for the first time, looked upon the tiny, perfect features of his daughter.

"Oh, honey."

Lara smiled and her eyes sparkled as she watched Cap's face. Without a word, she held out her arms and watched as he reached for the baby. She seemed even tinier as Cap held her to his broad chest. The baby uttered a soft mewing noise, and they both smiled as she raised her fist to her mouth and found her thumb. The perfectly formed rosebud lips closed contentedly around the wee appendage.

Lara and Cap both watched the satisfied look on their daughter's face as she happily sucked her thumb. Lara scooted up in the bed. She took the baby from Cap and laid her on her own lap. Then she patted the side of the bed and moved over for Cap to sit beside her. Together they spent the next half hour cooing over the baby, talking to her, laughing, and sharing the wonder of their daughter. Lara teased Cap as he counted each tiny finger and toe, and Cap laughed at Lara when she wrinkled up her nose as she changed the baby's diaper for the first time.

The warmth of their happiness wrapped the small family in a cloak of love as they spent their first hours together as father, mother, and daughter. And later, while the baby lay sleeping in Lara's arms, replete and content after having been fed, Cap lay stretched out on the bed beside Lara, holding his two girls in his embrace. He knew he would have to leave soon, and the thought brought a slight ache to his chest. With a groan, he rolled off the bed and leaned down to kiss the downy-soft head of his daughter before gently capturing a kiss from his sleepy wife.

"I love you, honey."

"I love you too, Cap."

"I'll stop by in the morning on my way to work."

Lara smiled sleepily at him and murmured her good-bye as Cap turned and left the room. A moment later, the nurse walked through the door and removed the slumbering baby from Lara's arms. She encouraged Lara to get some rest and left with the baby.

As Lara drifted off, she couldn't remember having ever felt so complete, so fulfilled. With a groan she turned on her side. She couldn't remember having ever felt so tired! But the fatigue was worth the happiness, she thought as a smile touched her lips in sleep. She knew that her baby girl and her husband's love would greet her with the morning's sun.

* * *

"Mrs. Martin, please wake up. Mrs. Martin."

Lara stirred as the nurse gently shook her by the arm, and she slowly opened her eyes in confusion. Her body ached, and even though it was dark, she could tell she was in a strange place. Her hands went automatically to her stomach, and as she felt its tender, slightly swollen surface, she remembered where she was, and she smiled in anticipation. It must be time to feed the baby.

She sat up, and as the nurse turned on the overhead light, Lara looked into the anxious eyes of the woman standing by her bed. Suddenly Lara felt frightened. She couldn't explain why, but there was something about the look in the nurse's eyes. Her face was calm and her voice quiet, but her eyes were sad. Lara felt fear take hold as the nurse said, "Mrs. Martin, I'm so sorry to have to tell you this, but your baby isn't doing well."

Lara groped for the nurse's hand and said, "I don't understand. She was fine just a short time ago." Looking at the clock on the wall opposite her bed, Lara said, "She was fine just two hours ago. What happened?"

The nurse, Mrs. Carlisle, returned the pressure of Lara's grip and said, "The doctors aren't sure exactly, but they think it's her heart."

"Cap!" Lara whispered. "I've got to call Cap."

"Your husband is on his way, Mrs. Martin. He'll be here soon."

Lara looked stunned, and as she climbed out of bed and reached for her robe, she felt weak and frail, unable to face what was happening. For a moment she felt unable to move, unable to think or feel. Her baby was sick. She might die. They hadn't even given the baby a name yet.

With a sob, Lara buried her face in her hands, unaware of the physical pain and discomfort that arose from moving around so soon after giving birth. All she felt was the anguish and the fear and the sorrow that the nurse's announcement had brought.

Desperately trying to pull herself together, Lara lowered her hands and looked at the nurse. "I want to see her. Please take me to her."

Without arguing, the nurse led the way. The walk to the nursery wasn't far, and as they approached the glass-enclosed cubicle, Lara could see that it was empty.

Their baby's empty incubator was the only one in the sterile surroundings of the nursery, and the sight of it pierced Lara's already-bleeding heart. With her fear lodged in her throat, Lara followed Mrs. Carlisle down the hall and through a set of double doors. Behind the doors, Lara could see a gleaming metal table surrounded by men and women scurrying around, dressed in green scrubs. A confusing assortment of tubes, wires, and equipment made Lara shiver as she drew closer and saw the tiny body of her daughter in the middle of the medical maze. She dropped into the chair that had been hastily pushed to the side of the table, her whole body shaking uncontrollably.

Lara could see the bluish pallor of her tiny daughter's face. The baby had patches attached to her chest, and IV needles pierced her delicate flesh. Lara felt warm tears sliding down her face as she reached a shaking hand out to her baby. The baby's skin was as cold as it was blue, and Lara ached for her as she watched the tiny infant struggling for breath. Lara could see the baby's chest rise and fall as the little body tried to compensate for the lack of oxygen. Lara could also see the veins in the baby's neck pulsing as her heart worked overtime to pump the life-giving blood through her body.

Lara looked into the face of the doctor standing opposite her, and her eyes pled for an answer. She wanted to hear him say that it was a mistake, that the baby was going to be fine. But as she looked into his face, she saw her answer in the weary, saddened shake of his head.

Lara was about to ask him the first of a thousand questions when the double doors opened once more and she turned to see Cap, his face mirroring her anxiety and her fear. His hair was rumpled and uncombed, and he was dressed in gray sweatpants and an old T-shirt. With tears streaming down her cheeks, she reached for him, and he walked across the room, taking her outstretched hand. He had eyes only for the baby girl, and as he searched for the tiny form, he saw what his wife had seen. And he knew what Lara knew.

With a cry of despair, he dropped to his knees and buried his head in Lara's lap. Lara wrapped her arms around him and leaned over him, trying to surround him with her love, knowing that it was futile to try to slow the flood of grief.

The only sound was their muffled sobs. The room slowly emptied except for the doctor, the grieving couple, and the tiny body of the dying infant.

Cap lifted his head, and as unexpected darts of anger lit his brown eyes, he drew in a shuddering breath. "Why aren't you doing something?" He rose from his knees, his voice quiet and controlled, masking the anger and the fear and the despair.

His question, fired at the silent doctor, stabbed Lara's heart as she realized that she hadn't thought to ask. She had unquestioningly accepted the fate of her daughter, and she felt a pang of guilt for having given her daughter up to death without a fight. She swallowed the lump of guilt as she, along with Cap, waited for the doctor's answer.

When it came, it brought no hope. His explanation was filled with medical terminology that left Lara and Cap with a sense of deepened hopelessness. Despite his professional bearing and the proficient explanation, both Lara and Cap were able to read beyond the words and the demeanor, and they could sense the doctor's hopelessness as he turned away from their dying daughter.

As he reached the doors, he said over his shoulder, "You need this time alone with her. I'm sorry."

In the quiet of the small room, Cap and Lara froze, caught in the middle of a horrendous nightmare. It was inconceivable that the tiny, warm body of the baby they had both recently held was now lying still and cold on the metal examining table, wrapped in warming blankets that had no impact on her condition.

Slowly, Lara reached out a hand and began to remove the patches from off the baby's chest. Cap gathered up the blanket and its tiny contents. He wrapped the soft material tightly around the frail body and gently picked her up, careful not to pull out the IV needle.

Lara stood and placed her arm around Cap's waist as she leaned against him, wrapping her other arm around the bundle in Cap's arms. As she and Cap wept their good-byes, Lara murmured, "Christine Marie."

Cap nodded his head, agreeing with the name that Lara had given their daughter. And as Christine drew her last breath, he cried.

CHAPTER 14

The next two days passed in a blur of painful activity for Cap and Lara. The medical inquest proved that the doctor had been right. Christine Marie was found to have an inoperable heart defect.

The military base on Guam wasn't designed for the interment of deceased loved ones, so Cap and Lara had the heartbreaking task of arranging for their daughter to be buried elsewhere, knowing that they would be unable to accompany her to wherever that was. Arrangements were made to ship the little body home to Idaho, and it was with numbness born of sorrow and grief that Lara and Cap stood on the dock and watched as their daughter, Christine Marie, was taken away from them.

Lara turned into Cap's embrace and sobbed as if she would never stop. "I can't bear it, Cap. I just can't bear it."

Cap swallowed his own grief as he pulled her close and offered his body and his strength for her to lean on. He knew Lara's pain. They had made the painful choice not to go with her because of the difficult financial circumstances they faced. The funeral costs and the travel costs to accompany Christine home were simply too much—it wasn't a choice. They could only do one. As Cap held his grieving wife, his shirt sodden with her tears, his own sorrow welled in his eyes, and he wondered if the emotional cost of not going with her would prove too great.

So they sent her home alone, and could only pray that their families would receive Christine with enough love to span the miles of the great ocean, that their support would be strong enough to bridge the distance of separation. Cap was grateful that Lara's parents had responded so quickly to their devastating news. He hadn't had any response at all from his mother, yet he didn't dwell on the pain that Pearl's apparent indifference had caused. It just didn't seem to matter in light of the earth-shattering experience he and Lara had shared in the death of their baby.

He hurt for Lara. And he felt so inadequate because he knew there was nothing he could do to protect her from the devastating pain.

As they stood and watched the ship vanish on the horizon, they said one final farewell to Christine Marie, and they knew that their lives would never be the same again. She had been with them such a short period of time, but she had touched their hearts and had brought them joy.

Lara lifted her face away from Cap's damp shirtfront and shielded her eyes as she gazed at the far horizon. She and Cap were wrapped in each other's arms, in the seemingly inadequate cloak of their mutual love and grief. As they stood watching the ship slowly fade into the distance, a light breeze ruffled their hair, and their eyes were drawn upward as the ship and the ocean and the sky merged in the far distance.

The sun was setting low on the sky's horizon, its golden light filtered through a bank of voluminous clouds. Cap and Lara watched as a split in the clouds opened the windows of heaven, sending down a dozen silvery rays, highlighting the ship's disappearance with a beautiful, iridescent fan of light.

"The fingers of God." Cap looked at Lara as she spoke, and then she continued, "I remember hearing someone describe the sun's rays shining through the clouds as the fingers of God."

The beauty of the sky, the clouds, and God's light brought a glimmer of peace to their aching hearts as tears streamed from their eyes. Neither Lara nor Cap was religious, but somehow they felt that God had spoken to them, and they felt a measure of comfort tempering their grief. Lara knew that she would remember the light that had surrounded the ship bearing their daughter home.

While Cap and Lara dealt with their grief, thousands of miles away Pearl Martin Aldrich sat in the darkness of her home. The curtains were tightly drawn against any light that might encroach on the shadows of her unlit house. Pearl sat silent and unmoving, the telegram informing her of her first granddaughter's birth and death lying crumpled in her lap. The gloominess of the house mirrored the darkness in her heart. William sat beside her, his eyes sad as he attempted to comfort his wife.

Pearl's icy demeanor deflected the warmth of his concern as she masked the anguish in her heart with the cloak of indifference that had shrouded her feelings for so many years. The sudden storm of sadness that had engulfed her as she read the words of the telegram had shaken her with the intensity of her feelings. The welling of grief had come as an unpleasant and unwelcome sensation to her hardened heart. She had fought back the feelings, determined not to give in to the weakness racking her composure. Pearl ignored William, knowing that if she were to acknowledge the glistening sadness in his eyes, she would be risking the total breakdown of her emotional shell. And she wasn't willing to take that risk. She couldn't.

So she sat, silent and cold, the only sign of her grief being the crumpled and torn paper lying in her lap.

CHAPTER 15

December 1956
San Diego, California

Lara Martin stretched lazily as she slowly came awake. Cap lay beside her, his face youthful and relaxed in sleep. He had come home the night before, tired but excited. This would be his first Christmas home since the girls had been born. He had missed Lisa's first Christmas last year. She had been seven months old, and even though Lara had sent him pictures, he still felt the loss of having missed such a memory.

Lisa had been born the year after Christine Marie. Cap and Lara had both faced the advent of her birth with a mixture of hopeful joy and fear. After Christine's death, they had both decided that they wouldn't wait to try for another baby, and were pleasantly surprised when Lara quickly became pregnant with Lisa. They had been transferred from Guam to San Diego, California, just before Lara's due date in May 1955.

Cap had been present for her birth, grateful for the modern medical facility at San Diego's community hospital. Unlike Christine, Lisa had quickly blossomed with health and vigor. She had been a good baby, cheerful and friendly. She rarely cried, even when hungry or tired. She would simply fall asleep, waiting patiently for food while filling her other need for rest.

In October 1955 Cap had been transferred overseas to Korea for an eight-month tour of duty. He had turned twenty-one the September before his departure, and even though he was so young, he had already lived a lifetime of tragedy and heartache. But he had left his family hopeful for the future. He knew as he boarded the ship that would carry him so far away that he would miss them terribly. He also knew that his absence would be difficult for Lara as she struggled with managing their small apartment, paying their bills, and raising their daughter. But he knew Lara had an inner core that was strong and vital. She had already proven herself, just as Cap had proven himself a survivor. As he had left his family, Cap had turned and waved at Lara, standing bravely alone on the dock, holding Lisa in her arms.

She and Lisa had worn matching dresses of floral cotton calico. Lara's dark hair gleamed richly in the morning sun, and Lisa's cap of short, curly hair reflected the chestnut tint of her mother's, her eyes already a dark, chocolate brown. Cap had smiled, emotion choking his throat as he gazed at his wife and daughter, knowing that he would firmly cement that picture in his memory. It was a picture that he had carried with him during the eight-month tour of duty to Korea.

Even though he had left them confident in Lara's abilities to cope and to manage during his absence, he had been worried about one thing— Lara's pregnancy with their third child. Yet to his relief, the pregnancy had been normal. The new baby had been born the following May, one month before his return to stateside duty in San Diego.

As Lara awakened on Christmas morning of 1956, she knew that it was probably the last Christmas morning that they would be allowed to sleep in. Lisa was barely eighteen months old, and Rachel was seven months old. By Christmas the next year, Lisa would be old enough to feel the pre-Christmas excitement and anticipation and would probably be awake before the sun. Lara reached over with a gentle hand and brushed a lock of hair off Cap's forehead. The warmth of her touch penetrated his haze of sleep when she replaced the stroke of her fingers with the caress of her lips.

Cap reached for her with a smile on his face, pulling her close and savoring the reality that he was home on this special day. Several minutes later, they both slid from the bed, hair rumpled from sleep, their eyes reflecting the light of the love they shared.

With a grin, Cap said, "I'll bet those babies are wide awake!" And as he sprinted through the door into the hallway of their small trailer, he said, "If not, they will be soon!"

"Cap Martin!" Lara squealed as she chased after him. "Don't you wake those babies up. We've got all morning!"

"I've waited too many days for this, Lara Bell."

Lara grinned at his use of the pet name and came to a skidding stop inside the doorway of the small room the two babies shared. Her grin turned to laughter when she watched her husband bend over the crib of their second daughter as he tickled her awake. Lisa's eyes popped open, a startled squeak of surprise turning quickly to giggles as she caught hold of her daddy's hand and he tickled her under the chin.

Cap's heart melted when his little girl's innocent, laughing face beamed up at him, her arms reaching up to him. He picked her up and held her close, breathing in the sweet smell of powder and lotion that lingered from her bedtime bath the night before. As Lisa's giggles quieted, she snuggled in Cap's arms and laid her head on his shoulder. His large hand gently stroked the downy softness of her brown curls as he held her close.

Cap turned from Lisa's bed and watched Lara reach down and pick up Rachel. He was awestruck by the feelings of wonderment and overwhelming love that flooded his entire being as he stood there, holding one daughter in his arms, watching his beautiful wife gently cradle their third daughter. He felt a poignant tug on his heart as he remembered Christine Marie. She should be there with them, toddling around on the floor, excitedly anticipating the hidden treasures lying under the gaily decorated Christmas tree. He silently whispered an "I love you, Christine" while Lisa stirred and stretched in his arms.

Lara was smiling down into the delicate face of her youngest child, amazed at the fair, exquisite prettiness of the baby. Lisa was already showing the dramatic, dark good looks of her father, his Native American heritage evident in the dark coloring and striking bone structure of her face. The soft roundness of her baby years would soon give way to the softness of girlhood, and Lara knew that Lisa was going to be a strikingly beautiful girl.

Rachel's fairness was a contrast to Lisa's complexion, reflecting the distant Scandinavian ancestry of the Straddler family. Lara often thought of Christine, wondering if she would have been dark like Lisa, fair like Rachel, or somewhere in between. Lara enjoyed the feelings of awe that her children evoked in her heart, and as Rachel opened her sleepy, blue eyes, Lara smiled tenderly at the baby in her arms.

Rachel was different from Lisa in many ways other than her looks. While Lisa was warm, friendly, and outgoing, Rachel was very quiet and shy, smiling happily at those familiar to her, but wary of strange faces. She had taken several days to warm up to Cap, but he had been patient with her, sitting next to Lara on the small couch as she fed the baby or standing next to her at the kitchen sink during bath time. Occasionally he would reach out and touch her hair or hold her hand while Lara was close. And this Christmas morning, as the small family stood by the Christmas tree, Rachel came fully awake in Lara's arms and fastened her blue-eyed gaze on Cap's face while he stood nearby, holding Lisa.

He noticed her attention and flashed her a gentle smile as he reached out to stroke her soft cheek. "Happy Christmas, my little bugaboo." His breath caught in his throat when her serious gaze suddenly lit up with a happy, toothless grin. She wiggled in Lara's arms and waved her hands at Cap.

"I think she wants her daddy," Lara said, her eyes shining brightly as the baby responded so warmly to Cap.

Carefully setting Lisa on the floor, gently swatting her padded behind, he straightened up and took a step toward Lara and Rachel. He reached out and took his youngest daughter, surprised at her lightness. As Lara shepherded Lisa to the presents under the tree, Cap tickled and played with the baby in his arms, knowing that she had just given him the best present ever. Her trust and affection were all that he needed to complete the scene of his family gathered around the tree.

He sat down on the floor next to Lara, and together they supervised the girls and the presents. Lisa had great fun ripping the paper off each package set before her, and she giggled and squealed as Lara helped her with the difficult patches of tape. Rachel seemed more interested in the paper itself, and happily sat between Cap's legs as she eagerly crumpled pieces of torn wrapping paper, chewing and tasting each one that came within reach.

Lara and Cap laughed, their joy complete. As the mound of wrapped presents dwindled, they shared intimate looks and reveled in the cozy happiness of their family's first Christmas together. Cap couldn't help but anticipate the next year, knowing that their numbers would increase by one as he reached over and laid a caressing hand on the gentle bulge barely noticeable under Lara's cotton nightgown.

"How are you feeling, babe?" he asked with concern. He didn't want her getting too tired. He knew that pregnancy made her feel fatigued and that she had problems with her back and legs during the latter months. He felt a twinge of guilt, thinking that they should have taken it slower, perhaps waited awhile before getting pregnant again. Lara wanted a large family, though, and had happily received the news regarding their fourth child.

"I'm doing good. How about you?" Lara knew that Cap was concerned, and even though she wearied more easily than before, she felt fine, and she smiled at him, hoping to ease his concerns.

Leaning across Lisa, who had wedged herself between her parents, and careful not to kick Rachel, who had toppled over onto her side in front of his legs, Cap cupped the back of Lara's head with his hand. He pulled her toward him and kissed her with all the tenderness that he could express. Despite the circumstances, with two babies and a mountain of toys between them, their shared love was very effectively communicated. Lara started to smile as Cap's lips teased hers, and they broke apart, laughing as Lisa climbed between their intertwined arms. They were sitting unbalanced, and her added weight sent them tumbling to the floor. Cap scooped Rachel into his arms, and the four of them lay on the floor, laughing and tickling and loving each other amidst the clutter and the glitter of their Christmas morning.

Later that day with both girls bedded down for a much-needed nap, Cap and Lara sat nestled together on the couch. They had enjoyed a simple, quiet dinner, and were relishing a few minutes of peaceful togetherness.

"Let's call our folks, Cap."

"Sounds good to me. Do you want to go first?"

Lara responded to Cap's invitation by sitting up and stretching her arms overhead. She grinned as she reached across him and picked up the telephone, stringing the phone cord across his chest as she settled back against the couch. She giggled as he tickled her side, and quickly kissed his cheek as he nuzzled the side of her neck.

"Behave yourself, young man. What would my daddy say if he knew you were smooching his daughter?"

Lara didn't catch Cap's laughing reply, as the ringing at the other end of the phone line was interrupted and she heard the happy voice of her youngest brother, Matthew.

"Hi, kiddo. Merry Christmas!"

"Lara! Hi! Guess what I got from Mom and Dad?" Lara smiled as eleven-year-old Matthew eagerly told her about the BB gun he had received from their parents. At the end of his animated narrative, Lara asked to speak to her dad.

Sam, always loving and warm, quizzed her eagerly about the girls and filled her in on recent family events, including the birth of her eldest brother's third child, a boy. Her father's voice was filled with laughter as he related some of Matthew's adventures with the BB gun. Lara smiled because she knew that even though he was precocious and spoiled, Matthew was a good boy. He was a handful for her aging parents, who'd been surprised by his coming, but they loved him deeply and cherished his youthful antics.

Lara talked to her mother, surprised by the lilting warmth she heard in Lily Straddler's voice as she asked about the girls and thanked Lara for the recent pictures of her granddaughters. Lara realized that somehow adulthood had brought her onto a plane familiar to her parents, a point that allowed the doors of communication and affection to open wider. Lara felt tenderness as she and her mom whispered their good-byes and her mom said, "I love you, Lara."

"I love you too, Mom," Lara choked out.

As she hung up the phone, she felt her heart swell knowing that she'd just been given a priceless gift, the gift of hearing those sweet words from a woman who, for reasons of her own, had a difficult time expressing them. It meant so much to Lara to actually hear the words.

"Here, babe. Your turn."

"Hey, bro!" Cap laughingly greeted John as he heard the familiar, deep voice on the other end of the phone.

"Hey yourself! Merry Christmas!"

"Merry Christmas, John! How's everyone doing?"

"Couldn't be better. How 'bout you?"

Cap filled John in on recent events in his family's lives. He congratulated John when told about his brother's plans to marry his girlfriend.

"Yeah, Sue and I are gonna get married next week."

"Next week! How come so soon?"

"Well . . ." John's voice trailed off, and Cap could almost picture his embarrassed face, "Sue's pregnant."

Cap kept the worry out of his voice as he offered congratulations. Even though John was twenty, he still seemed so young. Cap wondered if he truly was ready to take this step, to become a husband and a father. But he realized the futility of his worry and instead chose to be grateful that John was at least willing to be responsible for his unborn child.

Cap asked about Sandy and felt his heart drop when John said in a quieter, more serious voice, "Sis isn't here, Cap. She and the baby left two days ago. Mom and William tried to stop her, but she insisted she needed to be with Carl for Christmas."

Cap knew that their sister had some pretty serious problems. Of the three Martin siblings, she was the one who struggled the most with the impact of their childhood. Cap felt that while he had made some positive steps by leaving Idaho and by falling in love with a strong, caring woman like Lara, Sandy had chosen poorly in becoming involved with an older man.

Carl Wilkins was a drifter, a ranch hand who moved from ranch to ranch and state to state, the only constant in his life being a bottomless bottle of beer. He had drifted into Sandy's life, sworn his undying love to her, gotten her pregnant, married her, and then left her, drifting on to another temporary ranch job.

"Sandy heard from him a couple of months ago," John shared. "He wrote from a place in Montana, so as Christmas drew closer, she felt that she needed to go to him so that he and his son could be together for Christmas."

"Have you heard from her? Did she find him?" Cap asked.

"Yeah, she phoned last night. I guess he was surprised to see them, but it sounds like his boss's wife decided that Sandy and the baby should be there, and she moved 'em all into a small cabin that was available." John laughed, the sound more incredulous than humorous. "I don't think ol' Carl had much choice. Sandy and the rancher's wife just made up his mind for him."

Just then Cap heard a muffled voice on the other end of the phone. "Hey, Cap? Dad wants to talk to you. Thanks for calling, and Merry Christmas! Give Lara and the girls a kiss for me."

"Hey, you too, little brother!"

"Merry Christmas, Cap!"

Cap grinned at the husky voice of his stepfather. "Merry Christmas, Dad!"

"Hey, son, how are those sweet girlies doin'?"

Cap spent the next ten minutes visiting with William, filling him in on that morning's activities, laughingly describing the antics of the girls and cherishing William's hunger for news of his granddaughters.

"How's Ma?"

"She's good." William paused, and Cap heard him clear his throat. "She's takin' a nap right now. I don't think I should wake her."

No words were needed to convey Cap's understanding of William's unspoken message. "Not a problem, Dad. Let her know I called. I better go now, though. I hear the girls waking up, and they're gonna want to play some more."

"Give those girlies a kiss and a hug for me."

"I will, Dad. We love you."

"I love you too, son. Give Lara my best."

"I will. Merry Christmas."

Cap hung up, the lingering sadness over not being able to talk to Pearl fading quickly as he and Lara headed for the back of the trailer, where they could hear the movements of their awakening daughters.

He treasured the love he shared with his sister, brother, and stepfather, yet somehow there was always a gray shadow casting a pall over his dealings with his family. That pall stemmed from his worry for John and Sandy. They both showed the early signs of alcoholism, and Cap ached with the fear that they would follow the path taken by their father, Jake Martin. He also continued to yearn for some sign from Pearl indicating a softening toward him and his family. So far that hadn't happened.

Cap had learned, however, to push aside that yearning, knowing that it would eat him up if he let it. Instead, he focused on the joy of being with his wife and daughters.

Later that night, as he and Lara prepared for bed, he turned to her, grateful for her loving presence. Her love had helped the healing begin. He knew that he still carried some of the raw, open wounds of his past, but they no longer festered. And he felt that some plan greater than his own was in motion, moving him forward to a brighter future. His wife, his daughters, and his unborn baby were part of that future, and he relished the knowledge that they would have a lifetime of Christmases to share and to treasure.

CHAPTER 16

October 1957
San Diego, California

"Yes, Mama, we'll be there. The girls and I will be on the train tomorrow morning. It leaves here at six-thirty. I think with all the stops, we should be in early the next morning. I'll call you when we get in to town."

As Lara bid her mother good-bye, Lily's softly spoken "I love you, girl" ringing in her ears, tears gathered in her large blue eyes. She dropped onto the vinyl-covered kitchen chair that stood by the small table and buried her face in her hands as grief welled in her heart. Her mother's second call of the morning, confirming Lara's plans to come home, bore the mark of a testimony that Lily's earlier call had been real—and that the terrible news she passed on was real.

Lara's father, Sam Straddler, was dead at the age of forty-eight. He had woken up that morning not feeling well but convinced that he was just suffering a slight case of indigestion. Ignoring the tightness in his chest, he had started the day as he always did—with a large country breakfast consisting of ham, eggs, hotcakes smothered in home-churned butter and maple syrup, and lots of strong, hot coffee.

He'd gone out a little earlier than usual that morning because he had a young heifer with mastitis and needed to treat her before he could start the regular chore of milking his small herd of cows. He'd only been out a few minutes when the tightness in his chest became an intense, burning pain, and before he could cry out for help, he had collapsed on the barn floor, his face dark and dusky with death. His heart had literally exploded in his chest. He wasn't found until later that morning when his son Luke went to the barn to do his morning chores.

Lily's second call to Lara had been laced with grief, but she had been composed. As she spoke however, the composure seemed to become more set, the grief buried a little deeper. Lara sensed her mother's unspoken, underlying feelings, and as she hung up the phone and gave in to her own grief, her heart sent out a plea for guidance and strength for herself and for her family.

A twinge in her stomach reminded her that it was past lunchtime, and she had three daughters to care for. Slowly rising to her feet, she called to Lisa, who came running on her sturdy two-and-a-half-year-old legs, her dark hair a riot of curls, her eyes bright and expectant, and her giggles filling the silence of the small trailer. Lara scooped the little girl into her arms and hugged her tight, feeling the sweet return of Lisa's embrace.

"You hungry, bugaboo?" Lara smiled wanly as she used her husband's favorite nickname for the girls.

Lisa chirped, "Yup, hungwy, Mommy."

"How about Rachel?"

"Yup, Wachee hungwy too." And with a small, pointed finger, Lisa poked at Lara's chest, hitting her on her left collarbone, and said, "Sammy hungwy too." Lisa giggled as Lara grabbed the little finger and pretended to bite the tip.

"Mommy's hungry too, bugaboo, and you taste so good." Lara laughed as she pretended to gnaw on Lisa's sweet-smelling shoulder. The laughter felt good as she set her daughter on the floor and patted her behind. "Go find Rachel and bring her to the table."

As Lisa trotted down the hall, Lara heard her bossily tell Rachel to put her doll away and to come eat lunch. Lara reached into the cupboard and pulled out bread and peanut butter for sandwiches, her heart constricting with the love she felt for her daughters. And she thought about Cap, who was once again away from home. He'd be back in a few weeks, but she longed for him now.

Especially considering the heartbreaking news she had just received. Tears welled in her eyes again as she thought about her father, knowing that she would never see him again. And as her two little girls trotted down the hall toward her, Lisa pulling and tugging on Rachel's hand, the tears spilled over and ran down her cheeks as she realized her girls would grow up without their grandpa. They were so young they would probably not even remember him.

"Mommy sad?" Lisa asked, her little voice quavering as tears of sympathy gathered in her cocoa-brown eyes.

"Yes, sweetie, Mommy's sad. But I'm okay." Lara wiped at her eyes, drying her tears as she reached down and gently wiped Lisa's tears away.

"No more cry, Mommy," Lisa demanded as she turned and gave Rachel one last tug. Rachel, unsteady on her legs, toppled over and lay there with a puzzled look on her face.

"No!" she demanded of her sister, her blue eyes troubled and glaring as she stared at Lisa. Lara smiled, the glower leaving as quickly as it had appeared. The sweet, blue-eyed toddler, her fair hair wispy and straight, noticed her mommy and smiled up at her, arms outstretched for a hug. Lara picked up Rachel and hugged her tight, feeling the love for her girls mask the grief she felt for her dad.

Quickly she set both girls at the table, Lisa on an upturned pan placed on a chair, and Rachel in the high chair. She set their peanut butter sandwiches in front of them, cut into manageable quarters, and gave each girl a half a banana and a cup of milk. Both toddlers quickly became involved in their simple lunch as Lara went to the back of the trailer where baby Samantha lay in her crib.

Bending over the crib, she saw that her five-month-old baby was awake, lying happily on her back, playing with the little terry cloth rabbit that had become her favorite toy. "How's my Sammy girl?" Lara cooed at her.

Sammy's eyes followed Lara's face as Lara gathered what she needed to change the baby. "Baby's soaking wet, huh, sweetie?"

Sammy grinned, one tiny, white tooth poking through her bottom gum, and Lara realized how lucky she was. All three of her girls had been such good babies. And Sammy was the easiest of them all. Even though she was teething, she very seldom fussed or cried. Sammy was simply sweet, a gentle-natured baby who returned her mother's love with snuggles and sweet smiles.

As Lara gathered Sammy into her arms and sat with her in the wooden rocking chair that Cap had given her after Sammy's birth, she held the baby to her breast. The baby hungrily nursed as Lara closed her eyes and let the memories of her father play through her mind. She rocked gently, holding her child close and gathering comfort from her warm, sweet presence.

Lara allowed herself a moment alone to grieve as she rocked the sleeping, contented baby. A few minutes later, however, sounds from the kitchen roused her, and Lara realized that she needed to put her grief on hold. Wiping her cheeks, she stood up and gently laid the baby in the crib, placing her on her tummy. Covering Sammy with a light blanket, Lara went back to the kitchen.

She smiled involuntarily as she spied the sticky, peanut butter–smeared faces and hands of the other girls. "My goodness! You two look like you really enjoyed your lunch!" Lisa and Rachel both smiled at her as Lara quickly wiped up the sticky mess.

Lifting Lisa down from the table, she sent her to use the bathroom while she picked Rachel up and carried her to the girls' bedroom. As soon as Lisa was done, Lara tucked her into bed and then took Rachel into the bathroom for her turn. Lisa had been toilet trained by the time she was eighteen months old, but Rachel wasn't quite there. She still had a few daytime accidents, and had to wear diapers during naps and through the night. As Lara took care of Rachel's needs and fastened a diaper on her, she sighed, realizing that by this time next year she would be potty training Sammy. *Oh, well,* she told herself, *you're the one who had these three little tikes so close together. Just think—if Christine were here, you'd have had four straight years of potty training!*

A momentary sadness gripped her at the thought of her oldest daughter. Christine would have been three and a half years old. Lara swallowed the lump of grief that welled in her throat, wondering why the sadness and feeling of loss should still feel as fresh and as deep as it had during those first horrendous days and weeks after Christine's death. As she tried to control the painful memories that were mixing with the sadness she felt over the loss of her father, Lara whispered out loud, "Oh, how I would have relished that fourth year of potty training." Before the melancholy could get its hold on her again, Lara took Rachel by the hand and led the tired little girl into the bedroom. She tucked her in next to Lisa, who was already sound asleep, snoring softly.

Lara allowed herself to smile despite the ache in her heart, knowing that Lisa would sleep all afternoon, but she would be lucky if Rachel slept for just one hour. She watched as Rachel snuggled down under the blanket and closed her eyes. Lara's heart swelled with emotion as she gazed on the sweet, sleeping faces. She stood by their bed for a few minutes, garnering strength from the sight of her napping daughters.

Finally, she turned with a determined air. She would not give in to the emotions again. She had too much to do. The next couple of days were going to be busy and difficult.

The thought of going on the train ride alone seemed overwhelming. She had three children, the oldest being two and a half, with the youngest a baby of five months. She knew that she would have her hands full. She always had her hands full, but at least at home they had their little routine, their toys, and their beds. Lara grimaced as she hurriedly started to set out clothes, diapers, toys, and food for the trip.

By the time she finished packing, she had two large suitcases, a bulging diaper bag, and a paper sack filled with food. She had several peanut butter sandwiches, crackers and cookies, bananas, apple juice, and several jars of baby food. She would buy the girls milk from the train steward, and she would try to nurse the baby as discreetly as possible on the train.

The rest of the evening went by very quickly, and with the packing done and the girls playing quietly before bedtime, Lara sat down to write Cap a letter. She wished she could call him, but they couldn't afford the long distance charges. So she wrote him about her father's death, sharing with him the hurt and the loss she felt, but expressing her gratitude for the years she'd known her father's love.

> *You know, darling, losing Dad like this has made me think about Christine. Sometimes I wonder about what happens to us after we die. When someone you love dies, it just seems so unfinished. It doesn't matter if it's a tiny baby or an older man; I wonder what it's all about, but I don't think I have the energy to worry about it right now. I need to save all my energy for getting the girls and*

myself to Idaho. So, my darling husband, I better close. I feel like I could write books and books to you and still not be able to adequately express my love for you and my love for our daughters. Thank you for them, and thank you for loving me. I miss you desperately and wish you were here to hold me tonight and every other night. You are in my dreams constantly. I love you. Lara

Lara slowly reread her letter to Cap and realized again just how much she loved him—and how much she missed him. Her heart hurt with the loneliness—a literal, physical pain—and it was compounded by the pain of her father's death and the anxiety she felt about the coming days.

* * *

While talking to her mother earlier that day, Lara had made the decision to spend some time in Idaho. She felt the need to be close to her family, especially with Cap overseas and so far away. She dreaded the idea of returning to California to the lonely little trailer they called home, and as she made her final preparations to leave, Lara knew that her decision to stay in Idaho through the upcoming holiday months was a wise choice. It had meant a little more preparation before they could leave, but she had the arrangements finalized and she and the girls were ready to leave in the morning.

Once there, and after the days of mourning were past, she and the girls would be able to relax into a routine that would give them the gift of time—time for the girls to get to know their grandmother, aunts, uncles, and cousins. Lara felt tears form once again behind her tired eyes at the realization that it was too late for them to get to know their Grandpa Sam.

With a sudden and surprising shift of thought, Lara found herself thinking about Pearl Aldrich. Pearl had yet to meet her granddaughters, a fact that caused a maelstrom of conflicting emotions within Lara's aching breast. She was frustrated at Pearl's seeming indifference and coldness towards her eldest son and his family, and yet Lara felt her heart softening with sadness at the idea that Pearl had three granddaughters she had never met. Lara knew that the time in Idaho would offer her the opportunity to have Pearl meet them. She was going to make sure her daughters came to know not only their maternal grandmother, but also their father's mother.

CHAPTER 17

Thanksgiving Day 1957
Wendell, Idaho

Cap wearily dismounted from the steps of the train, his journey almost complete. He had arrived three days earlier in San Diego, free for two weeks. He was so eager to see his family, and he fumed at the seemingly endless delays as he had been checked in and then released on furlough. He had all that he would need in his duffel bag, and he hefted it to his shoulders as he left the train station, determined to reach his family in time to share Thanksgiving with them. He smiled as he pictured Lara's surprise.

He hadn't told her he was coming. She was aware that he was due for a furlough, but he had given her no details. As soon as he was released in San Diego, he had caught the next train headed for Idaho. He'd had enough money to get him within twenty miles of home. He would hitch the remaining distance, and with that thought in mind, he strode out of the train station, his step light and his shoulders straight.

It wasn't long before Cap heard a vehicle pull up behind him. The middle-aged farmer driving the well-worn truck waved him in with a smile. "Where ya headed, son?"

"Home," Cap said.

"I kinda figured that. But where's home?"

Smiling sheepishly, Cap said, "Wendell."

The farmer smiled and launched a quizzing dialogue as they drove down the country lanes, past the brown patches of dormant farmland. Before long, the old truck pulled into the familiar drive, and Cap jumped out with a smile and a sincere, "Thank you, sir. Sure do appreciate the ride."

As he smiled and pulled away, the farmer felt a small surge of happiness lodge in his throat as he watched the handsome young man eagerly run up the front walk towards the large, white farmhouse.

Lara was inside the kitchen and didn't hear the knock on the front door. Her hands were submerged in a sink full of soapy water, washing the bowls and pans used thus far in the preparation of their Thanksgiving meal. Lily was basting the turkey, her face flushed from the heat of the oven, and Carol and Nell, Lara's sisters-in-law, were busy at the counter, talking and laughing as they chopped and peeled potatoes. The sound of raised voices in the hallway caught the women's attention, and they looked at each other, puzzled. The family gathering was complete as far as they knew, and Lily frowned as she heard an unfamiliar voice.

Lara suddenly dropped a pan into the sink, bubbles flying upward and settling in her hair as she heard the excited squeal of her oldest daughter followed by a high-pitched giggle. Her mouth dropped open, and surprise widened her eyes as Rachel, who had been playing on the floor near Lara, suddenly crawled up onto her feet and ran to the man standing in the kitchen doorway. She ran as fast as her chubby legs could carry her, arms outstretched. She was calling out "Da-da," her words a song of joy to Lara.

As Cap scooped Rachel up, her arms thrown around his neck in an impulsive hug, Lara stood back and watched. Her joy held her spellbound as she watched the magic of Cap's return unfold before her eyes. Lisa was dancing around him, tugging on his pant leg, laughing and clapping her hands gleefully. Rachel, her first impulsive response leaving her suddenly shy, pulled back from Cap. His encircling arms cradled her, and she dropped her chin, looking up at him through her long, curling eyelashes. With a shy smile, she reached up and placed her hands on his cheeks, the soft whiteness of her fingers an alluring contrast to the weathered tan of his face. As her fingers stroked his cheek she whispered, "Da-da."

Happiness bubbled inside Lara as she raised her hands to her mouth, smothering the cries of tenderness that overwhelmed her. Cap stared into the loving gaze of his daughter and finally tore his eyes away from her, catching Lara's steady stare. Lily, Carol, and Nell all wiped quietly at their eyes as Lara's stillness was finally broken. With a sharp cry of joy, she flung herself across the room and into Cap's embrace. They were both laughing and talking as they held each other, Rachel caught in the middle of their clutching arms. With a wiggle and a matching giggle, Rachel wormed her way out of the hug as she slid down her daddy's leg and joined Lisa on the floor, where they danced and hopped around like two elves.

Cap and Lara were aware of the children, but were so lost in the joy of holding each other that the sound of their daughters faded as their lips met. Cap tightened his hold on Lara, relishing her warmth and her closeness. With a soft whisper, Lily, Carol, and Nell slipped from the room, urging Rachel and Lisa to follow them, leaving Lara and Cap alone.

After a few more moments of tender greeting, Lara nestled in Cap's embrace and softly asked, "Why didn't you tell me?"

"I wanted to surprise you!"

Lara murmured a soft comment about surprises, and Cap chuckled as he continued, "And I wanted to be sure I could make it here. I would have hated to disappoint you if something had happened to prevent me making it in on time." He paused as he smiled down into her eyes. "And I wanted to make sure you had something to give thanks for today!"

"I thank God every day and night for you and the girls." Before Cap could respond, they were interrupted by a quiet hiccuping sound. With a quiet laugh, Lara turned as the baby in the crib awakened from her nap and started to fuss. Cap stood spellbound, listening to the sound of his youngest daughter. As Lara started to go to her, Cap reached out with a gentle hand and held her back. "I'll get her."

Cap stepped up to the crib and stared down into the miniature bed. The baby, her large brown eyes and curly dark hair reminding him of Lisa, stared back up at him, a puzzled look on her face. She lay there, kicking her legs and chewing on her thumb, gazing at Cap for a moment before deciding that she trusted him. Cap felt a well of emotion as she grinned at him, her cheeks dimpling as she waved her hands.

"Hey there, my newest bugaboo." Cap reached down and pulled the baby into his arms, marveling at how much she had grown over the last six months. The last time he had seen her had been just after she and Lara had come home from the hospital. He was thrilled to hold her in his arms, to feel her healthy, solid weight, and to see the glow of joy and health on her face. Lara came up next to him and put her arm around his waist as she reached out and caught Sammy's tiny fingers in hers. Lara laughed when Sammy gleefully slapped at both of her parents, her sunny nature evident as she played with her daddy.

"It's as if I've never been gone," marveled Cap. "She seems to know who I am, to accept me without needing to know me."

"She's just a girl with good taste," Lara replied.

"She's just like her mama," Cap murmured as he gently kissed the top of baby Sammy's head. He then leaned in and kissed Lara's cheek. Lara trembled as butterfly wings seemed to flutter in her stomach at Cap's gentle caress. She smiled when Cap murmured, "You're both just so sweet!"

Lara giggled as she put her arms around Cap, their fourth daughter curled up between them. Lara felt as though she could stay wrapped in the warmth of Cap's embrace forever, but the awkward sound of someone clearing his throat brought her back to the present, and she reluctantly stepped back slightly, breaking the full embrace she loved so much.

Tom, Lara's oldest brother, was standing in the door, grinning sheepishly as he came into the room. "Sorry to interrupt, but Ma said to come in and tell you that the rest of us are hungry, and unless you want to be eating burned turkey, we best get on with dinner."

Laughing, Cap handed Sammy to Lara and moved toward Tom, clapping him on the shoulder and, with a teasing look at Lara, said, "I can't think of anything that I'm hungrier for than a plateful of good old roasted turkey."

Lara pushed the baby back into his arms and said, "Here, Sammy wants her daddy. I think she's in need of some attention."

Lara's saucy look was accompanied by a pungent odor, and Cap said, "That's definitely not roasted turkey I'm smelling."

Lara playfully ignored him as his look turned first pleading and then resigned. He held the baby out at arm's length and said, "Okey dokey, bugaboo, I guess this is what being a daddy is all about."

Lara laughed as Cap left the room, and as Lily, Carol, and Nell returned to the kitchen they teasingly hooted and razzed Cap. By the time he returned with a clean, sweet-smelling baby, the sumptuous feast was spread out on the table. The large kitchen table barely seated the entire family, but they were cheerfully crowded together, and as Lily asked Cap to offer grace, the rambunctious laughter gave way to a quiet reverence. The act of praying together as a family, even over their food, was a new experience for everyone gathered at the table, and Lara was surprised by her mother's request. But she felt a quickening of her spirit as her eyes softened, and she quietly bowed her head.

As Cap felt the spirit of the moment touch his heart, he felt warmth spread throughout his whole body. It was a warmth he had experienced before on rare occasions. Even though he didn't know its source, he welcomed the encompassing spirit, and his voice choked slightly as he said a simple, but humble prayer.

When he finished, he felt Lara's gentle squeeze on his fingers. He gazed for a moment into her loving eyes, wondering at the sudden sense of spirituality that wrapped the two of them in its safe cocoon. While neither of them recognized its origin, it was a shared feeling they had experienced before during special moments of their marriage. And it was a feeling that they both wished they could hold onto forever.

With a smile, Lara let go of Cap's hand, and they immersed themselves in the joy and the bustle of sharing their Thanksgiving with Lara's family. Cap felt overcome by their friendship, and he offered a silent tribute of thanks for the absence of loneliness.

He thought briefly about his mother and William and wondered how their day was going. He and Lara would call them later. Pearl and William were still living in Hailey, and he knew that sometime during the next two weeks, he and Lara and the girls would make the drive north to see them.

He also knew that Lara had made a couple of day trips to visit Pearl and William since she had been in Idaho. He was grateful for her determination to open the door into their grandmother's life for the girls. Lara had written him that the visits had appeared to be successful. He felt that in some unknown way, the addition of the girls to their family had touched Pearl's heart. Cap was looking forward to visiting her himself. He had never lost the hidden childhood desire to be accepted by his mother. Maybe the entrance of her granddaughters into her life would open the way for her estranged son.

Later that night, replete and satisfied from the day spent with the family and the turkey dinner, Cap helped Lara bed the girls down. They had moved Sammy's crib into the room Rachel and Lisa shared. It was crowded, but the girls didn't need much room.

What Cap and Lara needed was some quiet time together, and as Lara closed the thin wooden door and turned down the light, she moved quietly toward the bed, where Cap waited for her. Cap welcomed Lara into his arms, and as they drifted toward sleep, holding each other close, Cap relished the tender feelings of love that banished his loneliness.

CHAPTER 18

December 1, 1957
Hailey, Idaho

"Son," Pearl paused as an unfamiliar feeling of tenderness towards her eldest child touched her heart, "thank you."

Cap swallowed a lump in his own throat as he looked into Pearl's eyes, sensing the softening of her attitude toward him. He nodded and said quietly, "You're welcome."

As Cap and Lara and the three little girls drove away, Cap carried with him the image of his mother holding baby Sammy in her arms, a small smile softening the otherwise stern features. She had smiled, and actually laughed aloud a time or two at the antics of Rachel and Lisa. As for William, the babies had been drawn to him from the first time they had met him. His weathered, aging face had shone with an inner joy and peace, and his work-roughened hands had been gentle as he had played with the girls, teasing them and inciting their giggling responses.

The girls had warmed up more slowly to their grandmother, especially Rachel, who was naturally very shy. Lisa, on the other hand, was ruled by an outgoing and sunny nature, and it hadn't been long before she had been tugging at Pearl's pant leg, calling her "Gamma" and insisting on Pearl's undivided attention. The baby, Sammy, had instantly won her grandmother over by accepting Pearl as quickly as she had accepted her daddy on Thanksgiving Day.

The weekend had been full of laughter—the laughter of the three girls, the quiet laughter of Lara, Cap, and William as they drank in the

antics of the girls, and the subtle, almost hidden smiles of Pearl. Cap
was still amazed at the success of their visit. There had been restraint
between himself and his mother, a restraint born of years of emotional
neglect, but Cap had long ago put aside his pride and his hurt. He was
instead overwhelmed with the sense of hope that this visit had given
him. He and William had sat on the couch, quietly conversing as Lara
and Pearl had put together a simple meal. Their talk had been interrupted by the girls seeking attention, but at one point William had put
his hand on Cap's shoulder, looked him straight in the eye, and said,
"Give her time, son. I think she's coming around."

Cap had felt his emotions swell as he nodded in response to
William's words. And now, as he drove away, he felt again that sense of
hope as he reflected on Pearl's last words. He had almost taken her in
his arms, had almost felt a mutual desire for an embrace. But he had
held back, still held in a haze of doubt and the fear of further rejection.
It seemed, though, that the haze was lifting. He chuckled to himself as
he remembered an exchange between his mother and Sammy.

Sammy was just learning to crawl, pulling herself short distances
across the floor. Pearl's living room had polished hardwood floors
that made it easier for the baby to scoot. Her light blue dress of
dotted Swiss cotton had trailed behind her as she maneuvered across
the floor, prompting her Grandpa William to start calling her Sweet
Pea, after the baby in the popular cartoon *Popeye.* One day, William
and Cap had become engrossed in their conversation, Lara and Pearl
were busy in the kitchen, and so the baby, left to her own devices,
had her attention caught by the wooden cuckoo clock hanging on
the front room wall.

The singing cuckoo bird had just announced the noon hour, and
while the grown-ups barely registered its chiming, Sammy became
entranced with the bobbing bird. As it disappeared behind its
wooden door, Sammy began scooting across the floor, intent on
finding out more about the mysterious little bird. She came to a stop
under the clock and gazed upward, her head tilted back as she
studied the situation. Unbalanced, she rocked back onto her bottom,
and her searching hands suddenly found something that she could
hang onto—the wooden pinecone dangling at the end of the chain
that hung from the bottom of the clock.

With a squeal that caught the attention of her grandmother, Sammy gave the pinecone a tug, attempting to pull herself upright. Her balance, unsure and unsteady, caused her to reflexively fling out her other arm. Gleefully, she caught hold of the pinecone's mate and, with a squeal of achievement, gave both pinecones a solid tug.

"Sammy! No!" Pearl's exclamation came too late as the baby lost her balance and toppled sideways, her fingers still tightly curled around the twin pinecones. As she landed on her side, the chains and pinecones popped free from her grasp, the impetus of their release causing the entire clock to rock precariously on the wall. Pearl's exclamation had caught both William's and Cap's attention, and they had watched Pearl valiantly try to save both the baby and the clock. It had first appeared that she was more concerned with the clock as she had lunged for its perch on the wall, steadying its rocking movement. But then she had dropped to the floor and picked up the surprised baby, who was staring wide-eyed and confused, not sure if she should laugh or cry.

Pearl had gently scolded the baby, "You silly child, you almost got yourself beaned with that old cuckoo!" Her emotions almost got the best of her as her voice cracked on the last word, and she laughed out loud in an apparent attempt not to cry.

Sammy, hearing her grandmother's laugh, decided that she should laugh too, and her cheerful squeal joined Pearl's relieved chuckles.

A remnant of that merriment returned as Cap reflected on the incident. Lara looked at him quizzically and asked, "What?"

Cap glanced over at her, his warm brown eyes sparkling. "Oh, nothin' really. I'm just glad how this weekend turned out."

Lara smiled, pleased for Cap but feeling a flicker of doubt lingering in her thoughts. She didn't trust Pearl not to hurt Cap again. But if he was happy, she would try to set those doubts aside. "The girls really seemed to like their grandma and grandpa."

"And vice versa," Cap replied. "I don't remember Ma ever being so warm and open with her affections." Cap frowned slightly as his thoughts turned to the past and he pictured himself, a young child of four, standing in the corner of the kitchen, where he had been banished for some minor rule infraction. He saw himself surreptitiously looking over his shoulder at his mother, a thin, overworked woman with a strained and angry look on her face. She held John in her arms, her mouth curled into a grimace of distaste at the soggy state of his diaper. Sandy had been sitting on the floor, her small face grimy, her hair uncombed. The house reeked of dirty diapers and neglect, and Cap was having a hard time connecting the woman and children of that memory with the woman he had just left. He suddenly realized that he still retained a large portion of the doubt and mistrust that had always ruled his relationship with his mother.

He sighed as he realized that the weekend had probably just been a fluke, an unexpected lapse into emotional warmth on the part of his mother. But looking over at his wife and sleeping babies, he couldn't help but hold onto that dim flame of hope that had touched his heart as he had turned and walked away from his mother, her door standing open instead of being firmly shut in his face.

CHAPTER 19

March 1958
San Diego, California

Lara lounged on a towel spread on the warm, white sand of a San Diego beach. Sammy played in the sand a few feet away from her, her hands busy with a pair of small, plastic rings. For some reason, she had grown unusually attached to the set of graduating rings that fit over a plastic post anchored on a wooden rocking board. Her Grandmother Pearl had given them to her for Christmas, and she had immediately become enamored with the toy set. The red and green rings that she played with now were her favorite. Lara smiled at her youngest and marveled at the impact the girls, especially Sammy, had on their grandmother.

As she transferred her gaze to Rachel and Lisa playing nearby with their pails and shovels, Lara's thoughts went back to the last few months. During the last few days of their Thanksgiving holiday, she and Cap had talked about her staying in Idaho. But the time seemed right for her to return to California with the girls, to return to their life there.

Cap had used the last few days of his leave helping repack their possessions. Before returning to California, they had visited Pearl and William for an entire weekend, celebrating an early Christmas. It had been beautiful in the mountains around Hailey. Freshly fallen snow blanketed the mountain valley in a mantle of pristine, sparkling white, the purity of the newly fallen snow heightening the season of goodwill. The mountains rose majestically, the snowcapped peaks changing colors with the advent of day. The early morning sun, rising over the eastern peaks, bathed the mountains with a rosy, golden hue as if to welcome the new day with its bright, color-spangled aura. At night, the shadows of the western peaks cast violet hues back toward the purple sky as the sun slowly sank behind the cradle of the western horizon, bidding the sleepy valley eventide.

Lara had risen before dawn that Saturday and had stood at the bedroom window that faced the eastern mountains. She had watched, entranced, as the sun greeted the valley, bathing it with the glory of morning, and she had felt a spiritual awareness of the majesty and splendor surrounding her. The light from the sun and the snowcapped mountains cast a glow on her face, mirroring the radiance in her eyes. It seemed as if she and Cap had reached a new stage of closeness with both their families, and her heart ached with the bittersweet knowledge that life was ever changing. Even though some of the changes they had experienced during their marriage had been fraught with anguish, Lara could see how the tragedies had strengthened them. And those difficult times made the recent closeness with their families that much more precious.

Now, as she sat lost in her musings, her eyes distant and her thoughts faraway, she was suddenly brought back to the present by the high-pitched squeal of her oldest daughter.

"Mommy, Sammy's being waved at!"

Lara quickly focused on her eldest daughter, confused by her words. "What . . ."

"Oh, dear heaven . . . NO!" Lara shot to her feet, her shouted prayer propelling her toward the edge of the water, where Sammy had crawled and was in danger of being swept away by the increasingly powerful waves hitting the shore.

Sammy's face was filled with fear as she struggled to sit up after being knocked over by a wave. She opened her mouth to scream, but was suddenly buried by a large wall of water that pounded into her small body, knocking her face first into the sand. Her choking, sputtering cry was silent, lost in the cacophony of ocean noises.

Lara, running madly for her baby, was aware of the suddenly nightmarish sounds of the gulls, the waves, and the roar of blood pounding in her ears. She couldn't hear her daughter's cries. She could only see the tiny, innocent face screwed up in terror, eyes wide and confused.

Lara reached Sammy just as another incoming wave, powerful with the change in tide, coursed towards the helpless child. She fell to her knees, lowering her center of gravity as she seized the struggling baby, the powerful waves crashing around them. She held Sammy to her breast, conscious of the baby's cold skin.

As the wave receded, Lara pushed herself to her feet and ran toward the dry sand and the blankets, where Lisa was holding Rachel back. Lara dropped to her knees once more, this time on firmer sand. She held Sammy away from her and turned the sputtering baby across her forearm facedown. Sammy coughed and choked up a small amount of water. As she gulped in a breath of air, she let loose with a screeching wail born first of terror, and then of anger.

Lara brought Sammy up against her shoulder and hugged her close. She was crying, tears running down her face as she knelt on the sand, rocking back and forth. Lisa and Rachel were crying and leaning against her. Holding the baby with one arm, Lara reached around and gathered Lisa and Rachel to her. The four of them sat that way for several seconds as they contemplated the terror that had engulfed them just moments before.

"Miss, excuse me." An unfamiliar male voice broke through the trance of Lara's tears, and she raised a ravaged face to look at a tall, suntanned teenager. "I saw what happened and came as quickly as I could. I called the beach patrol for you. My dad'll be here soon. He's with the first aid squad."

Before Lara had a chance to reply, she heard the approach of a vehicle and turned her gaze to the open jeep pulling up a few feet away. Two men jumped out of the jeep and ran to Lara and her family. The older man, Jed Baker, dropped to his knees next to Lara, and after introducing himself, he gently took Sammy from her arms. The second man was beside them, opening a waterproof bag with a large red and white cross sewn on its flap.

Lara barely registered when the boy, who had introduced himself as Jason Baker, coaxed Rachel and Lisa away from her side. She was too busy watching the two medics as they worked with Sammy.

Jason took Rachel and Lisa a few feet away and settled them in the sand, enticing them to play with their buckets and shovels. While he played with the girls, he kept an eye on the trio of adults working with the baby.

Jason swallowed hard, his tender heart hurting for the young mother. He was a sensitive boy, and he didn't want to see her afraid. He could read the guilt in her eyes, the self-recrimination for having put her baby in danger's way.

Quietly he bowed his head, closed his eyes, and murmured, "Dear Heavenly Father, please help the baby to be okay. And help her mama to be strong. Bless her for her courage and quick action, and help her realize Thy love for her."

Jason opened his eyes and saw Lisa and Rachel both watching him. Rachel was staring at him with a fierce concentration that caught him by surprise, while Lisa had a quizzical look on her face, her rosy lips pursed as if to ask a question. Her dark brown eyes studied him, and she finally asked, "What you do?"

"I just said a prayer."

"Who you talk to?"

"I was talking to my Heavenly Father," Jason answered her, his voice gentle with the cadence of someone born to teach.

"Jesus?" Lisa asked.

"Yes, I was asking Jesus and God, His father, to help your mom and your sister."

"Oh," Lisa said. Her eyes suddenly sparkled at him as her lips curved into a sweet smile. "Jesus loves Mommy."

It was more a comment than a question, and Jason felt his heart stir at the simple faith of this little girl. He glanced at her sister and saw that Rachel's intense look had lost its ferocity and had been replaced by a soft shyness. She bobbed her head, making her straight, blond locks dance around her face. "Jesus loves me."

Jason reached over and picked Rachel up, her sand bucket and shovel clutched in her hands and said, "Yes, cutie pie, Jesus does love you! How did you know that?"

As he asked the question, he saw a luminosity brighten her blue eyes, and she leaned forward, bringing her face close to his. Her tiny button nose almost touched his as her eyes looked unwaveringly, all shyness gone, into his. The tip of her tongue moistened her lips as she whispered, her voice soft but sure, "He tol' me."

He hugged her close and closed his eyes, grateful for the sweet knowledge that Jesus truly did love this sweet girl. He felt as if the

Master Himself was teaching him as Rachel's and Lisa's faith touched his heart. He held Rachel close and looked over at the trio of adults, sighing with relief as he saw his father, Jed, holding the squirmy baby.

Lara's face was white and pinched as Jed handed Sammy to her. "She's going to be okay. She swallowed some of the water, so she might feel a little sick to her stomach. But her lungs sound clear."

Lara's eyes were fastened on his face as she tried with all her might to concentrate on the meaning of his words. She felt the deadly fear loosening its viselike grip, and she clung to his assurance as if it were a lifeline. She was overwhelmed with guilt. She had been so lost in her thoughts that she had almost lost her baby. If something were to happen to Sammy, she knew that she would never forgive herself. As she rocked Sammy close, Lara tried to concentrate on the instructions being issued by Jed's partner.

"You probably should take her to the doctor just to be sure she's okay." His voice was calm but authoritative. "He'll probably want you to keep an eye on her, keep her quiet for a day or two." A skeptical expression broke through the tightly pinched look on Lara's face, and he grinned and continued, "I know that'll be hard to do. She seems like a pretty active baby."

Lara found her voice, her throat dry and swollen. "So are her two sisters."

Jed laughed softly as he looked over at the two youngsters romping on the sand with his son. A look of pride shone in his eyes as he watched his handsome boy who would soon be leaving on his mission. They belonged to The Church of Jesus Christ of Latter-day Saints, and Jed knew that the Lord had blessed him and his wife with a special child.

He felt the twinge of an old hurt as he remembered another blond, brown-eyed boy who should have been by his brother's side. His two boys had been close in age, just like the three sisters, and they had been inseparable until Tim had taken ill with pneumonia. He'd never recovered from the sickness, and the pain of losing his son still pierced Jed's heart.

Jed looked back at Lara, who was starting to recover. She was such a pretty woman, but there was something in her eyes that spoke of past pain and loss. Jed withdrew his billfold from his pocket and said,

"My name's Jed Baker. Here's a card with my phone number. My home number and my office number are both on there." At Lara's questioning look, Jed said, "I only do the beach patrol a couple times a week. I practically grew up playing in the ocean, and I love it. I do this more for play than for work." Looking down at Sammy, Jed's voice took on a husky quality. "Sometimes, though, it's not so fun."

Gathering his emotions, Jed smiled at Lara. "Please give me a call in a day or two. I'll rest a whole lot easier if I know everything is okay with this little one." His hand reached out and caressed the soft, downy hair of Sammy, who was finally lying quietly in her mother's arms.

"Thank you, Mr. Baker." Lara smiled at him and turned her eyes to include Jed's partner and son in her gratitude. "I will call you."

Jason began helping the girls gather up their toys, and as he reached down and picked up Lara's blanket, he said, "I'll help you to your car."

Jed and his partner also helped gather the young family's belongings, and soon Lara and her girls were waving good-bye. "Wave bye-bye," Lara said, suddenly reminded of what Lisa had screamed—something about Sammy being "waved at." Her smile of farewell was wide and genuine, but suddenly she found herself fighting back tears as she relived the horror of watching her baby being washed away from her, carried on the threatening waves. Guilt flooded through her as she turned the car onto the freeway, headed for the base. She was going to take Sammy directly to the doctor, knowing that she needed his reassurance that Sammy was going to be okay.

Meanwhile, back on the beach, Jed and Jason stood talking. Jason was expressing his impressions of Lara and the girls, and his father was touched by the boy's insight. "You know what, Dad? We didn't get their names."

Jed shook his head regretfully. In his heart he knew that he had let an important opportunity pass by, and he saw his remorse mirrored in Jason's eyes.

"Sure were cute little girls," Jason murmured.

"Yes, son, they are cute." As he turned to leave, Jed issued a silent prayer that the girls' mother would call him as she had promised. The whispering of the Spirit told him that she was going to need his help.

He looked over his shoulder and watched the distant road, as if hoping to see Lara and her car returning. He breathed deeply and sighed again as he prayed for her.

CHAPTER 20

Two days later

Abruptly awakened, her heart thundering and a hovering cloud of fear choking her, Lara threw back the light bedcovers and swung her legs over the edge of the bed. Sitting there in the dark, the hands of the illuminated clock pointing to the time, 4:15 A.M., Lara knew that something was wrong. She immediately thought of Cap. Was he in danger? Had something happened to him?

Almost as quickly, her fear shifted to her children. With a sense of dread, she stood and started walking through the small apartment, her movements slow and dreamlike. She moved to the door of the small room shared by the three girls, then stood in the early morning gloom of the hallway just outside the room. With her eyes adjusting to the dim light from a streetlamp outside, Lara held her breath, listening to the silence. She could hear Lisa's gentle snore, and as her gaze shifted to the room's second bed, she saw a slight movement as Rachel turned over.

She transferred her gaze to Sammy's crib, and as she moved across to her youngest daughter's side, her fear escalated, choking her breath and making her tremble. She reached into the crib and drew away the light blanket, and then Lara closed her eyes in agony. She clutched at the baby, pulling the still, silent form into her arms. She sank to the floor, her thin nightgown shrouding her as she rocked back and forth, her grief and anger and guilt bubbling into her throat like vomit. She rocked in silence, lost in an isolated world of death that separated her from her sleeping children, and locked her in with the dead baby clutched in her arms.

CHAPTER 21

March 1958
San Diego, California

The small chapel was sparsely filled. The bishop of the ward stood in front of the congregation, a simple wooden lectern offering him support. He looked with sorrow upon the young couple sitting in the front row. Their grief was firmly etched on their faces. Bishop Lang was especially concerned for the mother, Lara Martin. He had known her for just a few days, but he felt drawn to her, touched by the courage she showed in forging ahead with the funeral arrangements for her baby. He had been called a week earlier by a ward member, Jed Baker. Jed, his voice cracking with emotion, had told him of a young woman in desperate need of help.

"Her husband is overseas. The American Red Cross and local naval authorities are trying to cut through the red tape in order to get him home, but for now she's on her own."

"How did she come to meet you, Jed?"

Bishop Lang's question had filled Jed with a sense of wonder at the workings of the Lord. Humbly, he had told the bishop about Lara's experience on the beach and his subsequent meeting with her and the girls. Jed had sensed that his introduction to Lara and the girls had a purpose, and when Lara called him early that dreadful morning, her voice carefully modulated and in control, Jed had recognized the desperation and the hysteria lurking behind her quiet words.

As the bishop opened the funeral service, Jed's eyes rested on the tiny white casket sitting at the front of the room. His heart nearly broke as he heard Lara's sobs, quietly controlled but filled with such grief-stricken intensity that Jed felt tears well in his own eyes. He glanced at Lara and then at her husband. Cap sat still, his face rocky, molded by shock. He sat, pale and disbelieving, staring at the casket. Jed saw him swallow hard, the muscles of his neck and throat working as he fought to maintain his composure.

Jed felt for the young father. It had been only fifteen years since he had sat in Cap's place, his own red-rimmed eyes fastened on a small, pine box—the resting place for the small body inside. Jed's tears began to flow without restraint as he groped for his wife's hand.

Jason sat on his other side, next to Lara Martin. He looked pale and confused. This was the first time in maturity that he had come face-to-face with death, and even though he had only seen Lara and her girls that one time on the beach, Jason had been drawn to them, feeling a connection of spirit, and he was grieving.

He had been too young at the time of his brother's death to remember more than a sense of loss and wonder as he had searched the house the day after the funeral for his playmate. The intervening years had dimmed the memory of that search, and his testimony of the gospel plan had buoyed up any lingering sadness. He took it on faith that his brother was happy and safe and that one day they would be reunited.

Jason longed to reach over and take Lara's hand, to bear to her his testimony of eternal life and eternal families. He couldn't fathom the sadness she must be feeling. He knew that she wasn't a member of the Church, that she didn't have much of a religious background. And he knew that her husband was in a similar position. In his heart he prayed for the parents, that they might be comforted and come to know that they had a Heavenly Father who loved them and who knew how much they hurt. He wanted them to know that He was there for them, loving them and willing to take away their pain.

Cap was in shock. He could barely absorb what was taking place. He felt as if he were in a nightmare. The bishop's words scarcely registered. He grasped Lara's trembling fingers in his, drawing strength from her. He felt a tremble in his breast and fought harder than he ever had to control and to conceal his emotion. He had to. Giving in to the emotions meant incapacity, and he had to be strong for Lara. He felt her frailty, and he sensed that it was only by a single, tiny thread that she was holding on to her sanity.

He had been devastated by the news delivered to him by telegram. But after the long flight home, he had been shocked even more by the sight of Lara's pale face, her blank eyes, and her monotone voice as she recited the torturous events of the previous few days. She had told him of Sammy's horrifying experience on the beach, of their visit to the doctor's office and his assurance that all was well and the baby would be fine. Then she had told him, her voice not matching the change of emotion that flashed in her eyes, of the morning she had awakened so abruptly, her heart pounding with an unknown fear. She had described finding the baby, cold and still in her crib, and then of her phone call to Jed Baker.

What she couldn't tell Cap about were the hours she had sat on the floor rocking the lifeless body of their youngest daughter, crying silent tears and alternating between cursing God and pleading with Him to make it different. By the time the sun had risen fully in the sky, Lara had managed to pull herself together physically if not emotionally. She had laid the baby down, but her eyes had remained fastened on the beautiful features, so still and white with death. She had lost track of the time as she stood there, her tears drying on her cheeks but the pain still raging within her heart. It had been the slight sounds of rustling bedclothes and the cheerful voices of Rachel and Lisa that had propelled her forward into the day.

Later, Lara had realized she had to call someone. She didn't know who. She had no close friends, having only lived in the apartment a few short months. After returning to San Diego from their holiday visit to Idaho, Cap and Lara had decided to move from the small trailer that had been their home. They needed more room and had found an inexpensive apartment that offered them additional living space. Since moving in, Lara had kept to herself, concentrating on her girls for company. Her family was too far away. But she knew she had to call someone, do something. The image of her dead daughter had flashed in her mind, and she had caught a rush of emotion with her clenched fist and pushed it against her mouth as if she could smother the scream that threatened to erupt out of her chest.

She had turned abruptly and left the room, not wanting to alarm Lisa and Rachel. Running to her room, she had stood in front of the mirrored dressing table. Her tortured gaze had fallen on a small piece of paper stuck in the corner of the mirror. Reaching for it with shaking hands, she recognized the card given to her by the man from the beach patrol. He had been so kind and so comforting. Maybe he would be able to help her again.

He and his wife had responded immediately to her cry for help. They had known, through their own experience, what to do and what lay ahead for Lara. They had kindly taken her under their wing, comforting and guiding her through the harrowing days that followed. The medical examiner had issued a death certificate stating that the cause of death was quick pneumonia possibly caused by a minute amount of water that could have trickled into Sammy's lungs during her experience at the beach. Lara had blanched, her pale features going even more alabaster as the coroner's words pierced her heart. Jed's wife, Alice, had taken Lara into her arms, holding her close, trying to reassure her that the baby's near drowning had been a tragic accident, that the baby's death was not her fault.

Lara had allowed their comforting words to flow around her, had felt their loving concern. She had appreciated their assistance in making the funeral arrangements with their bishop, but Lara hadn't cared which church provided the services. Her feelings for God were on hold, frozen by her grief. She heard their words and she felt their love, but it made no difference.

Under the layer of grief lay the real tragedy, the knowledge of her guilt and her responsibility for Sammy's death. No human words, no human kindness, could touch that hidden pain. Only God could do that, and she had turned from Him as surely as she felt herself withdrawing from Cap's love. As she and her husband sat side by side on the polished wooden pew, the bishop's words were meaningless to her, the music of the children singing as distant as the robin's sweet song in the tree outside the chapel. The prayers of the day were as fruitless as the prayers she had alternately shouted and whispered that morning she had sat with her dead baby in her arms.

As the funeral service moved forward, Lara sat locked in time, her emotions, her spirits, and her heart encapsulated in an ever-thickening shell of grief and guilt and pain. She was like a living statue of marble, cold and unfeeling. Only the blink of her eyes, the flow of her tears, and the gentle rise and fall of her chest symbolized the life that lurked beneath the pale and wintering wasteland of her face.

Cap knew that his own emotions were close to the surface. He felt Lara's cold hands as they lay in his. There was no return to the grasping squeeze of his fingers. And as he finally tore his eyes away from the tiny, flower-covered casket, he rested his gaze on her pale features and felt her withdrawal. He ached inside as he felt the familiar distancing of her emotions.

He felt his spirit stir in his heart, but it was as if the pathway that had always bound his heart to Lara's was blocked. He didn't know if there was any way to break through to her, but as he looked at her averted face and saw the blank expression in the blue eyes that he loved so much, he made a secret promise to her that his love, his strength, and his faith would be strong enough to see them both through the dark days that lay ahead. As he made this promise, he suddenly sensed a light growing within his mind.

He looked to the front of the chapel, confused about what he was feeling. It was soft and sweet and much stronger than those sweet, tranquil moments he had occasionally shared with Lara. It was as if someone had taken all of his pain, anger, and confusion and had lifted it from his heart. He felt enveloped with a sense of warmth and well-being. With a start, he recognized what it was.

Peace.

Peace descended on him, and finally his stony countenance changed and softened, bringing tenderness to his eyes, allowing the tears to flow over his brown cheeks. As sobs shook his shoulders, he listened to the music being played. The voices of the six children singing at the front of the chapel sounded like a chorus of heavenly angels singing their praises to God. Their music found rest in his heart and soul, and he felt as if he had found another missing part of himself.

He started to listen to the words and felt his heart warm as the message of the simple song awakened his spirit. *Am I really a child of God? Does He really know my needs? Will He . . . can He lead me and guide me back home to Him someday?*

As the children's voices reverently sang the final verse, Cap listened in awe and wonderment, realizing that the burning within him was confirming to him that he truly was a child of God. He listened intently to the closing of the song, and Cap realized that even though the first verse spoke of a loving home and parents, a sentiment that pierced his heart with longing and sadness, the final words brought him a stronger sense of peace. And he felt a wellspring of joy that came from knowing God and His role as a heavenly parent.

Cap prayed with all his heart that it wasn't too late for him. And as the Spirit washed over him, bathing him with the warmth of God's love, he looked into Lara's face and prayed that it wasn't too late for his beloved wife.

CHAPTER 22

June 1959
San Diego, California

The day started out as all the other mornings of the past year had—with silence. The morning passed slowly as Cap and Lara mechanically completed their chores. After lunch, the girls went down for a nap. Lara disappeared into her bedroom, and a few minutes later Cap followed her.

"Lara?" he called, a question in his voice.

Lara's only response to her name was a slight shift of her shoulders and a minute turn of her head. She sat at the dressing table, where she had been for more than fifteen minutes, a hairbrush grasped loosely in her hand while she stared with unseeing eyes at her reflection in the mirror.

"The elders are coming over in a little while, about an hour before I have to leave for work."

Lara met Cap's announcement that he was meeting with the Mormon missionaries with a steely, unforgiving stare. Cap had been trying to convince her to join him in his investigation of The Church of Jesus Christ of Latter-day Saints, but she had adamantly refused. The look she gave him stopped him in his tracks, the invitation to join him dying on his lips.

Suddenly, his patience snapped. "Lara, I've had it with your moping around. Darn it, I lost a daughter too."

His anger quickly faded at the stricken look on Lara's face. He reached for her and pulled her to her feet, drawing her into his arms.

She didn't fight the embrace, but merely remained stiff and unbending. Cap let his arms fall to his sides.

"Lara, something has to give. You can't go on like this," Cap continued in the face of her steely silence. "If you would only give the elders a chance. Pray with us." He reached out and touched her. "Honey, if only you would pray with us, I know it would help. It's helped me so many times."

Ever since the day of the funeral, when he had experienced the first taste of the Spirit blessing him with peace and comfort, Cap had diligently sought to retain that special feeling. He had become a firm friend of Jed Baker and his family. Jed and Alice had embraced Cap and Lara and the girls. They hadn't pushed their religion; they simply lived what they believed, and their example, more than anything else, had convinced Cap to start taking the missionary lessons.

He was halfway through with the discussions, and he knew the Church was true. He had even given up smoking, which was something he had wanted to do for a long time. When the missionaries had asked if he felt he could live the Lord's law of health, the Word of Wisdom, Cap had readily committed to do so. Smoking had merely been a habit of convenience and comfort anyway. He had always tried to avoid the lure of alcohol, and he had only struggled for a few days after cutting himself off from drinking coffee. He wanted to be baptized, but he wanted to wait until Lara had reached the same decision.

He felt that he was being patient and supportive, lovingly giving Lara the space and time she seemed to need. But this evening, he felt as if he had taken several steps backward.

Sensing what seemed to be a softening in her response to his plea for her to join him in prayer, Cap pulled Lara into his arms again, his lips seeking hers in a loving kiss. Breaking his lips away from hers, Cap was oblivious to the lack of reaction from Lara as he buried his face in her sweet-smelling hair. "Oh, Lara, I miss you so much. I need you. Won't you please come back to me?"

He took her silence as a reluctant acquiescence, and he wished she could sense even a small part of what he felt about the Church.

"Stop it, Cap. I can't do this. Not now."

"Then when?"

"I don't know when."

Lara's hurtful words caused a look of such intense anguish to wash over Cap's face that she stopped her tirade and cried with anguish, "What do you want from me?"

"I want you to smile again. I want to hear your laughter. I want to love you."

"Oh, Cap."

Her soft reply gave Cap the encouragement he needed and he reached for her again. This time she went into his arms, but as soon as she did, Lara started to cry, and her body trembled as she pushed herself away. Suddenly, she turned away and cried out, "Get away from me!"

The hostility of her demand shocked Cap. His passion died, leaving him feeling bewildered, rejected, and angry.

"You want me to get away from you. Fine, I'll leave. It's obvious you don't want me around, and to tell you the truth, right now, I don't want to be here."

"I'm glad you finally got the message. I can't stand having you here." Lara's harsh words masked the true meaning of her message. What she couldn't say, what she kept hidden, was the fact that Cap's presence reminded her of what they had lost—what she felt responsible for. Her grief was locked in with her guilt, binding her in a never-ending prison of self-hatred that made it impossible for her to love. Even her relationship with Rachel and Lisa was being affected. Lara was aware of their drifting away from her, and she saw it as another indication of her guilt. She accepted the loss of their love as another part of her sentence for putting Sammy in danger, for causing her death.

As Cap recoiled from her angry words, Lara felt compelled to shout, "I don't know what you want from me!"

Cap's response, shouted over his shoulder as he turned his back on her was, "I want you to be my wife!"

Cap's heartfelt plea fell on deaf ears. He knew by the silence that followed his response that Lara had left the room, her departure merely a symbol of her emotional abandonment. It had been a little over a year since the tragedy of Sammy's death, and the silent vow he had made to Lara on the day of the funeral was being tested. And he felt as if he were going to fail.

This afternoon's fight with Lara was just one of a hundred. They never talked anymore. They conversed, passed information back and forth regarding the girls and the activities of the day, but the deep, soul-searching talks that had bonded them so closely together were a thing of the past, dead and buried, it seemed, with their daughter Sammy.

Angrily, Cap stalked from the room, grabbing the hat for his uniform and automatically checking his pants pockets for his keys and wallet. Without another word to Lara, he slammed out the door, leaving her behind in her world of silent self-recrimination. Cap was so hurt and bewildered that he forgot about the missionaries. He forgot the spirit of peace they brought and taught. And he forgot how much he loved his wife.

Several hours later, as he wandered the dimly lit streets of San Diego's waterfront district, he felt the ire still burning in the pit of his stomach. He felt the absence of the sweet feelings that he had become used to in response to his prayers and his study of the gospel. Yet he was so immersed in his own hurt and anger that he barely registered the loss.

The night sounds of the seedier part of the city intruded on his thoughts. Absentmindedly he reached up and tugged on the MP armband that seemed to constrict his upper arm. He had been assigned to the military police just after Sammy's funeral, and he appreciated the new work. It kept him in San Diego, where he needed to be, but lately it had offered him an escape from the turmoil at home and helped occupy his time as he volunteered for extra duty more and more frequently.

The raucous music and loud voices coming from the many bars that he passed called to him, and he found himself searching the faces in the crowd. They were the faces of laughing men and women who seemed to be having a great time. He caught sight of his reflection in a window, and he realized that he looked out of place, not because of his uniform—most of the other men on the streets were in uniform also—but because of his ghostlike and lonely countenance. Looking at his watch, he saw that it was late, past eleven o'clock, which meant his patrol was over. Reaching up, he grabbed the MP armband and wrenched it off his arm, stuffing it into his pocket. He then spied a pay phone on the corner of the street. He stalked over to it and placed a call to the military police headquarters and verbally signed himself off duty.

With no other thought than to escape the pain, Cap turned into the next doorway and found himself in the smoky interior of a dimly lit bar. It was crowded, but Cap pushed his way through the horde of people crushed around the tables. After ordering a beer, he grabbed the cold bottle and found a seat at a vacant table located at the back of the noisy, smoke-filled room. The loud music reverberated through the room, and Cap allowed himself to feel the deep throbbing of the bass. He felt an answering throb in the pit of his stomach that seemed to amplify the black rage descending upon him.

He lifted the beer bottle to his lips and drained it in one shot. Wiping his moist mouth, he signaled to the waitress for another. Forgotten was his repulsion for beer and getting drunk. Right now it seemed to offer the only solace for his hurting heart. "What heart?" he muttered to himself.

As the waitress deposited his beer, Cap reached into his pocket for the money to pay her when a soft, sultry voice whispered behind him, "Never mind, sailor, this one's on me."

He turned his head and looked up at the woman standing by his side, studying her face as she paid the waitress. She had dark red—almost auburn—hair, and strong facial features that were at once imposing and feminine. Her heavily lashed dark eyes were made up with thick makeup, and her full, pouty lips were painted a dark red. Her skin was smooth, the color of honey. She wore a tight black dress with a high neckline and long sleeves, but still somehow managed to leave little to the imagination. Cap felt his stomach tighten with tension as she trailed soft fingertips along the back of his hand.

Knowing he was doing wrong, but with his senses and his conscience dulled by the two beers he had consumed, Cap smiled at her and stood as he pulled out a chair for her to sit down. For the next hour, they sat close together, drinking beer and exchanging inebriated small talk.

Cap was lost in an alcoholic haze, and he finally felt as if he had let go of his anger. At least this woman made him feel like he had something to give. He had a dim image of his wife in the back of his mind, but pain and a resurgence of anger blurred her reflection, and he blocked the image further by downing another bottle of beer. The woman stood and ran her fingers through his hair as she whispered, "Come on, sailor, I know someplace where we can have some privacy."

Following her out of the bar and into the street, Cap allowed himself to be led further into the darkness of the night. He laughed and spun her around, unsteady on his feet, lurching and stumbling as he tried to turn her into his arms. As he lurched, his feet became entangled together, and Cap fell and found himself facedown in the gutter.

As Cap looked up at the woman, the drunken haze momentarily cleared. In a flash, the specter of Jake Martin rose before his eyes, and he realized that he was behaving just like his father. The thought was so painful and so nauseating that Cap grabbed his stomach and hunched over on his knees into the gutter. The combination of beer, self-loathing, and pain had him retching his guts out. He vaguely heard the woman cursing and screaming at him, but then she was gone. He was too ill, however, to really notice.

Several minutes later, Cap sat sprawled in the street, smelling of beer and vomit and tears. He buried his head in his hands and gave in to his grief. Soberness was slow in coming, but finally he was able to rise to his feet. Walking unsteadily, Cap made his way up the street, feeling lost and out of place. He knew that he had come close to making the worst mistake of his life, and he ached with remorse and confusion.

So he prayed. It was the only thing he could think of to do, although he felt undeserving of help from the Lord considering his actions that night. Looking at his watch, squinting in the dim light of the street, Cap saw that it was almost three o'clock in the morning. He wondered if Lara missed him, and with a groan of remorse, he cried out in his soul for forgiveness. He knew how much Lara was hurting, hurting where no one could reach her. Cap wanted so badly to be able to take it from her.

What had he done instead? He had gotten drunk and acted stupid, and he knew that all his stupidity was going to do was cause her more grief. He didn't know what to do. His heart ached as he searched his soul and prayed ceaselessly for guidance and forgiveness. "Oh, Heavenly Father, I know I am unworthy of Thy love tonight. I don't know what I'm doing here or what could have possessed me to come here. But I was wrong. I was wrong to leave Lara tonight with so much anger in my heart. Please forgive me."

His emotions were so fraught with regret and his tears were coming so hard and so heavy that Cap could go no farther. He turned into a dark, narrow alley and dropped to his knees, wrapping his arms around himself. He rocked back and forth as the tears and the emotions spent themselves and his spirit cried heavenward.

Time passed, and he continued to kneel in the dark. Just as he felt himself sinking further into the abyss of pain, he suddenly became aware of warmth touching his heart. It spread into his chest and soon encompassed his entire body. The anguish of his soul gave way to lightness, a lifting of the burden that had him pressed to the ground. And as light filled his mind, he knew that he had been forgiven, and he knew that he needed to forgive himself. Several minutes passed as he savored the enveloping warmth. Soon he found the strength to rise, and he began to walk home.

He opened the front door to the apartment as the hall clock struck five-thirty. He had been out all night, and he felt ravaged. He set aside his hat, and part of him wondered how he had managed to hang on to it through all that had happened that night.

He slowly walked through the apartment as he headed for the bedroom. Before opening the door into his room, he peeked in on the girls. The sweetness of their spirits greeted him as he stood and gazed down on their sleeping faces. He loved them so much. And no matter what he and Lara had to do to make it through this, he vowed to work it out.

He again felt the regret of his choices earlier that night, and he shuddered to think about what he had almost done. Before the regret could consume him, however, he felt the reassurance of forgiveness, and he knew that he needed to forge ahead and do whatever he could to forgive himself and gain absolution from Lara.

As he stepped through the door into his room, he watched Lara for a moment, unable to tell if she slept. With sadness in his heart, he turned from her and rummaged in the dresser for clean clothes. In the bathroom, he shed his outer clothing, disgusted with the smell that seemed to permeate the fibers. He wished it were as easy to shed the stench of sin as it was to discard his clothes.

Yet he was learning that there was a stronger force, a stronger love that could take it from him. And it was becoming easier to trust that love. He stared at his tired face in the mirror and was able to look at himself, seeing the man without the deeper regret he would have known had he completed the downward path he had been on a few hours earlier. Pushing the dirty clothes into the hamper, Cap stepped into the bathtub and turned on the water. He stood still under the shower and allowed the hot, steaming water to cleanse his outer being even as he attempted to allow the Lord to cleanse the inner. He reveled in the clean smell of the soap and felt his anger and hurt begin to dissolve. He could almost picture the anguish washing down the drain along with the soapsuds.

"Cap?"

Lara's soft voice startled Cap, and he quickly reached for the shower nozzle to turn off the cascade of soothing water. As he stepped from the shower stall, Lara handed him a towel. He wrapped the towel around his hips as she looked at him, and her eyes seemed to bore into his. He returned her gaze, grateful that he could do so without the burden of a heavier guilt. Her eyes looked softer, and there was sadness in their blue depths that seemed more human. It was a look that lived, and Cap reached for her, grateful that she had lost the look of one who walked with death.

Lara buried her face against Cap's damp chest, saying over and over again, "I'm so sorry."

"Honey, I'll never leave you. Please forgive me."

"I love you so much, Cap. I don't know why I said all those horrible things."

"I love you too, Lara. We both have said and done some hurtful things." All Cap wanted to do was to gather her in his arms and hold her close forever, but he knew that he had to be honest with her, to tell her where he had been all night. Pulling back, Cap took Lara by the hand. Leading her to the bed, he sat down with her and looked her in the eye. "Lara, we need to talk . . . I mean, I need to talk. I need to tell you something."

As he concluded his story, Lara wiped tears from her eyes. "Cap, I can't begin to imagine the type of healing you felt tonight. All I can do is try to understand."

Cap looked amazed. "But, Lara, what about the woman? What about what I almost did with her?"

A momentary hurt flickered in Lara's eyes, but she continued, "Cap, that's not the point. It was your love for me that made you stop. It was your love for our family that brought you back to me this morning." While Lara was human enough to feel the sting of betrayal, and she almost cried at the thought of Cap with another woman, it was her love for him that allowed her to release that sense of betrayal even as she shouldered the responsibility of her own actions from the night before. Her forgiveness for Cap's mistake was almost instantaneous.

Cap swallowed his emotion as Lara softly continued, "I'm so sorry I haven't been here for you, Cap. I never meant to hurt you or the girls."

Cap kissed away her tears, and their early morning togetherness proved to Lara that the forgiveness was mutual. She recognized that she was on the road to recovery. Even though she still hurt, and the longing for her daughter would always be a part of her, she had at last broken through the black, heavy veil of guilt. And she knew that she had to rid herself of the self-loathing that had buried her in a grave as real and as confining as the tomb that held the body of their baby. She was able to see, at last, the needs and the longings of her husband and her two living daughters. She still had Cap and Lisa and Rachel, and they were worth living for.

CHAPTER 23

August 1959
San Diego, California

Lara watched as her husband, dressed all in white, was lowered into the waist-deep water, their friend Jed Baker supporting him as the clear water enveloped Cap, burying him in its crystal depths. Lara felt a stirring in her heart that she had noticed on occasion during the missionary discussions. She knew that the missionaries and Cap believed it to be the Spirit of God, but she herself still wasn't sure. She had watched Cap change as he learned about The Church of Jesus Christ of Latter-day Saints, and she had to admit to herself that he seemed at peace. There was a new light that seemed to shine from his eyes, yet her heart lurched painfully with the sadness that still encompassed her. She felt tears gather in her eyes as Cap rose from the water, looking happy and complete. Lara's tears were a manifestation of the strange stirrings of her spirit mixed with the sadness that never left her.

Lara became aware of sweet young voices singing, and she smiled as she recognized Lisa's sweet voice among the other children gathered at the front of the room. They were singing "I Am a Child of God." Cap had requested this song be a part of his baptismal program.

Lara and the girls had accompanied Cap when he attended the local ward of Latter-day Saints, and Lisa had immediately become attached to her junior Sunday School teacher. She loved listening to the stories about Jesus Christ and the ancient prophets, and she joined in singing the songs as if she had been waiting for this experience the whole of her four years of life.

Cap and the girls had immediately fit in while Lara had struggled with her shyness and the uncertainty of what the Mormon gospel taught. The concepts taught by the missionaries were new to Lara, and while a part of her hungered for the knowledge they seemed to possess and the surety of their testimonies, there was also something that Lara just couldn't let go of. And as she watched Cap and Jed climb the stairs out of the baptismal font and disappear into the dressing room, Lara settled back to listen to the children sing, content for the moment to let the sweetness of their voices wash over her.

She felt some of the cleansing spirit that she was sure Cap had felt during his baptism. There was something about it all that reassured Lara, and she hoped that eventually she would find her answers. As she listened to the young voices, she felt that same, strange stirring, and she knew that somehow with time she, too, would come to know the peace and assurance that had been given to Cap. She sensed that one day, the understanding that she had already gained would be added upon.

CHAPTER 24

January 1960
Wendell, Idaho

"Lara, honey, are you okay?"

Cap's voice was quiet and filled with concern. They were driving away from Lara's childhood home, their two girls lying on the back-seat, napping away their exhaustion from the past three days' whirl-wind activities. They were heading back to San Diego, leaving behind what remained of Lara's family. The unexpected death of Lily Straddler had shaken Lara and left her feeling like the orphan she suddenly was. She had shed quiet tears on the drive up to Idaho and during the simple graveside ceremony. But the wrenching grief she had shown over the deaths of her daughters and her father was missing.

Cap knew she was grieving, and he was worried that she seemed so introspective. He reached over and touched her hand, feeling a modicum of reassurance as her fingers curled around his. They had been through so much in such a short period of time. He and Lara had experienced the most devastating depths of grief over the loss of their two daughters, and they both grieved the deaths of Lara's parents. But the gospel had given Cap the gift and promise of peace, and he wanted so desperately to share that peace with Lara.

Cap squeezed her fingers and gave a gentle tug on her hand. Lara responded to his cue by sliding across the front seat of the car until she was sitting next to him. She kept hold of his hand and leaned her head on his shoulder. Her quiet sigh accompanied the relaxation of her body as Cap felt Lara lean against him. "I love you, honey," he said.

"I love you too, Cap."

"Are you okay?"

Lara responded to Cap's question by nodding her head. "I'm okay. Just really tired."

"Why don't you try and rest," Cap suggested. "We're going to be on the road for a long time."

"How far are we going to drive today? You don't have to be on base until the day after tomorrow. Are you going to try and drive straight through again?"

Lara's question was asked in a voice husky with fatigue and accompanied by a wide yawn. She was remembering the horrendously long drive from San Diego to Wendell. After they'd received word that Lily Straddler had died unexpectedly, they had hurriedly made arrangements for Cap's emergency leave from the base. They had then driven straight through, a drive that had taken almost thirty-five hours. It had been exhausting for them all, and Cap knew that the return drive would be just as debilitating, if not more so, considering the harrowing days spent in Wendell. Cap knew that Lara was not only physically tired, but emotionally drained as well.

"We'll stop in Sacramento for the night." He smiled as Lara groaned her relief. "That's still a long way to go, though, so why don't you go ahead and try to get some sleep."

Lara's answer was to snuggle closer to Cap's side, her head resting on his shoulder as he encircled her with his strong arm, pulling her close. Turning his head, Cap placed a gentle kiss on her forehead and whispered, "I love you, Lara."

He grinned again, as the only response to his whispered endearment was a soft mewing sound that came from her lips, slack in sleep. Cap felt his heart turn over as he gently removed his arm from around Lara's shoulders. He needed it free to shift the car during the drive. His movement only slightly disturbed the sleeping woman as she moved in her sleep and slid down into a semireclined position on the wide front seat, her head resting against his hip.

The big Rambler station wagon ate up the miles as they traveled through the flat, seemingly never-ending deserts of northern Nevada. It was a tedious drive, but Cap seemed immune to the boredom as he drove. His family slept for hours, and he found himself free to think about all the changes that had come into his life since leaving Hailey that long-ago spring after he graduated from high school.

That had been nine years ago. He would turn twenty-six on his next birthday. He was a seasoned Seabee in the United States Navy. He had a wife. They'd had four daughters. They'd buried two of them. Both of Lara's parents were dead.

Cap and Lara had talked about having more children. When they had first married, they had both wanted a large family. But Lara felt the need to rest and heal for a time. She had been through so much, both physically and emotionally. They decided to leave it in the Lord's hands. If they were meant to have more children, they would welcome them into their home. If not, they had Lisa and Rachel and the memories of Christine and Sammy.

Cap's thoughts then turned to his brother and sister. John and Sandy had both married young, had children of their own, then divorced and remarried, their saga following the unhappy pattern of their parents. Cap, on the other hand, had made friends with his stepfather, William Aldrich, and with a start of surprise, Cap realized that he had even started to develop a relationship with his mother. He felt a calm sense of thankfulness in his heart as he realized that his lifelong search for his mother was finally seeing some results.

As he thought about the wonder of the blessings that had filled his life, he suddenly stilled, holding his breath as the warmth of a loving spirit washed over him. He realized that his search for his mother had actually brought him so much more than the fledgling start of a relationship with the woman who had given him life.

It had given him his career. It had brought him his wife and his children. But most important, it had brought him the gospel of Jesus Christ. Cap realized anew that the greatest reward to his search had been coming to know and understand the greater love of his Heavenly Father and his Savior, Jesus Christ. That love was the true gift, and that love had made possible the strengthening of his love for his wife and children. And he knew that it was the advent of the gospel in his life that had strengthened the beginnings of his relationship with his mother.

He whispered a silent, grateful prayer for all that he had found. His prayer included an entreaty for the woman who was sleeping so quietly by his side, that one day she would join him in the quest for eternity that he had embarked upon at the time of his baptism. He had recently started to learn about the temple and the ordinance of eternal marriage and eternal families. His heart was anchored in the testimony he had received that families could be together forever, and he yearned for the day when Lara would know the same things he did.

Cap found his thoughts wandering to the more distant past. He felt the healing of the gospel in his heart, lending him the ability to begin to forgive his mother, to seek a greater love for her. And he was grateful that he was finding it easier to displace the pain of rejection that had surrounded him for so many years. The stirring of compassion for his mother was making the healing a reality.

His thoughts then turned to the man who had caused Pearl so much pain. He frowned as darker thoughts and a hardening of his heart intruded upon his former joy. The image that came to him was of a brutally abusive man, drunken and cruel, and Cap found himself seemingly incapable of forgiveness.

As he recognized the harshness of his own feelings, Cap realized that he still had a long way to go. He had forgiven his mother. In fact, he had forgiven her a long time ago, recognizing through his own pain as her young son, rejected time and again, the depths of her pain and the anguish that had driven him out of her life.

And the source of that pain was Jake Martin. In Cap's mind, Jake was the source and the root of all the misery that he and his mother and his brother and sister had ever experienced. And as his anger and resentment rose to the forefront, Cap's brown eyes darkened. He knew it was wrong to hold on to the anger and the hate. Hate was a cankerous emotion that would eat away at him if not dealt with. Through his hurt and sorrow, Cap struggled to utter another prayer, a prayer of supplication founded in desperation. His prayer encompassed the hurt and the anger and the hate he felt blackening his heart, and he asked for it to be taken away.

Sacramento, California

It was late when Cap pulled the car into the parking lot of a small motel. The girls and Lara had awakened as they passed through Reno,

Nevada, so they had stopped to fill the car with gas and take a potty break. Since they had slept past the noon hour, the girls had awakened hungry, so he and Lara had treated the family to a rare extravagance of lunch out, which included hamburgers, french fries, and milk shakes.

Rachel had been so funny. She was a picky eater and had proceeded to tear her hamburger apart, peeling away the pickle and wrinkling her nose over the pungent scent of ketchup and mustard. She had nibbled at the hamburger patty until Lara wiped away the condiments with a paper napkin. She had then gobbled the meat and bun hungrily along with her fries.

Lisa and Rachel had been given a chocolate milk shake to share, a first for them both. Lisa enjoyed the shake, but was more interested in her sandwich and fries. Lara had held the shake back from Rachel until she had eaten a good portion of her lunch, knowing that her younger daughter had a definite sweet tooth. Lara knew that once Rachel tasted the creamy goodness of the shake, she wouldn't want anything else. Lara had also made sure Lisa had her fair share of the ice cream before allowing Rachel to finish devouring it. And as expected, once Rachel tasted the frosty sweetness, she hadn't once removed her lips from the straw until the very last drop was gone. Cap had watched the girls, delighted that they were enjoying their treat and grateful that he could occasionally give his young daughters such simple pleasures.

As the car came to a stop near the motel office, Cap climbed out from behind the wheel and wearily stretched. He felt cramped from the long drive and was happy to stop for the night. As Lara tried to restrain the girls from crawling out of the car, Cap went into the office to check in for the night.

Lara felt tired and weary, her heart heavy with the loneliness she felt for her parents. She didn't know how long it would take for her to get over feeling like an orphan. At twenty-five, with a family of her own, all she felt was the sadness of a little girl suddenly left alone and lost in the great big world. She was physically tired, and longed to stretch out on a soft mattress with a fluffy, clean pillow under her head. She felt like she could sleep for hours, and she recognized the early signs of depression. After Sammy's death, she had sunk into those depths for several months, and though she had worked through those dark days, she still recognized the shadows that lurked beneath the surface of her emotions.

She, too, was anxious to get home. Lara knew that Cap was tired, and she was grateful he had so selflessly allowed her the time to rest. The last few hours on the road had passed quickly. The girls had awakened with a boost in their energy level. Lara and Cap had been pushed to keep them occupied with toys and games and songs.

It had been fun, though, and Lara smiled as she listened to the giggles and whispers coming from the backseat. Her daughters were truly good girls. They were growing so fast. Lisa would be five that year, and Rachel four, but they still seemed so little. Lara again felt the sadness overwhelm her, knowing that they would grow up without knowing their grandparents. She was grateful when the driver's side door opened, interrupting her thoughts.

Cap climbed into the car announcing, "We've got us a double room down at the end of the building."

The sky was dark and clear as they pulled into the parking space in front of their room. Lara and Cap both took a deep breath, appreciating the softly scented night air. As Lara got out of the car, she paused for a moment to enjoy the balmy breeze of a California night.

Cap gathered their suitcases, and Lara and the girls followed him into the plainly furnished but clean room. Lisa and Rachel quickly amused themselves by bouncing on the beds. Lisa leaped from the edge of one bed and landed in a tumbled heap on the other, giggling and squealing. She looked quickly at her mom, knowing that she would never have been allowed to do that at home, but she saw Lara and Cap watching her with smiles on their faces. She started to bounce on the middle of the mattress, her knees tucked under her, arms flapping up and down like she was trying to fly away. Rachel was in the middle of the other bed, laughing and mimicking her older sister. Cap and Lara both stretched their arms overhead as they chuckled and turned toward each other.

Cap took Lara in his arms and held her close, drinking in the lightly perfumed scent of her soft, brown hair. It felt so good just to hold her. In the midst of his family—his daughters playing happily on the beds and his beautiful wife in his arms—he was able to forget the anger that had so unexpectedly erupted in his heart, spurred by the memories of his father.

"Lara Bell, I am so tired!"

"I'm sure you are. Why don't we call it a night?" Lara asked.

"Sounds good to me. Are you hungry?"

"I'm not, but the girls should probably have something."

Cap groaned as he released Lara and picked up the keys. "I think I saw a small grocery store just down the road. I'll see what I can find."

Lara reminded Cap that her sister-in-law had packed a small cooler for them. "I think it's still in the car. She put in leftovers from the family dinner yesterday."

Cap sighed with relief and smiled as he left the room only to return seconds later carrying the small cooler packed with food. As they dug into its contents, they found the makings for turkey sandwiches, as well as carrot sticks, juice, and cookies. The girls ate their simple meal hurriedly, and even Cap and Lara found their appetites. Soon, all that remained were a few slices of bread, a couple of carrot sticks, and some cookie crumbs.

While Cap cleaned away the leftovers, Lara got the girls ready for bed. Lisa was whining that she wasn't tired, and Rachel was sitting on the floor, her usually cheerful face sullen and pouty. Lara patiently dealt with the children as she got them into their pajamas, coaxing them to brush their teeth, wash their faces, and hop into bed. Lara knelt beside them, as did Cap, and she listened as Cap offered a simple family prayer. Since Cap had been baptized, Lara had to admit that this one ritual was something she found pleasant.

Usually they had the girls utter their own simple prayers, but they were so tired Cap was the one who prayed that night. Lara allowed the comforting spirit to settle not only on her shoulders, but also in her heart. And as Cap's quiet voice, reverent and loving, asked for God's blessings to rest upon their loved ones that night, Lara again felt a stirring in her heart and she welcomed the relief it brought.

She had become much more accustomed to those feelings, and she had even started to admit that the missionaries probably knew what they had been talking about when they shared their testimonies. As Cap closed his prayer and kissed the soft cheeks of the girls, Lara slowly rose from her knees and looked at the sleeping faces of her two angels. They had quickly succumbed to slumber and truly looked like cherubs, their hair softly askew, their cheeks flushed pink, and their sweet mouths looking like rosebuds. Lara leaned over and kissed their cheeks, tucked them in, and turned out the light between the two beds.

She and Cap prepared to retire, moving quietly about the room and whispering, their voices soft and hushed. Lara recognized a feeling almost of reverence. It was as if God had sent angels to wrap them in their arms, and as she and Cap lay down, she whispered her own silent prayer of thanks. Cap pulled her into his arms, kissed her fervently, told her he loved her, then closed his eyes and fell soundly asleep.

Lara lay in his arms, her lips tingling from his kiss, her eyes shining with the love she felt for him, and suddenly and inexplicably, she was fully awake. *It was probably that long nap I took in the car,* Lara thought to herself. Turning a little in Cap's embrace, Lara made herself more comfortable and let her mind drift to the past.

She thought back on her brothers and herself during their childhood, of her parents, quiet and strong, distant but loving. She especially cherished the rare words of love that had passed between herself and her mother over the last few years. It had seemed easier for them both to express their love as Lara had entered adulthood, and Lara was grateful for the gradual ease. She felt again the loneliness for her parents, and then she felt the sadness and emptiness of a parent herself, the longing she felt for the two little girls who should have been tucked up in the bed with Lisa and Rachel.

As she thought of her two missing daughters, Lara felt warmth spreading through her entire being. It surpassed the warmth and the light she had felt earlier during Cap's prayer. It surpassed any of the feelings she had come to welcome over the past few months. Cap's baptism had not only brought change to Cap, it had also wrought a change in Lara's heart. She had welcomed those moments of light and had been toying with the idea of inviting the missionaries back into their home. She just hadn't done it yet.

As she lay in the quiet motel room far from home, she listened to the quiet sounds coming from her sleeping daughters in the other bed. She listened to Cap's quiet snoring, and she felt the warmth of his body pressed against hers. Suddenly her senses seemed heightened to all of the loveliness in that shabby room. The exquisiteness stemmed from her daughters and her husband, their love for her and her love for them. It stemmed also from her husband's faith and his love for a

God that Lara was just coming to know. And as she admitted to herself that his God was real, Lara felt again the overwhelming warmth and light surrounding her. And suddenly she knew.

She felt as if she were lying directly in a ray of heaven's light. The sensation and beauty were so real and so pronounced that Lara found herself crying out with delight. The feeling of loving arms wrapped around her was a tangible, physical impression.

At first she thought it was Cap's arms she was feeling, but she realized that he had turned from her and was facing away from her. She wrapped her own arms around her chest, hugging herself tightly as if to enfold closer the awareness of being held by one whose love was so great and all encompassing.

The next morning they arose and made an early start. They stopped at a grocery store to pick up donuts, bananas, and milk for breakfast. Lara also chose the fixings for a picnic lunch, which she packed in the cooler. While she knew that Cap wouldn't mind spending the extra money for breakfast and lunch out, Lara felt strongly that they should be frugal. Her thrifty meal planning was born of necessity and of habit.

One of the few issues she and Cap had experienced dissension over in their marriage had been money. Lara was careful of spending, remembering all too clearly how it had been when Cap was overseas and the money he sent home hadn't spread far enough. There had been many days she had eaten very lightly, and she had frequently given up drinking milk. But the girls had never gone wanting. She had always made sure there was food and milk on the table for them. Since Cap had been stationed stateside in San Diego, she had come to realize that his spending wasn't nearly as frugal or as budget conscious as she felt necessary. He always liked to have cash in his pocket. He called it his "mad" money.

Lara smiled to herself as she remembered how she had retaliated and told him that it was indeed "mad" money because it made her madder than an old wet hen when he insisted on taking money out of the household budget just so he could have some loose change in his pocket. The argument had ended with laughter and Cap's promise to be more careful. Lara smiled as she thought about their marriage, growing stronger every day. It was the little incidents like the "mad" money experience that helped them learn as individuals and as a couple.

A sparkle came into her eyes as she recalled the breathtaking feelings from the night before. She knew that she still had a long road to travel when it came to spiritual awareness and understanding, but she was thrilled to have received such a resounding testimony. And she knew that her answered prayer was also an answer to Cap's prayers. She was debating on when to tell him when he said, "All right, Lara. What's going on with you?"

Lara pretended to look surprised and innocent as she said, "What do you mean?"

"You look like a pampered cat who's just lapped up a bowl of cream. What gives?"

"I guess I'm just happy to be heading home."

Cap took his eyes off the road long enough to look at her, and for a moment he almost bought her reply. Then he said, "Uh-uh. There's something more."

Lara looked at him and raised her eyebrows, her eyes soft with love but twinkling with her secret.

"Come on, honey, I can tell something is going on." Cap's voice turned soft and serious. "I mean, we buried your mom the day before yesterday, and even though you seemed to handle it okay, there was a bruised look in your eyes. You didn't say much to me, but I could tell you were hurting."

"I'm still hurting, Cap. I miss her very, very much."

"I know, Bell. I didn't mean to imply that you didn't. It's just that the bruised look and that deep sadness I could see in your eyes are gone."

Lara didn't respond for a few minutes. It was early afternoon, and she turned to the girls and asked if they were ready for lunch. Lisa and Rachel, who were playing happily in the backseat with their toys, excitedly agreed that they were hungry. "Cap, let's pull over, and while we eat we can talk."

Cap drove until he found a turnoff into a small town. They found a municipal park where they could set the girls up with their picnic, and once they were happily munching their sandwiches, Lara turned to Cap and said, "When we get home, I'd like to call Jed and have him come over."

"Okay, that would be great. We haven't seen Jed for a while. I'd like to see him myself."

"That's not all. I'd like to invite the missionaries to come over too."

Cap's eyes widened, and his lower jaw dropped as he said, "Okay . . .?"

Lara smiled, looking deeply into Cap's eyes. Then she turned and looked up at the sky. It was a beautiful, deep shade of blue, dotted with cumulus clouds. The sun felt warm and balmy, and Lara basked in the warmth of it as she continued, "I want to be baptized."

"Oh, honey."

At Cap's softly whispered endearment, Lara looked at him, her eyes swimming in tears as she said, "I've been fighting it for a while, and I'm not sure why. But after losing Mom, I realized that I need whatever anchor is holding you safely in place." Lara gulped her tears down as she said, "I feel as if I've been buffeted by an unending hurricane. Your love has helped, and somehow I've been given the strength to ride the waves. And I've finally been able to see why that is."

Cap reached for Lara and took both of her hands in his, holding them tightly as she continued, "Your love has been strong enough to help me because you are anchored by your faith in Jesus and in Heavenly Father. You've had such a rough life, but you are so strong and so good. I can't believe my fortune in having you for my husband. I know why you accepted the gospel first."

"Why?" Cap murmured, his hands trembling slightly as he gripped her fingers even tighter, his eyes set on hers as he gazed into her soul.

"Because spiritually, you've been prepared for it. And your heart was open and willing to learn. It's like you had to learn, like you had to grasp ahold of what the gospel offers because you've been waiting for it all your life. And I couldn't do that. I don't know why I've been so stubborn, but, honey, I'm ready now. I know that I'll see Mama and Daddy again. And I know that Christine Marie and Sammy are still mine, still ours, and that they are waiting for us to make our family complete."

All of a sudden, Cap dropped her hands and stepped back. Then he turned and started gathering up the items from their lunch. He urged the girls to hurry and finish their juice as he started tossing paper plates and napkins into a nearby trash can. Lara was stunned by his sudden activity. She sat and watched him, puzzled and a little perturbed at his reaction to her words.

"Cap?" she said, his name a question left hanging in the air.

Cap stopped his frantic movements, facing away from Lara, his head tilted back, his face turned toward the brightness of the noonday sun. Suddenly he jumped in the air and let out a mighty shout, his voice echoing across the park. Lara started to laugh as he turned and ran to her, his arms outstretched. When Cap reached her, instead of gathering her in a big hug, he stooped down, put his arms around her hips and lifted her high in the air. He started to spin in circles, his laughter ringing in the trees. Lara threw her head back and flung her arms wide as she, too, started to laugh and shout without inhibition. Lisa and Rachel stared, their mouths open as they watched their parents. They started to giggle, not sure why Mommy and Daddy were acting so crazy, but soon unable to restrain themselves from joining in the fun.

Lisa jumped up from the picnic table and ran over to her parents, launching herself at Cap's legs. She caught him around the knees, knocking him off balance as all three of them tumbled to the ground. Rachel decided she couldn't be left out of the merriment and scampered over to jump in the middle of the pile of arms and legs. After a few seconds of tickling and laughing, Cap withdrew the two little girls from the dog pile and told them to go finish their juice.

"We are done, Daddy."

"Wanna play some more!"

Lisa and Rachel tried once again to join the fun, but Cap laughingly pushed them away and said, "Then you girls run over to the bathroom and go potty. And be quick about it. We need to get headed home."

As the two girls took off, skipping to the nearby bathrooms, Cap looked down at Lara, who still lay flat on her back, looking up at him. "We've got some important business to attend to."

A moment of stillness settled over Cap and Lara as they looked at each other, awed by the emotions and the events of the day. Cap's face shone with the radiance reflected from the happiness in Lara's eyes. He took her by the hand and helped her sit up before he raised her hands to his lips, kissing her knuckles as he continued to gaze into her eyes. He knew that the oneness they shared as husband and wife would soon be an eternal bond that no man on earth could break, and that knowledge fanned the flame of their love. Lara and Cap were locked in a spiritual embrace stronger than any physical contact.

They sat quietly together, their hearts joined as the sun shone brighter, the breeze softened, and the music of the robins perched in the tree branches high overhead celebrated the beauty of the moment. Soon the musical cadence of the girls' laughter joined the song of the day, and Cap and Lara quickly arose to clean away the refuse of their lunch. It wasn't long before the girls were settled on the backseat of the car for a nap. Lara and Cap spoke quietly of their future as they drove toward the sun, knowing that in reality a greater light was drawing them toward home and eternity.

CHAPTER 25

June 1962
Simm's Canyon, Idaho

"Cap, are you sure you want to do this?" Lara's voice was anxious as she watched her husband's face and saw him tensing his jaw muscles.

"I have to do this, babe." Cap quickly took his eyes off the road and looked at Lara. He smiled into her anxious face and said, "I can't move away without trying."

Lara reached over and took ahold of his hand as Cap turned his attention back to the road. "I know the turnoff is here soon." With a grunt of satisfaction, Cap saw the small, weathered sign that pointed down a narrow dirt lane.

Simm's Canyon. Cap's thoughts turned to the tiny encampment where he had spent his early years. He had been surprised but not shocked when his sister-in-law Karen had told him that Jake had moved back to Simm's Canyon. The little town was no more than a deserted ghost town, but for Jake it had offered a refuge when he found the loneliness of his life in Boise too difficult to continue. He had moved back in June 1960 and soon after had met his current wife, Pat.

"Daddy, is Grandpa Jake really a gold miner?"

"Yes, bugaboo, he is."

Rachel giggled at the silly nickname as she tried to picture her unknown grandpa, the gold miner.

While Rachel and Lisa appeared to adapt easily to the many moves as a result of Cap's naval career, the one major drawback was the lack of opportunity to spend time with their extended families.

Cap and Lara had both tried to make sure the girls knew their grand-parents, aunts, uncles, and cousins through letters, phone calls, and stories—all in an attempt to make up for the infrequent visits. But this trip to visit Jake was a new adventure.

"Rachel," Lisa whispered to her sister, trying to keep from drawing her parents' attention, "maybe Grandpa Jake will give us a gold nugget."

"Our very own gold nugget?" Rachel echoed, her eyes large and shiny with excitement.

"Shush, don't say it so loud. Daddy might not let us keep it. I don't think he likes Grandpa Jake very much."

"Don't shush me, Lisa! And you just better shush yourself. Daddy loves ever' body, so of course he loves his daddy."

Before Lisa could respond, Cap said, "Girls, if Grandpa Jake gives you a piece of gold, of course you may keep it."

"But, Daddy, Lisa said you don't like your daddy. Is she right?"

Cap flinched. He still wasn't dealing with his feelings about his father very successfully. He found himself unable to answer Rachel's innocent question. "You girls need to settle down. We'll be there soon."

Both girls settled back in their seats, their enthusiasm only slightly diminished by Cap's sudden gruffness. With a twinkle in her eye, Lisa reached over and tickled Rachel. "We might get our very own gold nugget!" Rachel held her hands to her mouth, muffling her excited giggles.

While the girls whispered in the backseat, Cap let his mind wander to the past. He hurt with the knowledge that his daughters had picked up on his feelings of animosity toward Jake. He wondered if he would ever win the struggle that continued to rage in his heart and mind. Lately it seemed to be a struggle that was escalating, and he recognized that ever since he and Lara had gone to the temple, his thoughts turned more and more to his father.

Cap still choked up when he remembered the day they had gone through the Salt Lake Temple. It had been so beautiful. The spirit of reverence had permeated his very soul, and he could see the same light of testimony reflected in Lara's eyes. When they had knelt across from each other at the altar in the sealing room and had been sealed for time and all eternity, Cap had felt that life couldn't get any better—until Lisa and Rachel walked into the room, holding hands and looking angelic in their white dresses. Then their friend Alice Baker and her daughter June knelt across from them, taking the place of their two daughters Christine and Samantha, completing their family circle. As they were sealed together, Cap and Lara had felt the holiness of their union and a completeness of their family that they never had before.

Soon after that momentous event, Cap and Lara became interested in family history. The classes they took on genealogy reinforced the importance of families in Heavenly Father's eternal plan. It made Cap feel more grateful than ever for his blossoming relationship with his mother. Pearl still kept him at a distance emotionally, and Cap somehow knew that she always would.

It was his growing acceptance of Pearl's weaknesses that made him start to question his relationship with his father. He tried to dampen down the old, familiar feelings of anger and hurt just as he tried to ignore the prompting in his heart to do something about it. He felt he was succeeding until they started attending the genealogy class at Sunday School. And then the girls started asking questions about their grandparents, and Cap knew that the time had come for him to address his past and the role his father had in that past. Cap knew that John's new wife, Karen, had befriended Jake, and as long as there was no indication that Jake had been drinking, John allowed Karen and their children to visit him. Karen also felt it important for Cap's girls to have a chance to meet their grandpa, so she convinced Lara to speak to Cap about it, and surprisingly, he had agreed. Sandy, on the other hand, flatly refused to allow her two children to have anything to do with their grandfather.

As they moved closer to Simm's Canyon, Cap felt the stirrings of painful memories. In the furthest reach of his memory, he could see the shadowy figures of his mother and father always accompanied by memories of violence.

It had been at the end of his third year of school that he had stood in the shadows and watched his mother leave him. She hadn't looked back, nor had she said a word to the three children standing huddled in the corner of the one-room shanty as she walked out the door. Jake hadn't been home at the time of her departure, but Cap had known what would happen once he arrived home and discovered that Pearl had left. Cap blanched and refused to pursue his memories beyond that point. That summer had been the beginning of his personal hell on earth. The imprisonment to which his mother had sentenced him had ended twelve years ago. He had left his father behind, but the memories and emotions evoked by that man were still an integral part of who Cap was.

The anger that he still harbored in his heart made him feel almost physically ill as they traveled down the rutted, narrow road leading into Simm's Canyon. Lara reached over and squeezed Cap's hand tightly as she watched pallor overcome his ruddy complexion. She realized that confronting his father, as well as bringing his children to meet their grandfather, was probably costing him more than having had to bury two young babies. She slid across the seat, sitting close to him as the car crested a small hill and the dilapidated and deserted buildings of the once-prosperous mining camp came into view. As they pulled closer, Cap and Lara could see a lone figure standing outside the door of a shabby trailer, its exterior weathered by the elements.

Lara was startled as she got her first good look at her father-in-law. It was like looking at an aged, withered, and very ill ghost of the man sitting at her side. She felt an inkling of understanding for the pain Pearl must have felt every time she looked at Cap. Her eldest son was the spitting image of the man who had married her as a young girl, and who had then robbed her of her ability to love.

The man was stooped, his broad shoulders rounded in fatigue. His dark hair was streaked with gray, and Lara could tell that he had attempted to comb it and hold it in place with water. He was clean shaven, but the color of his face was ashen and gray, almost the color of clay. His shirt was tucked into the waist of faded blue jeans, and he wore stained, heavy work boots. His hands were gnarled with arthritis and shook as he pocketed a cigarette lighter. His eyes were red rimmed, and his lips trembled as he tried to smile at the approaching family.

For Cap, it was like a dream. Only it wasn't a dream. Slowly he emerged from the car, the sounds of Lara and the girls following him hidden by the thrumming in his ears. He was then aware of Lara at his side, her left arm encircling his waist as she shepherded the two girls to stand in front of her. Jake's eyes rested on his son, and though Cap may not have been aware of it, Lara could see the pleading in the old man's faded brown eyes, a glimmer of moisture in the dull mahogany depths that were a dim reflection of her husband's. She knew that Jake was pleading for forgiveness.

And as he dropped to one knee, his joints cracking, Jake Martin held a trembling hand out to his granddaughters. Shy at first but then with a trust that was natural and sweet, both girls stepped forward. Ignoring his outstretched hands, they threw themselves against Jake's chest, wrapping their arms around his neck. The embrace lasted only a moment, but as the girls stepped away, they eagerly introduced themselves and started asking questions.

"Hi, Grandpa Jake! I'm Lisa."

"Grandpa, Daddy said that you have a gold mine!" Rachel's voice cracked with excitement.

"Do you live in that little trailer?"

"We used to live in a trailer too. Only it wasn't so small."

"Where do you go to the bathroom, cuz I gotta go!"

"Where's your mine, Grandpa? Can we see it?"

As their girlish voices tickled his ears, Jake laughed. He looked at Cap and met his son's steady gaze. "Thank you, son." Cap needed no explanation as Jake softly stroked the hair of the two girls dancing around him.

Lara watched as a moment of healing took place. She knew that the past could never be changed, but the look that father and son shared at that moment promised an easier future. She knew that the seed of forgiveness had been planted in Cap's heart.

"Jake, hi. My name is Lara."

Lara stepped forward, and like the girls, put her arms around the old man and hugged him briefly. She felt the trembling in his frail frame as he returned her embrace, and she realized that Jake Martin was a sick man.

"It's good to meet you, Lara." Jake returned Lara's embrace and then turned to shepherd his visitors inside. "Come on in the house."

Watching her squirming daughters, Lara smiled and said, "I think we need to make a visit to the facilities."

"All I have is an old outhouse. No indoor plumbing."

Lara smiled gently, recognizing Jake's embarrassment. "That's okay. We're not picky."

Jake pointed Lara and the girls towards the wooden structure that stood several yards away, the weathered boards and the moon-shaped cutout identifying it as "the facilities."

During the course of the afternoon, the reunited family had a chance to catch up on the last few years of their lives. Lara and Cap were introduced to Pat, Jake's new wife. They liked her immediately and could tell that her love for Jake went deep. Cap and Lara discovered that Pat had been baptized a member of The Church of Jesus Christ of Latter-day Saints and that she was faithful and devoted to her beliefs. It was her testimony of the healing power of the gospel that had given her the strength to overcome her own past. And it was her belief in the gift of repentance that allowed her to love Jake so deeply.

Cap was able to see the changes in Jake that Karen had spoken of, and he whispered a silent prayer that the seedling of forgiveness already planted in his heart would remain in fertile ground.

As evening approached, the adults in the group grew quiet. Rachel and Lisa were tired and, when instructed, clambered into the car. They hugged and kissed their newfound grandpa and grandma, thanking them for their gold nuggets. Jake held the girls for several seconds, knowing that these two precious granddaughters were a treasure that he might never have known. He hugged Lara and thanked her for coming.

Lara stepped out of the old man's embrace and stood beside Cap for a moment as the silence between father and son thickened. Lara glanced at Cap and, with a small smile of understanding, placed a gentle hand on his forearm, squeezing it softly before stepping back and joining the girls in the car.

Cap watched Lara leave, providing him and Jake a moment of privacy. With a sigh and a lifting of his chin, Cap turned back to Jake. He felt the conflict of his emotions boiling inside. The visit had gone well, but as the girls had chattered and giggled through the afternoon and the adults had talked and laughed, they all knew that the ease masked the deeper emotions of the two men.

They stood facing each other in the deepening twilight of the rolling hills, the years melting away, leaving the two men facing the past. Cap felt the old anger and hurt and loathing. And he felt the pride that had kept him a prisoner of the past. He didn't want to be the first one to reach out—he was the one who was injured. He was the victim of Jake's drunken abuse. And scene upon scene of encounters with his father's fists and hateful words replayed themselves in the window of his mind. He felt the tightening of his throat and the tensing of his muscles, and he clenched his hands almost as if he had to defend himself.

He knew the pride was choking him. He knew that he had to free the seedling of forgiveness from the roots of his pride and hurt. And as he struggled to do so, he prayed. Suddenly, he felt the weight of the years of hurt lift, almost imperceptibly, from his shoulders. He felt the freedom in his heart, and his hands relaxed, opening and reaching for his father.

Jake watched the play of emotions cross his son's face. He saw the clouds of darkness and despair encompassing the light in Cap's eyes, and he felt his own heart constrict with sadness. Over the years, he had come to realize how alone he was. He had allowed his anger and pride to cut him off from everyone in his past, not wanting to admit to the responsibilities of his choices. He had drowned himself further and further in the depths of drunken forgetfulness. He had welcomed the familiar feelings of rage and violence, and then the blessed numbness of forgetfulness found at the bottom of endless bottles of liquor.

He didn't know why he drank. He couldn't remember a time in his life when he hadn't turned to the solace of liquor. Pearl and their children, as well as the subsequent women in his life, could never know the demons that chased him to the bottle. They could only know the effects.

And once he found himself completely alone, he knew that the destruction was almost complete. One drunken, lonely night, he had come face-to-face with his own blameworthiness. And in a sudden, foreign moment of self-disclosure, Jake had admitted to himself that he had destroyed any chance he may have had for happiness. He had searched for it in all the wrong places—the gold mines, the gambling halls, the brothels and beds of too many women to count, and most destructive of all, the amber depths of liquor bottles.

He had shouted to the skies and had smashed the bottle of whiskey on the jutting rocks at the mouth of his nearly depleted mine. It was his third bottle of the night, and he had suddenly become sick of it. He was sick of the whiskey, he was sick of the violence, and he was sick of being alone. More than anything, he was sick of what he had become.

The previous two bottles of whiskey had hardly caused a stumble in his step, so used was he to its poisonous effects. As the glass shards splintered in the moonlight and the amber liquid melted harmlessly into the ground, Jake had fallen to his knees. He'd sat there for hours, alternately burying his head in his gnarled hands and throwing it back, screaming into the night skies. Finally exhaustion overtook him, and he fell to his side, curled in the fetal position on the stony ground. For the first time in years, he had fallen asleep out of exhaustion rather than from the stupefying effects of drink. And when he had awakened the next morning, it had been with a clear mind—another first. He had felt lost, unsure what to do, but he knew that he had to try to salvage something of his life.

His search had brought him into the company of Pat, a woman he had met previously but whom he had bypassed with little regard because of her stand on drinking. She was a woman with a past of her own, a woman who had traveled a road similar to Jake's, a woman who understood the torment of his alcoholic world. When she met Jake one afternoon at a small café, a bond had formed, and she had turned into his salvation. She had walked with him through the first hellish weeks of withdrawal, and she had been the first to contact John and Karen, inviting them back into Jake's life. Karen had responded to the invitation, and that had been the beginning of Jake's tenuous return into the lives of his children.

As he stood watching his eldest son, Jake saw again the gangly, dark-haired child whom he had tormented and eventually driven away. He felt the regret that stung his heart, regret for all the lost years, for all of the abuse and hateful behavior. Tears of shame fought to escape, but Jake held on to them, longing for Cap's forgiveness.

Now, he stood in the deepening twilight, the wind brushing the overhead trees with a soft whisper and the cicadas singing their evening chorus, and he saw Cap's arms reaching out to him. He felt himself move in time with Cap, and as he pulled his son into his embrace, Jake cried.

CHAPTER 26

July 1962
Wyoming

Muttering a mild expletive, Cap slowly released the pressure on the Rambler station wagon's accelerator. Lara looked at him, a question on her lips as Cap pulled the car to the side of the road. Before the question could be uttered, however, she heard the wail of a siren, and she murmured a little "Oh, dear" as she turned in her seat and looked out the rear window.

The flashing lights of a state trooper's car were almost indiscernible in the glaring sunshine that cast the rolling plains of rural Wyoming in a blinding white haze. Cap leaned across Lara's lap as he rummaged in the glove compartment for the vehicle registration. By the time the uniformed officer appeared at the driver's window, Cap had his driver's license and registration papers ready. He rolled the window down, ready to explain—if he could—why he had been going faster than the posted speed limit. Much to his amazement, the young officer didn't ask for his license. Nor did he appear to have a ticket in hand. Cap's bewilderment increased when the officer addressed him by name.

"Cap Martin?" the young officer queried.

"Yes, that's me, Officer. Um, is everything okay?"

With a sense of premonition, Lara reached for Cap's hands. To be stopped on the freeway in the middle of nowhere without any apparent cause made Lara's chest constrict with concern. They were on their way to Colorado, Cap's next assignment. He was being stationed at the naval reserve station located in Denver. During his early days in the navy, he had quickly discovered that he suffered from motion sickness, and was therefore less likely to be given sea duty. He often found his assignments situated far from the ocean. They had been on the road for two days, having left Idaho after a monthlong visit with their families. As Lara peered up at the young officer, she noted the gravity of his expression, and she knew that Cap was starting to feel the same sense of apprehension. He gripped her fingers.

"I hope I didn't startle you too badly, sir. I've been trying to get your attention for a few minutes, but you didn't seem to notice my lights."

Cap looked slightly startled as he answered, "I'm sorry. The glare of the sun was so bright in the rearview mirror. I didn't see you."

"I thought it must be something like that." The officer smiled slightly. "I hated to turn on the siren. You didn't do anything wrong, but I had to get your attention."

Cap just stared at the young man, his mouth going dry with increased concern.

"Mr. Martin, sir, I'm sorry to be the one to tell you. I mean, out here like this." The young officer was clearly ill at ease as he waved his hand toward the bland expanse of rangeland. "The American Red Cross put out a notice to watch for you, sir."

Cap sat up straighter, his sense of foreboding increasing at the mention of the Red Cross. That organization had already been the conduit of too many messages of grief. He nodded as he said, "Go on, son."

"Well, sir, is your father Jake Martin?"

"Yes." Gulping around the knot that suddenly tightened his throat, Cap continued, "Yes, my father is Jake Martin."

The state trooper straightened his hat and squared his shoulders, but his voice softened with sympathy. "I'm sorry, Mr. Martin, but your father died unexpectedly late last night. A heart attack."

Lara felt tears well in her eyes, and she saw Cap's face tighten. He clenched his jaw in an effort to control whatever emotions were arising in him. She barely heard the police officer as he said, "If you'll follow me, I'll escort you to the next town. You'll be able to call your family from there."

Thirty minutes later, Cap placed the phone receiver back in its cradle and turned to Lara. Both girls were playing at a nearby table.

The local police had been very kind to Cap and Lara, and had attempted to engage the girls with paper and crayons while their parents made the difficult phone call.

Cap reached for Lara's hands and said, "He died right away. He and Pat were having dinner, and he just keeled over." Cap fought to maintain his composure as he continued, "Pat was all alone. She had to drive into town and get help. She had to leave him there alone. There wasn't any way she could get him to the car."

Lara silently nodded, slipping her arms around Cap's waist. She cried for Pat. She couldn't imagine being in Pat's position, having to leave the side of the man she loved, not knowing for sure whether he was dead or alive, while she went for help.

Cap tightened his hold on Lara as he continued, "We have to go back. The Red Cross has arranged for me to have family emergency leave." Lara felt her stomach heave with sadness, churning with the memories of the other times Cap had been granted emergency leave.

Cap continued as Lara wrestled with her sadness and the painful memories, "They've given me ten days before I have to report. Karen said the funeral would be in three days. We should be able to get there late tomorrow if we drive straight through.

The next twenty-four hours passed in a blur for Cap and Lara. The drive seemed endless, and neither of them slept. The girls slept only fitfully, waking up cranky and grumpy. Lara was patient with them, somehow finding a reservoir of tolerance hidden beneath her own weariness.

As they drew closer to Boise, Lara remembered with gladness the parting from their family just a few short days ago. They had made a second visit to Jake and Pat's trailer, letting the girls have another few hours to get to know their Grandpa Jake and allowing Cap another opportunity to lay to rest some of the pain he still carried in his heart.

She hoped that he would be able to find a measure of comfort in knowing that he and Jake had found their way to a new beginning. Though their journey had been brief, at least it had commenced. Lara wondered if Jake's death would be difficult for John and Sandy. They had lost the opportunity to make peace with Jake, and Lara worried how it would affect them. She had come to love John and Sandy as though they were her brother and sister.

As if he were reading her mind, Cap broke the silence as he said, "You know what, honey?"

"What?"

"I'm so glad I had a chance to see Dad before we left."

"I know, babe."

"I mean, what if this had happened and I'd never had the chance see him again?" Pausing and shaking his head in disbelief, he continued, "I guess I would feel like I'd lost something forever. And now it's like I've only lost it for a little while."

As Cap spoke, a sweet stillness filled the interior of the car. The dusky light of the setting sun reflected its glow on Cap's face, and his eyes filled with tears. He wiped them away, then smiled and looked at Lara as she, too, dabbed at moist eyes. "It seems like all we've done over the last few years is say good-bye to people."

They thought of the two babies they had buried, as well as both of Lara's parents, and now Cap's father. Struggling to control his grief, Cap said, "We've cried at so many gravesides. At first I thought I was going to die right along with our babies."

He looked at Lara, whose emotions were still close to the surface, and he squeezed her hand as the light of the setting sun seemed to glow brighter in the approaching darkness. He continued, "It's not so hard now, though. I mean, I'm grieving, but it's not like I'm lost, like I was before. I know something that is gonna see us through all this."

Lara understood what Cap was saying. She felt the stirring of her own testimony, comforting and bringing peace to her soul. And as they drove, following the winding road to the point where it met the horizon, she knew that the falling night's darkness would soon be dispelled by the warmth and the brilliance of tomorrow's rising sun. And even though they were again facing the shadows and the heartache of death, tomorrow would bring healing and light.

CHAPTER 27

Christmas 1965
White Mountain Lodge, Idaho

The log cabin rang with the excited voices of children. Pearl Aldrich sat back and felt a sense of contentment and peace that was strange and slightly uncomfortable. It was the first time that she could remember having all of her children and grandchildren with her at the same time. Cap and Lara were being transferred again, this time to Rhode Island. After hearing about Cap's latest orders, William voiced his wish to have his family together, even if for a few short days. So he invited them all to join Pearl and him for Christmas.

William was employed as the caretaker of White Mountain Lodge, a remote retreat located in the Stanley basin of south-central Idaho. The lodge was hard to access during the winter, so it was not opened to guests during that season, and William's days were spent maintaining and protecting it from the harsh Idaho winter. He had used his snowmobile to get the families to the lodge from the state highway three miles away. The lane leading to the lodge was covered in four feet of snow, and the grandchildren had loved the ride on "Rudolph," Grandpa's bright red snowmobile.

Now, as they gathered and warmed themselves by the fire, chattering happily, Pearl wondered if she dared let go of the shield that had encased and protected her heart for so many years. She felt the vague desire to reach for something more, but she was doubtful she could. Her doubts were especially strong as she watched her eldest son.

He was so good with the children. It was obvious how much his daughters adored him, and his nieces and nephews clung to him as he teased and roughhoused with them. His dark good looks had been hewn into a leaner, softer version of the man who had sired him, yet he had the same sculpted cheekbones and strong jawline. His jet-black hair, showing only a few strands of gray, was closely cropped and shiny clean. His eyes, a mixture of gold and brown and red, were sparkling clear and reflected the smile that creased his cheeks with deeply embedded grooves, mirroring the curve of his laughing mouth.

Yes, she could see Jake Martin in his son, but she saw something more, something different. She saw the kindness and the goodness that set him apart from his father. Pearl could finally look at him and see someone other than the man she so hated, even now that he was dead and buried. But even as she felt the stirring of love for the man her son had become, she felt a blanket of fear enshroud the beating of her maternal heart.

She couldn't do it. She couldn't trust him. He was Jake's son too, and there must be something there, hidden and waiting for her to let down her guard.

As the fire crackled and a log fell, sending a shower of sparks up the chimney, Pearl turned from the painful reminder of her past and held her arms out to Jason, her only grandson. Jason was Sandy's oldest child. He was eight; his younger sister, Maggie, was five. Jason was her special boy. He embodied the innocent love that Pearl had been unable to accept from her own children.

Pearl sat hugging Jason while the other children played quietly in front of the fire. William and John came stomping through the door, and everyone squealed at the Arctic blast of frigid air that entered the room with them. Ned, Rachel and Lisa's dog, came scampering inside with the two men, his silky black coat frosted with a layer of icy crystals. As soon as he felt the warmth of the room, he halted midstride. Lara, watching his antics with an indulgent smile on her face, realized what he was preparing to do. Before she could cry out a warning, Ned planted his feet, the vigorous shake starting at his head and traveling down the entire length of his strong, sinewy body. His face exhibited a doggy smile of glee as he showered everyone nearby with a cascade of wet droplets.

The squeals and giggles of the children and the shouted surprise of the adults made the big dog jump around with puppylike abandon, licking the faces of anyone he reached. Laughter accompanied Cap's reprimand, "Ned, down boy!" Ned subsided on the floor next to Cap's feet, panting with content, his momentary play over.

Rachel, who had been watching her pet with unabashed joy, suddenly became aware of William's approach. "Grandpa!" Rachel shouted, giggling as William came towards her, his bare head and jacket-clad shoulders covered with a thick layer of powdery, white snowflakes. He pretended to be a bear as he growled and stomped across the room.

The three girls sitting on the floor squealed and collapsed as their grandpa came and stood over them, shaking his head and shoulders, showering them with the tiny flecks of icy cold.

"Will, you're making a mess!" scolded Pearl, the smile on her face not quite reaching her eyes. She knew that William doted on his granddaughters, and she felt an unaccountable sense of jealousy because he was teasing all the children while appearing to ignore Jason, whom she held on her lap. Yet William would have been dismayed if he had known of his wife's thoughts. He never showed favoritism among the grandchildren, and he loved them all equally, including Jason.

"Oh, Ma, it'll clean up. It's only water."

Pearl shot John a withering glance when he defended his stepfather. The other adults laughed at William's antics, ignoring Pearl's brief outburst of irritation.

"It's snowing to beat the band out there!" John exclaimed as he walked over to Karen.

As he reached for her, she suddenly slapped at his hand, laughing, "Don't you dare, John Martin! You look like an icebound polar bear!" Karen's words were lost in a peal of laughter as John scooped her up and held her close and rubbed his wet, cold face into the crook of her neck.

Laughing at his brother, Cap looked at Lara, his eyes filled with happiness. Lara smiled, and her heart warmed knowing that the family gathering gave Cap a long-sought-after sense of closeness with his kin. Lara knew that being together, seeing his brother and sister happy in their current marriages, was allowing Cap to dispel some of the worry he felt for them.

Cap sensed that John had a strong and loving mate in Karen, and he saw the changes in Sandy's demeanor the moment he met her husband, Theo Clark. Theo was a gentle, kind man whose love went deep and encompassed Sandy's children. When he and William met, they had recognized a kindred spirit in each other.

"Did you get the firewood, Will?" Pearl's question refocused everyone's attention on her and the boy struggling to get down from her lap.

"Sure did. Hey, Spud!" William addressed Jason using his favorite nickname for the boy. "Why don't you climb down from Grandma's lap and come help me stoke up this fire?"

Jason gleefully broke free from Pearl's arms and dashed across the room toward William. Pearl huffed her irritation and then hid it behind a smile as she said, "Yes, son. Go help Grandpa. We need that fire built up good and high. It's going to be a cold, wet night, and we'll need it to keep this old lodge warm."

White Mountain Lodge was a large structure, sturdily built of closely hewn logs interlocking together after the art of frontier builders. Even though the lodge was solidly built, the frigid cold of the mountain nights had a way of seeping between minuscule cracks in the outer walls, stinging the homey interior with tiny fingers of drafty, cold air. Each of the large bedrooms upstairs had its own fireplace, and earlier that evening, Cap, John, and Theo had carted armfuls of sap-filled logs up to the rooms.

"It's getting late, Cap. We should be thinking about getting the girls to bed."

"Oh, Mommy, do we have to?" Lisa and Rachel both whined, their tired eyes belying their words of complaint.

"Not right away, girlies, but soon. Daddy needs to go light the fire in the bedroom so it'll get warm before you go to bed."

Bending down and tickling Lisa, Cap said, "That's right, bugaboo. If I took you in there and put you into bed right now, you'd turn into a little popsicle!"

Lisa laughed as Cap ruffled her hair. Turning to his brother, he said, "Shall we?"

John and Cap left the room and climbed the wide staircase leading to the loft. Their voices faded as they traversed the open, beamed corridor that encircled the perimeter of the bedrooms overhead. At

Sandy's urging, Theo arose from the deep, comfortable chair where he had been sitting quietly, observing the activity taking place in the room. "Honey, why don't you go help Cap and John get all those fires lit? It's about time for Maggie and Jason to hit the hay too."

Five-year-old Maggie, the youngest of the children, had remained lying on the hearth rug, where she had collapsed after William had romped and teased with them earlier.

"Look at that little girly." William squatted down beside her and gathered her into his big arms. He held her close and smiled gently as she snuggled into his embrace. Her face was content as she immediately fell back asleep. William walked over to the large armchair recently vacated by Theo and gently lowered himself, taking care not to awaken his Maggie as he settled into its soft depths.

"Rachel, Lisa, why don't you girls put the game away? It's time to start winding down," Lara said quietly.

The lodge, its rafters recently ringing with the laughter and voices of the children, suddenly seemed quiet and still as everyone settled down, sleepy and happily worn-out after their busy day. Rachel and Lisa climbed up beside Lara on the couch and snuggled against her. Karen's children, Kevin, Pete, and Shari, settled onto the rug in front of the blazing fire. Kevin and Pete, ages eleven and nine, lay down and immediately went to sleep. Shari, age thirteen, simply rested, quietly gazing into the fire's flames, lost in her daydreams.

Lara tiredly stroked the soft, silken hair of her girls, and she knew from their quiet, slow breathing that both girls had fallen asleep. Jason and Shari were the only children awake, but they, too, were getting heavy-eyed.

Cap, John, and Theo came down the stairs, quickly hushing their voices at a warning signal from Sandy. "Looks like we got those fires lit just in time," Theo whispered. He smiled warmly as Cap offered him a friendly clap on the shoulder.

"Yep, looks like we're going to have to pack these little bundles up the stairs. Come on, bugaboo," Cap whispered as he bent down and roused Lisa, urging her to get up from the couch. Lara followed him with Rachel in her arms. She struggled as she climbed the stairs. The girls were growing so fast. Lisa was ten years old and already too big for Lara to carry. Rachel was nine, and she, too, was too big to be carried, but Lara tightened her grip and shifted her hold on Rachel, determined that she wouldn't yet relinquish the joy of carrying her sleeping daughter to bed.

Sandy followed, leading Jason as Theo bent and took Maggie from William's lap. Karen shook her boys awake and urged Shari to her feet. "You don't need to come up with us, sweetie," Karen whispered to John. As his wife shepherded their drowsy children up the stairs, John settled himself in front of the fire, visiting quietly with Pearl and William.

It took fifteen minutes for the adults to get all of the children tucked into bed. Cap and Lara were the last to come back downstairs, and the scene that greeted them was warm and cozy. The arrangement of the furnishings formed a large semicircle, with the rock fireplace providing the focal point of the room. The sight of their loved ones gathered intimately in front of the crackling fire was pleasing.

William and Pearl relaxed on one of the large sofas while Sandy and Theo occupied the second. John and Karen were sitting sprawled on the floor, making the most of the sensuously furry rug. Cap led Lara to one of the chairs and eased her down into its soft, comfortable depths. He sat on the floor at her feet, his back resting against her legs. Lara's fingers teased Cap's dark hair as he settled back against her. She felt the comfort and the safety of his presence as his body's warmth penetrated the thin layer of denim covering her legs. Ned, who had accompanied them upstairs when they took the girls to bed, had followed them back down and now lay sleeping next to Cap, his soft muzzle resting on his thigh. Cap gently stroked the smooth, silky cap of the slumbering dog's ears.

The room was quiet and peaceful as the tired grownups sat in silence. The hiss and crackle from the roaring flames provided a gentle cadence to the flickering light that accompanied the warmth from the fireplace. Someone had pulled back the curtain from the large side window of the lodge and had dimmed the interior lights. From where Lara and Cap sat, they were able to see the gentle drift of snow filling the blackened surface of the window.

Cap's eyes closed as he laid his head against Lara's knees, his thoughts and senses focused on the heady feeling of family togetherness that filled the room. More than just their physical presence, it was a uniting of hearts and souls. The rest of the family felt the same sense of harmony. And for most, it went deep into their hearts.

For Pearl, though, it was a surface feeling, mercurial and unpredictable, as fleeting as the falling snow. Her heart had been armored for so many years that to let herself be vulnerable and open to love was an ability that was all but lost. Even though there were cracks in her armor, the cycling poison of her hatred and fear welled up and prevented the soothing and healing balm of love from seeping too deeply into her inner core. Her eyes, too, were closed, and on the surface she appeared calm and at peace.

Her husband, the man who had loved her through all the lonely years when she had been married to Jake, separated from her in body but always near in heart, knew the truth. The man who loved her still, despite the hardness and the coldness that was such an integral part of the woman, was the only person truly aware of the deceptive sense of serenity that appeared to rest on Pearl.

The woman who held his heart in her two selfish hands dismissed the love he so freely offered. But William, like the others, was willing to settle for what he saw and had in front of him. He had come to terms years ago with the fact that his love for Pearl would have to be enough for them both. And while his gentle heart hungered at times for Pearl to return his devotion, he found refuge in the love he shared with his children and grandchildren.

A quiet voice broke through the stillness in the room. "Cap, I think we'd better go on up. I'm going to fall asleep sitting here if I don't move soon."

A quiet snore echoed Lara's words, and everyone laughed as Karen poked John gently in the ribs. As he sleepily raised his head, Karen stood up and held her hands out to him. "Come on, sleepyhead. Let's go to bed."

Cap arose also and took Lara by the hand. "Yep. Tomorrow is almost here, and we've got a full day ahead of us."

"Those kids are sure excited about hunting for the Christmas tree." William's eyes sparkled with his own eagerness as he continued, "Us old folk are gonna need all our energy just to keep up with those youngsters! Come on, honey, let's hit the sack." Pearl rose at her husband's bidding and silently led the way to the stairs.

Theo was the last to rise. He tossed three large pieces of split log into the fire, then securely fastened the wire mesh and screen before rising and joining his wife. She had wandered over to the window to close the curtain, and she smiled contentedly when Theo came up behind her and put his arms around her. He pulled her close as they stood for a moment, gazing out at the beauty of the winter night. The snow that had been sifting softly through the ebony sky had subsided, and the clouds were passing, allowing the weak light of the winter moon to illuminate the outside yard. The wintry panorama sparkled in the dim moonbeams, and as Theo and Sandy turned away from the picturesque scene, a deepening peace descended on the household.

The fire crackled and hissed merrily as it threw out its flickering light and lent warmth and comfort to the empty room. Quiet voices echoed "good nights" along the balcony overhead. The gentle closing of a bedroom door left the lodge in silence and tranquility while cotton-soft clouds, heavy with winter's moisture, gathered once again, snuffing out the moon's incandescent light. The snow that began to fall whispered a lullaby to the sleeping family.

CHAPTER 28

"Come on, kids, get your winter gear on and let's go get us a tree!" Grandpa William's voice rang through the lodge, exciting the eager children to action.

"Shouldn't we stay and help Mommy clean up?" Rachel's worried voice asked quietly, her eyes shining with anticipation for the upcoming outing but her natural sense of responsibility holding her back from joining the other children in their madcap dash to the coat closet.

"It's okay, bugaboo. You go on and get ready to go with Grandpa. You've been waiting all morning for this!"

Rachel jumped up and down as her excitement got the best of her. But before running for her coat, she turned to Lara and wrapped her skinny arms around Lara's middle. "Thank you, Mommy. I love you!"

"I love you too, sis. Now go on. Scoot or you're going to be left behind."

Lara didn't have to repeat her warning twice. As Rachel ran after the others, Lara turned with a happy smile. "Are we ready, girls?" Lara and her sisters-in-law were going to spend the day baking and cooking. They had all the ingredients for a myriad of pies, cakes, cookies, and breads, as well as the makings for soups, salads, and side dishes to complement roast ham, turkey, and chicken.

Lara, Karen, Sandy, and Pearl busied themselves with their culinary activities while Cap, William, John, and Theo ushered the herd of excited children outside. Ned scampered joyfully through the snow and chased the children as they ran around the men in circles. The late morning hours were spent riding Rudolph, with everyone enjoying the heart-stopping rides through the snowy woods. William was an expert at maneuvering the snowmobile, slicing it through drifts and across open fields, causing the child riding with him to shriek with excitement. He made sure each of the children was given a fair turn on the machine, and he laughingly turned over the controls to Cap and John as they insisted on taking their turn operating Rudolph. Theo, after much cajoling, overcame his hesitancy and took a cautious turn around the field, arriving back at the group with a big grin on his face. When offered a second chance at operating the snow machine, he eagerly clambered aboard and laughed as Jason piled on behind him and they swept through the snowy terrain, racing the sun as it chased the few drifting clouds across the broad expanse of wintry blue sky.

While waiting their turns on the snowmobile, the remaining men and children gleefully built snow forts and engaged each other in a battle of icy orbs. Snowmen soon dotted the far reaches of the grounds, and the happy sounds of laughter rose to the skies with crystal clarity.

Finally, the men called the children close and passed out sandwiches and cups of hot soup. Everyone quickly finished their lunch. The men were eager to get on with the afternoon's activities. They knew how quickly the coming afternoon would pass as they watched the sun slowly track westward, and they also knew the time had come for them to start the search for their Christmas tree.

Gathering the children close, William issued a few words of caution. Each of the men had two of the children assigned to him as "buddies." Cap had Jason and Shari assigned to him; John was paired up with Rachel and Kevin; Theo had Pete and Lisa, with William taking charge of Maggie. Each of the children had been instructed to keep their adult buddy in sight at all times and to stay within arm's length of their "kid buddy." The whole group would stay together during the march to the nearby woods, but would separate once they reached the forest of trees. They all understood that they were to stay within hearing distance of the others, ensuring no one group or child could wander off.

Though the day was sunny and bright, the afternoon seemed to bring with it a downward plunge in the temperature as a light breeze swept across the mountain valley. The children already had rosy cheeks and runny noses from the hours spent playing in the snow, and even though they were bundled up in boots, hats, mittens, scarves, and heavy winter coats, the cold seemed to grab them with icy claws that made them shiver under the layers of warm clothing.

Maggie was riding on the sled pulled by William. She was wrapped in a heavy quilt that would be used to truss the tree once the group had decided on the perfect offering for their Christmas celebration. Rachel walked by the sled, worried that Maggie would feel left out if she were left alone while everyone but Grandpa played in the snow.

The men knew that after a full morning of play, the children would tire easily and the cold would soon overcome their eagerness. It was their plan to find the "perfect" tree quickly and head back to the lodge. William had previously scouted the forest for offerings, and he directed the group deep into the woods, following a logging trail that was easy to find and easy to follow. He had found a patch of lovely fir trees that would bear several options for the kids to choose from.

Shari, Pete, Kevin, Jason and Lisa were busy lobbing snowballs at each other while Ned jumped and pounced trying to catch the flying, frozen spheres. Rachel was trotting alongside the sled, her high, clear voice joining the deeper tones of William's and the lisping voice of Maggie in singing "Jingle Bells." Cap, John, and Theo were playfully shouting back and forth, occasionally tossing a carefully aimed missile at an unsuspecting child as they joined in the game of throwing snowballs. The laughter of the children added its own musical accompaniment to the song being sung by William and the two youngest girls.

With an abrupt stop, William shouted, "There!"

Excited shouts preceded a general stampede through the snow to the patch of fir trees to which William pointed.

"Hey, those are dandy trees!" John's judgment was greeted with shouts of agreement as everyone dashed among the snow-laden cones of green. Cries of "Here's one!" and "Look at this one!" rang across the frosty landscape as the children and the adults hunted and explored the forest glen. Forgotten in the excitement were the careful instructions and warnings about keeping everyone in sight.

William pulled the sled to the side of the logging road and loosened the quilt from around Maggie, who was eager to join her older cousins in their merry search. Shari took Maggie by the hand and pulled her along as she dashed from tree to tree. At one point she turned her over to Jason, who in turn took Maggie and pushed her in the direction of one of the other children. The other kids, however, were too busy and didn't notice the little girl in the dark blue parka wandering on her own.

The men took part in the hunt and soon realized that their buddy system had fallen apart. They watched the group and listened to the young voices, confident that they were keeping track of the seven small figures darting about the trees. Suddenly, the voices all quieted, and a hush fell across the mountain air. Cap and John hurried to join the others assembled in front of one particular tree. It appeared that they had found their perfect Christmas tree.

And it was grand. Perfectly shaped with heavy, dark green boughs, it smelled divine in the cold mountain air, and it rose to a majestic nine feet. William glanced around the group and asked, "Is it unanimous?" All heads nodded in assent, and as William picked up his ax, they stood in awe, watching as he worked. Cap noticed that Rachel and Lisa were shivering, and he was grateful they had found a tree so quickly. It was cold, and the wind was picking up. The shadows of evening were already creeping across the mountainside.

As they stood and watched William tackling the mighty tree, no one noticed the absence of one little girl, her dark blue parka missing from amongst the huddled group. The ax's blade bit into the resin-filled bark, and its sharp ring filled the air. Tiny footsteps in the snow became obliterated as the wind picked up and began to swirl the soft, loose snow in wild patterns of drifting cold.

A few minutes later, William yelled out, "Timber!" and all the children shouted with glee as their tree came crashing to the ground, its full branches sweeping through the air with flying snow and a whoosh of sound.

"Kevin, go get me the sled and the quilt!" shouted William.

A few minutes later, the tree was securely trussed and lashed to the sled. "Who's cold?" Cap shouted.

Cries of "Me!" echoed through the darkening grove of trees as everyone prepared to troop back to the lodge.

"Maggie sure is lucky! She gets to ride on top of the tree!" Jason cried with a hint of envy in his voice.

"That's right, because she's so little," Rachel defended her young cousin.

"Come on Maggie-girl, your carriage awaits you," invited William.

A few seconds of noisy chatter followed William's words, but when Maggie failed to come forward, the voices stilled. Silence surrounded the group, and frowns of concern began to crease the faces of the four men.

"Maggie! Come to Grandpa!" William shouted.

The faces and the voices of the children mirrored the concern and worry now firmly stamped on the faces of the adults. Maggie's name was shouted over and over as they all began to turn and search the darkening grove of trees.

"Daddy, where's Maggie?" Rachel's voice carried a hint of hysteria as she ran from tree to tree. "Maggie!" Tears began to trickle down her cold, red cheeks, and as she stopped in midstride, Rachel began to cry in earnest.

Maggie was missing. She wasn't in sight, nor did she appear to be within earshot. Lisa and Shari were crying too, while Pete, Kevin, and Jason tried to appear strong and calm. But their faces were twisted with fear and their eyes were glistening.

All of the children were shivering, the cold wind cutting through the layers of their outer clothing. Their frozen discomfort heightened the sense of devastation that stemmed from Maggie's disappearance. Cap, William, John, and Theo stood looking at each other, their faces stricken and white with shock. How could this have happened? Just the thought of the little girl lost and wandering in the world of frozen white made them cringe with despair.

Cap, used to making quick decisions, took charge. "William, you take the tree and the other kids on home."

"But Cap, I have to find her." William's voice was thick with emotion. "I was her buddy."

"I know we'll find her. We're all buddies now. And these kids need to go back home." Putting his arm around the shoulders of the older man, Cap reassured him, "We'll find her."

William nodded, his throat tight with emotion. "After you get the kids back home, gather up flashlights and blankets, and refill a couple of those thermoses with soup and hot chocolate. Then come back here," he said.

"We're going to need some light. And when we find her, she's going to be pretty cold." No one commented on Cap's optimistic use of the word *when*.

William set off, the children silent as they trailed after him. Their afternoon of fun had taken a disastrous turn, and their demeanors reflected the seriousness of the situation. William didn't know how he was going to tell Sandy. He was racked with self-accusation, and he felt responsible. He had been assigned as Maggie's buddy, and he had lost sight of her.

Shari felt her insides quake with guilt as she remembered how she had handed Maggie off to Jason because she was holding her back. And Jason wondered why he had been so quick to push her away. Why hadn't he been more careful about making sure someone else had Maggie by the hand when he had gotten tired of her short legs holding him back? Lisa had Rachel by the hand, their tears cool on their cheeks. Pete and Kevin both shared an understanding of the danger facing Maggie. They had been hunting a few times with John, and they knew how easy it was to get lost in the woods.

It was so cold. And it was getting dark.

Thirty minutes after he returned to join in the search, William still hurt from the experience of telling the women that Maggie was missing. He had left behind a solemn and terrified group. Sandy had been hysterical, inconsolable in spite of Karen's attempts to comfort her. Lara had busied herself getting the other children warmed up, and Pearl had turned white, her face stony and silent. William had left, his heart heavy and his ears ringing from the unspoken accusations.

He rejoined the other men, bringing with him blankets, matches, powerful flashlights, and thermoses filled with warm drinks and soup. Cap, John, and Theo each gulped down a cup of hot soup, needing its sustaining warmth before they continued their search. It was almost dark, and they knew if they didn't find Maggie soon, it was going to be too late.

Cap set them up to search in grids, starting with the area immediately surrounding the grove of trees where they had cut down the Christmas tree. Cap cursed the wind that blew away any traces of their footprints, and he prayed as the search continued. He calculated that Maggie had been missing for about an hour, so it might have already been too late. She was so little, and the elements were so overpowering for one unprepared to meet their challenge.

Cap could hear the voices of the other men as they searched and called for Maggie. He felt a sense of hopelessness as the wind blew and the snow swirled. The tall trees were dark and looming, and the sky was overcast with dark, snow-laden clouds, adding to the gloom.

With a groan, Cap sank to his knees and bowed his head. Ned, sensing the drama in the air, stayed close to his side, his ebony face worried as he trotted beside his master. He now sat on his haunches, leaning against Cap, his eyes soulful and beseeching as he watched his master.

Cap ruffled the top of Ned's head as he whispered, "Good boy. I sure wish you had some hound dog instincts."

Cap's heart felt like it could break as he began pleading with the Lord to help them in their search. "Please . . ." His voice caught in his throat. "Please, dear Heavenly Father, help us find Maggie. Keep her warm and safe. She's so little . . ." He was unable to finish the sentence. The words wouldn't come. But in his heart he pled with all the faith and yearning of his soul.

Back at the lodge, Lara and Karen were sitting with Sandy, whose silent sobs bespoke her worry and fear more poignantly than her earlier hysterics. Lara and Karen were quiet, knowing that there was nothing they could say to help make the waiting easier. The lodge was as silent as the night was dark.

The children were gathered in the dining room. Rachel was sitting apart from the others, listening to their hushed whispers. Her tears had long since dried on her cheeks, and her solemn face reflected her heartache. With a determined look in her eyes, Rachel suddenly rose from her seat and walked over to Lisa. As she stood in front of her sister, she said, "Lisa, we need to say a prayer."

Rachel had murmured many silent prayers during the long trek home through the snow and the cold, her tears and thoughts centered on the image of her cousin lost in the forest. She now felt an overwhelming urge to share a spoken prayer with her sister.

Lisa nodded her head and looked at their cousins. "We want to say a prayer for Maggie."

Kevin, Pete, Shari, and Jason all looked at Lisa and Rachel, uncertainty on their faces. "We don't know how to pray," murmured Jason.

"It's easy," answered Lisa. "You just kneel with us, and while one of us says the words, you guys say it in your hearts. You know, let God know you believe what we're saying, and He'll hear it."

"Okay, let's try," Shari agreed.

With great solemnity, the youngsters knelt in a circle, following Lisa's and Rachel's example by bowing their heads and folding their arms.

A hush settled in the room as Lisa spoke. "Dear Heavenly Father, Maggie is lost in the woods, and it's very cold out there. Please keep her safe. Help Daddy and Uncle John and Uncle Theo and Grandpa find her." A few sniffles could be heard in the stillness of the room as Lisa paused. Her voice choked up slightly as she continued, "We know You love her. We love her too. Thank You for helping bring her home safe. In the name of Jesus Christ, amen."

"Amen," Rachel echoed.

"Amen," whispered the other children. None of them doubted that Maggie would soon join them.

In the darkness of the woods, Cap, too, rose from his knees as the children finished their simple prayer. A sense of reassurance settled on his shoulders as he stood for a moment to gather his thoughts.

With a sense of surety, Cap retraced his steps and returned to the original grid where they had begun their search. John, following the arc of Cap's powerful torch, shouted, "Cap, we already searched back there!" Cap didn't answer as he strode purposefully through the deep snow. Suddenly the gloom of the night dispersed, and Cap glanced up at the sky. He saw the cloud cover breaking apart and drifting away, allowing the bright light of the stars and the moon to shimmer and gleam across the white expanse of the snow-shrouded forest. Cap felt as if the light had also filled his mind as he stopped on the logging road, his feet planted within inches of where the sled had rested earlier that day. He saw through the grove of trees the spot where they had cut down their Christmas tree, and he stood there and scanned the terrain, his eyes resting on each tree.

With a sense of wonder, Cap's gaze came to rest on one tree. It wasn't a particularly tall tree, but it was full and bushy, its heavy boughs brushing the ground. He noticed that some of the lower branches were bare of the thick layer of snow covering most of the tree, as if it had recently been disturbed. He walked to the tree and knelt down. Brushing aside some of the heavy boughs, he dropped to his hands and knees, shining the bright beam of his flashlight under the weight of green. The ground immediately under the tree was carpeted in a thick layer of soft, dry pine needles. The ground was free from snow, and the space beneath the branches was protected from the rustle of the winter wind.

"She's here," Cap called softly to the other men. Ned whined softly as Cap knelt in the snow, gazing at the tiny figure huddled beneath the protective branches of the large tree.

John, Theo, and William quickly joined Cap as they, too, knelt on the ground surrounding the shielding tree. They could barely see into the dark interior of the tree's undergrowth, but as Cap shined his light on the small figure lying beneath the tree, tears came to the eyes of all the men.

Cap reached out and handed his flashlight to John. He then reached for Maggie, his hands gentle as they shook her awake. "Maggie-girl. Come on, honey, wake up. It's Uncle Cap."

Maggie stirred as she felt Cap's hands. "Uncle Cap?"

"Yes, honey. It's me. Come on, baby, we need to get you home."

"I'm cold, Uncle Cap."

"I know. I've got a blanket here for you. Grandpa's got some hot chocolate for you too."

"Oooh, I love hot chocolate."

Maggie's voice was weak but clear. She seemed to move stiffly, and she cried out as she crawled towards Cap. As she came nearer, Cap reached for her and gently lifted her into his arms. Maggie was crying, but she came to him willingly, her arms circling his neck as he gathered her close.

"I'm so cold."

John draped a heavy quilt around her shoulders and tucked it under her chin as Cap turned her in his arms. She felt heavy with the cold, and he could feel her shivering. "Grandpa, let's get this bugaboo some of that cocoa."

William quickly wiped away the tears that were streaming down his weathered cheeks. His face looked gray and old as he battled with the feelings of guilt raging along with the overwhelming relief. "You bet, my little Maggie." With shaking hands, he poured a generous helping of steaming hot cocoa into a cup. "Here you go, baby. Grandpa will hold the cup for you."

Maggie eagerly sipped at the warming liquid, and she shivered violently as the first trickle of nourishing warmth tickled her tongue. Her shaking stilled slightly as she gulped down more and more of the hot drink. She quickly drained the cup and asked for more.

Grinning with relief, William quickly complied and poured another helping of cocoa into the cup. As he went to hold it to her lips, Maggie pushed aside the quilt and grabbed the cup from William. With a sigh, she again drained the cup and licked her lips as she finished, holding the cup out to William. "Thank you, Grandpa."

"You're welcome, sugar."

Maggie laid her head on Cap's shoulder, snuggling back into the folds of the quilt. She immediately fell asleep, her soft cheek resting against Cap's chest, her hair tickling his chin. Cap hugged her close as he whispered, "Let's get this baby back home."

It was a joyous reunion when the search party arrived back at the lodge. Sandy took Maggie away from Cap, hugging her close, tears falling unrestrained. Maggie awoke and, unsure why Sandy was crying, began to cry with her. Her face was red and chapped from the cold, but her tears soon decreased to an occasional hiccup. As the warmth of the room and the knowledge that she was safe permeated the previous cold, Maggie shrugged out of the quilt and very vehemently announced that she was hungry.

Laughter filled the room as the evening's tension gave way to the tremendous relief of having Maggie back with them, safe and unharmed. As the laughter died down, Lara ushered all the children to the bathroom to wash up as Sandy and Karen busied themselves with dishing up plates of hot stew and corn bread.

Soon everyone was gathered around the large dining room table. Before anyone could start to eat, Cap said, "I think we owe our Heavenly Father a prayer of thanksgiving." Even though John, Sandy, and Pearl and their families were not religious, they, too, felt the blessings of the evening's events and gratefully bowed their heads to join in the prayer of gratitude that Cap quietly and sincerely offered.

Soon the room rang with the chatter and laughter of the group hungrily and happily eating their meal. As they finished up and were devouring a plate of homemade oatmeal cookies, Pete asked if they were going to put up the tree.

Looking around at the tired faces, Pearl spoke up and unexpectedly made the decision. "I don't think so, son. Not tonight. Everyone's too tired."

As Pete's face fell with disappointment, William said, "Grandma's right. We're all too bushed. We'll all get a good night's sleep and put the tree up first thing in the morning."

There were a few grumbles from some of the children, but stern looks from their parents hushed them quickly. Everyone helped clear away the dishes and the supper mess, after which William and John went upstairs to light the bedroom fires. It wasn't long before the children were all settled in their warm beds, sound asleep.

The adults gathered in the family room, once again sprawled before the crackling warmth of the fire, Ned completing the postcard picture as he lay dozing on the hearth rug. Sandy was relating the events of the evening as she understood them from Maggie, shaking her head as she finished her story. "Maggie said that she just got tired and the wind was making her cold. She said that the tree looked like it had a 'cave,' and she crawled under there to take a nap."

"So she slept right through all the noise we were making while we were searching for her."

"I guess so, John," Sandy answered.

"I can't believe she's come through this without any apparent injury. She's so little, and she was missing for so long."

Theo's comment was met with several nods of agreement. "I think she had more than just the protection of that tree tonight." Lara's quiet words brought another round of nodding agreement.

William's voice cracked as he said, "Sandy, honey, I am so sorry this happened. It's my fault. She was my buddy, and I didn't do my job."

Sandy rose and went over to the older man, kneeling in front of him. "Oh, no, Dad. It isn't your fault. Please don't think that." She put her arms around him as they both cried.

Pearl's face looked hard and there was an accusatory tone in her voice as she asked, "Then whose fault was it?"

Everyone looked at her, appalled and surprised. William raised his head, tears drying on his stubbled cheeks as he looked sorrowfully at his wife. He read the clear condemnation in her eyes, and it broke his heart all over again. Sandy sat back on her heels, her eyes shooting sparks of anger.

"It wasn't anyone's fault, Mom. They were all out there together. They were all busy and having fun. Maggie wandered away. If it was anyone's fault, Maggie's to blame. She's old enough to know not to wander away like that."

John spoke up. "That's right, Mom. Dad has been tearing himself up over this long enough. He doesn't need to feel worse."

Pearl's face became even more hardened as she grimly sealed her lips. She looked at Sandy and John. Her eyes darkened as she shrugged her shoulders and stood up. "I'm going to bed."

"Dad, please don't feel bad." Sandy held on to William's hands as his sad eyes followed his wife's retreating back.

"It'll take some time, honey, but I'll be okay." What hurt him the most was knowing that even though Sandy didn't blame him, Pearl did. He knew that this was just one more brick that would be added to the wall that shut him out of her heart. "Guess I'll go to bed too."

"G'night, Dad," Sandy whispered as she put her arms around him and gave him one final squeeze.

After William left, the others sat for a few more minutes, quietly talking. They, too, were exhausted. Lara tugged on Cap's hand, and he silently followed her gentle command by rising and pulling her off the couch to stand by his side. As they climbed the graceful stairway to the overhead balcony, John and Karen, as well as Sandy and Theo, remained by the fire, their soft voices blending in with the musical crackle coming from the fireplace.

As Cap and Lara reached the door to their room, Cap stopped and said, "I'll be right back, hon. I want to . . . I need to go look in on Maggie." Cap's voice was gruff as Lara nodded her understanding.

"Go ahead, babe. I can't begin to imagine how it must have been for all of you looking for her. It was so cold and dark out there. And then, when you did find her . . . I don't know, I just can't imagine what it must have felt like."

Standing on her tiptoes, Lara reached up and put her arms around Cap's neck. Her gentle hands guided his head down to meet her loving lips, and after she kissed him, Lara whispered in his ear, "I love you so much. I know our Father in Heaven guided you to Maggie's hiding place tonight. He was the only one who could have known where she was in that great big forest. You did real good out there, honey."

Cap returned her embrace and held her close, his arms trembling with emotion. "I was so frightened that we wouldn't find her in time. But after I prayed, it's like a veil was lifted and I saw her. Even though I could hardly see my own shadow, I saw her."

"Go to her, Cap. Go give Maggie a kiss and then come back to me." Lara ushered Ned into the room before her as she lovingly waved Cap off on his mission to reassure himself that Maggie was tucked safely in her bed.

As Cap turned and left his wife, his heart was filled with gratitude for her love and support. He felt an overwhelming sense of relief and thankfulness that they had been able to overcome the hardships that they had encountered over the last few years. Since the beginning of their marriage, they had faced loss after loss, and it seemed as if a pattern of tragedy and heartache overlay the pattern of their everyday lives.

As Cap reflected further, he realized that his entire life had been spent facing tragedy or violence or loss in one form or another—from his early years when Pearl had abandoned him and John and Sandy, leaving them in the cruel care of their father, to tonight's events and their frantic search through the cold, dark wintry night. The reality of that day's fearful search seemed to be a mirror for the lifetime he had spent in the emotional search for his mother's love and the ability to forgive his father.

As these thoughts raced through his mind, Cap suddenly realized that the violence, the loss, and the searching had not only taken something from him, it had also given him a gift. The gift was the priceless knowledge he found in the gospel of light and hope. Cap felt the light fill him as he realized that the many tragic events had softened his heart to a point of yearning, a yearning so great that when the opportunity had come for him to hear the gospel of Jesus Christ and to open himself to the love of his Savior, he had been able to accept the message of love and hope with a faith born of trial and tears. And he also recognized that there was still a great yearning in his soul to continue growing in his faith.

Cap knew that even though he had overcome many obstacles, his learning was not complete. He realized that the trials he continued to experience were meant to strengthen him even more. The nature of his family and his past experiences with them allowed Cap the insight to accept that the future was not going to be smooth and free from conflict. But his faith told him that he would be able to overcome whatever came his way, and that if he remained true to his beliefs and allowed the Lord's Spirit to guide him, he and Lara and the girls would be okay.

Cap reached Maggie's bedroom and paused before turning the polished brass doorknob and pushing the door open. The small fire glowing in the hearth softly lit and warmed the room. Cap made his way though the shadows toward the far bed. He saw the small figures of Jason and Maggie curled under the heavy quilts, and he could hear the muffled snores coming from the sleeping figure closest to him. He knew it was Jason who was buried completely under the blankets. On the other side of the bed he could see the soft tendrils of Maggie's hair curling on her pillow. He walked around the far side of the bed and knelt down beside her.

He remained there, watching her face in quiet repose, and he felt a tenderness for the little girl who was his sister's daughter. She looked so small and fragile lying beneath the heavy quilts. She was only five, and she looked vulnerable lying in the soft cocoon formed by the pillow and quilt. He thought of how this evening might have turned out if he hadn't been in tune with the Spirit, letting it guide him through the dark and snowy night. He reached out a hand and gently brushed the curls from her forehead, then leaned close and placed a light but loving kiss on the smooth, white skin. She smelled so fresh and innocent.

"Uncle Cap?"

"Hi, baby. I'm sorry I woke you up."

"That's okay." Maggie's voice was tiny in the vast darkness of the room. "I wasn't really asleep."

"You weren't? Were you just resting your eyes?"

"Uh-huh." Maggie's answer was lost in a giant yawn. "Uncle Cap?"

"Yes, bugaboo?"

"Thank you for finding me."

"You're welcome, Maggie."

"Uncle Cap?"

"What, Maggie?"

"Would I have turned into a snowflake if you hadn't found me?"

Cap's heart turned over at her innocent question. "Yep, you would have been the prettiest little snowflake in the whole forest."

"I'm glad I didn't."

"Me too, baby. You're much prettier as a little girl. Snowflakes seem to melt away too quickly."

"Uncle Cap?"

"Yes?"

"I love you."

"I love you too, baby girl." Cap felt Maggie's hands slide around his neck, and he held her close for a moment.

Cap held Maggie for a few more minutes, relishing her closeness and thankful again that the day's earlier misadventure had turned out okay. He whispered a prayer of gratitude, kissed his niece's soft cheek, then laid her down to nestle in the cocoonlike softness of the bedding.

As he left the room, Cap met Sandy and Theo coming down the hall. Sandy's face mirrored immediate concern, but Cap's smile of reassurance quickly dispelled her worry.

"Cap," Sandy's voice was hoarse with emotion, "thank you again for finding my baby girl."

Cap smiled self-consciously. "You're welcome, sis. It wasn't really me, though. I couldn't have done it without some help."

"I know." Sandy's eyes softened for a moment, warmed with the fledgling birth of her own faith. "You know, I've never given much thought to God, but tonight . . ." Her voice trailed off for a moment as her emotions caught in her throat. "Tonight we saw a miracle."

Theo smiled warmly as he squeezed the shoulders of his wife. Cap leaned forward and kissed Sandy on the cheek. "God has many more miracles in store for you, sis. He loves you. So do I."

Sandy nodded, her eyes shining with unspoken emotions and her voice stilled by the sudden surge of feeling that warmed her heart.

"G'night, Theo."

"G'night, Cap. We'll see you in the morning."

Cap smiled as Theo led Sandy into their room. As the door closed behind them, Cap bowed his head as he strolled down the corridor. The old lodge was still and peaceful, and he felt himself enveloped by the Spirit. For at least one moment in time, all was well with his family.

CHAPTER 29

The next morning, everyone slept late, tired from the excitement of the previous day. Cap was the first one up. He had awakened earlier than the others, rested and surprised that he had been able to sleep at all. He quietly slipped out of bed and hurriedly dressed in warm clothes, shivering slightly in the cold morning air. A glance at the gray ash in the fireplace explained why the room was so chill. As quietly as he could, Cap rekindled the fire so that Lara and the girls wouldn't have to face the cold room when they arose.

Cap noiselessly opened the door, looking over his shoulder at his sleeping wife and daughters. He smiled at the contented sounds coming from the rumpled beds as he turned away from them and wandered down the stairs. By the time the others made an appearance, Cap had the fire rebuilt and had pulled in the large Christmas tree and mounted it in its stand. It was a large, beautiful tree, and would look lovely once decorated. It filled the room with its piney and resin-filled scent, and Cap hoped that they would all be able to enjoy the tree and its symbolism of the Christmas season without having the memories of the previous day cloud their enjoyment. He still shuddered when he thought about what could have happened, but then he felt an overwhelming sense of gratitude for the kind and loving hand that had protected Maggie and had guided him to her.

Cap was busy carrying in armloads of split wood to refill the wood box when Lara came downstairs. Rachel and Lisa, bouncing and eager to start their day, followed her. Lara and the girls greeted Cap with kisses and smiles before they went into the kitchen to start breakfast. Lara instructed Rachel to set out the dishes for the meal, and she had Lisa stir up the batter for pancakes.

Soon the kitchen was filled with the mouthwatering aroma of sizzling bacon. As if drawn by the rich scent wafting from the kitchen, the rest of the family soon made their appearance. By the time the bacon was crisp and the golden-brown pancakes came off the griddle, everyone was gathered around the table, hungry and eager to indulge their appetites.

That night was Christmas Eve, and many activities were planned for the day and the evening, including a special supper. A spirit of love and camaraderie filled the old lodge as voices were raised in happy song and much laughter. Hands were kept busy preparing for the upcoming festivities. Lara and Pearl worked side by side in the kitchen, finalizing the food preparations. Lara was surprised that she enjoyed the time spent with her mother-in-law. Pearl seemed to have overcome the hardness that had prevented her from comforting William the night before and was heard laughing with him. She even laid a gentle hand on his arm in a gesture that appeared loving.

Karen and Sandy helped supervise the children as they completed the Christmas projects they had started a few days earlier. Whispers and giggles accompanied handmade gifts gaily wrapped in colorful paper.

William, Cap, John, and Theo engaged themselves in various "honey-do" activities, including chopping wood and filling the wood boxes in all the bedrooms, stringing the lights on the Christmas tree, and hauling food around for the women.

The latter part of the morning was spent decorating the Christmas tree. The children eagerly participated, and once the last ornament had been hung, everyone oohed and aahed over the results. It was indeed a work of art, bright and cheery with the colorful orna-ments and the lights. Strings of popcorn and cranberries graced the branches, and tinsel shimmered on the tree, covering it in a sparkling veil of silver.

Lara, glancing at her watch, realized they had worked straight through the lunch hour.

"Is anyone else as hungry as I am?" she asked with a smile.

A resounding group "Yes!" answered her query. "Well, then, let's get lunch on the table."

"You know what, Lara?" Karen asked.

"What?"

"It's already almost three o'clock. Why don't we forget lunch and have an early dinner? We can just put out everything we had planned for both meals and let everyone go for the gusto!"

"Great idea. We'll have our own smorgasbord." Sandy grinned as she continued, "I'll bet these hungry kids will clear the table."

Amid much laughter, the dining room table was soon laid with a feast that would please any palate. There was sliced ham, baked beans, baked potatoes, hot rolls, leftover corn bread, pies, cookies, and much more.

Twenty minutes later, everyone agreed that it was the best meal they'd had—amidst groans of "I don't think I'll ever be able to eat again" mingled with "I don't want to ever look at food again."

Kevin wriggled his eyebrows as he said with a boyish grin, "Not me! I can hardly wait for the turkey tomorrow!"

The adults all groaned good-naturedly and laughed as John picked up a thick, knitted pot holder and heaved it across the table, hitting Kevin in the side of the head, "Be quiet, you!"

Pearl smiled, the usual tension in her face smoothed for once by the happy feelings of shared celebrations. "Kids, why don't you start clearing the table."

There were very few grumbles as the children hastened to do her bidding. They knew that Santa was coming that night and that now was not the time to be naughty or crabby about doing chores. As Rachel started carrying dishes to the sink, she started to sing. Soon the kitchen and dining hall were filled with young voices singing "Rudolph, the Red-Nosed Reindeer."

After the rooms were tidied, the children, along with Lara and Karen, trooped out to join the others by the fire, where they could relax and enjoy the warmth as well as the lights from the tree.

Lisa and Rachel had prepared a flannel-board presentation depicting the Christmas story, and they presented it with a sense of reverence and awe that settled the spirit of peace and goodwill in the hearts of all who listened. As they shared it, silence reigned in the old lodge. The spirit of the story touched the hearts of all present, but for Pearl, John, and Sandy, this was a first. They had never before given much thought to the real meaning behind the annual celebration.

Lisa and Rachel completed their story, and as the group joined in singing Christmas hymns, all felt the healing promise that accompanies a true understanding of the Christmas celebration. Even Pearl felt it, and as the last note of "Silent Night" faded, she gazed around the room, and for the first time in her life, she was able to admit to herself that she enjoyed having her children and grandchildren with her. Her eyes lingered on the face of her oldest son, and her countenance momentarily softened as she watched him help the girls pick up the props from their storyboard.

As if he sensed her gaze, Cap turned his head and met her eyes across the room. And for an infinitesimal moment, their souls connected. Cap smiled at his mother, his heart warmed from the unexpected gift of her momentary acceptance. She smiled back at him, but suddenly found herself unsure. And with regret, Cap saw the shadows again fall across her features as her smile faded and she turned away from him.

Cap felt the twinge of sadness that always lingered after each new moment of rejection, but as he heard the laughter and saw the loving faces of his family surrounding him, his heartache was replaced with understanding and acceptance. He smiled as Lara called his name and, turning to her, he put aside the sorrow.

The next half hour was spent shepherding the sleepy children off to bed. It wasn't difficult because they were all tired and anxious for the next eight hours to pass. They knew that morning would come soon, heralding another round of excitement as they explored Santa's offerings.

The adults spent the next hour quietly visiting while they waited for the children to fall asleep. Christmas gifts were then brought out and piled beneath the tree. When the last gift was placed, they all stood back and viewed the homey yet pleasing sight of the gaily decorated tree protecting the mounds of beribboned gifts beneath its boughs.

Lara sighed with contentment as she snuggled against Cap. His arm encircled her shoulders, and he squeezed her tight, murmuring, "Merry Christmas, Lara Bell."

"Merry Christmas, sweetheart," Lara responded with a hug and kiss.

William yawned loudly, making everyone chuckle. "I know, I'm an old man. I just wish I had a portion of them youngster's energy. I better get myself up to bed. They've got a head start on me, and I'll never be able to keep up with them tomorrow."

As he climbed the stairs, there was sadness in the stoop of the old man's shoulders. He knew that their time together was drawing to a close. After they all left, the lodge would seem hollow, echoing the silence of the empty bedrooms, bereft of the sparkle of his grandchildren's laughter.

With a start of surprise, William glanced down at Pearl, who had come up behind him and had taken him by the hand. There was gentleness in her eyes, a rare treat for William. He engulfed her hand in the warmth of his bearlike hand as they turned and waved a last good night to the three couples leaving their sight. As the last door closed, William turned and gently led his wife into their bedroom.

CHAPTER 30

June 1968
Davisville, Rhode Island

"Lara, honey, can you hear me? Over."

"I can hear you, but there's a lot of static. Over."

Lisa and Rachel sat on their parents' wide double bed, listening as Lara talked to Cap and intrigued by the frequent use of the word *over*. Cap was in Vietnam, and the call had been placed using shortwave radio.

"Lara, what's going on with Mom? Over."

"I don't know the specifics, Cap, just what the Red Cross told me. I couldn't get ahold of anyone back home. I assume they're all at the hospital with your mom. Over."

"She must really be sick. I'll be flying out of here in just a couple of hours. I've been given two weeks of emergency leave. I should be home in two days. My flight arrives at 0930 on Wednesday, your time. Over."

"We'll meet you at the base airport, Cap. I'll have everything ready to go. Do you want to spend the night here and leave for Idaho the next morning? Over."

"I'd like to, babe, but if Mom is as critical as it sounds, we'd better hit the road as soon as I get in. Over."

"Oh, Cap, you're going to be exhausted. Over."

"Yeah, but I'll be okay. We better end this, babe. I'm getting the signal to cut it short. I love you. Over."

"I love you too, sweetie. I can't wait to see you. The girls are excited to see you, and they say they love you too. Over."

"Tell them I love them and I'll be home with you all soon. Bye. I love you. Over."

"Bye, Cap. I love you. Over."

Tears streamed down Lara's cheeks at the silence on the other end of the phone. She missed Cap so much. Just as she had gotten used to having him home, he had been called up to go to Vietnam. The sudden loss was difficult. It had been years since he'd had to leave them for an overseas furlough.

Rachel and Lisa wrapped their arms around Lara as she cried. Her tears reminded them of the day Cap had left for Vietnam. He had left just before Christmas 1967, six long months ago.

They had waited in the small building just off the runway that served the naval personnel and their families during arrivals and departures from the busy naval airbase. The room had been crowded with the families of the men serving in the 51st Battalion of the Seabees. They were being sent to DaNang, Vietnam, and even though Cap's battalion wouldn't be involved in combat, he was still going to be near the front line, where ferocious battles were raging in the jungles. His battalion had been commissioned to construct a hospital for the naval base in DaNang.

Tension and sorrow had permeated the small room as families stood huddled together, talking quietly as the time of departure drew close. Finally, the moment they had been dreading was upon them, and the men gathered their belongings and headed for the waiting aircraft. Just before boarding, Cap threw his gear to the ground and turned to the girls. One by one, he gathered them close and hugged them tightly. They were growing up so fast, and he loved them so much. He hated having to be away from them. Lisa had been twelve; Rachel, eleven. By the time he returned home, they would be young ladies. Cap felt as if his heart were breaking, his lips trembling as he gently kissed their lips. Both girls were crying, their tears bathing their faces with sorrow as they clung to him.

Cap had to disentangle himself from their hold. Lara was standing behind the girls, her face composed, her dry eyes belying the anguish wrenching her heart. He stood in front of her, silently looking into her eyes. He had left her many times during the early years of their marriage, and while it had been difficult, those separations hadn't been this devastating. He was going to war, and they both knew there was a chance that he might not return. Their unspoken anguish bound them together as they stood apart, not touching.

As the last call to board was announced, Cap suddenly reached out and pulled Lara toward him. She threw herself into his arms and kissed him, unable to stifle a sob. Cap held her tightly, stroking her back and hair, wondering how he could be expected to say good-bye to this woman, his wife. She was already a part of his soul, and as he pulled himself away from her embrace, he turned and gathered up his belongings, gently stroking his daughters' wet cheeks in a final gesture of farewell before boarding the plane.

The girls' sobs were noisy as they waved good-bye. Lara stood, silent and dry-eyed, as she waved until the plane was out of sight. She then shepherded the girls into the car, and Rachel, whose sobs had quieted to noisy sniffles, asked, "Mommy, why aren't you crying?"

Lara thought a moment before answering. She settled herself behind the steering wheel and started the car, then said, her voice quiet and husky with emotion, "I didn't want your daddy to leave with the memory of me crying. I want him to remember my smile." And after saying that, Lara burst into tears and cried all the way home.

That had been six months ago, and now, as she sat on her bed with the girls, crying yet again, Lara realized that her tears were a mixture of loneliness, relief, and joy. Cap was coming home. Yes, it would only be for two weeks, and at the end of those two weeks there would be more good-byes. But at least he was coming home.

Even though his reason for coming home was an unhappy one, Lara was still grateful for the opportunity they would have to be together again. Finally she dried her eyes and said, "Girls, we need to get cracking! Daddy's coming home, and then we're going to Idaho! We need to clean the house, we have laundry to do, we need to pack clothes, and we need to let our neighbors know we're leaving so they can take in the mail. There's lots to do."

Lara gave the girls each a list of chores to do, and the remainder of the day passed in a whirl of activity. Lara called Idaho one more time that night, trying to get in touch with someone who knew what was going on with Pearl.

The Red Cross coordinator who had called Lara with the news that Pearl was ill and that arrangements were being made for Cap to come home had been able to give her just a thumbnail sketch of the situation. All Lara knew was that Pearl was ill and in the hospital, and there was a strong chance that she might not make it. Lara prayed that she would stay alive long enough for Cap to get home. He would be devastated if Pearl were to die before he had a chance to see her one last time.

Recently, Pearl had been in and out of the hospital, and was regularly going to the doctor at least once a week for one ailment or another. In their letters to Lara, Sandy and Karen had both expressed their belief that Pearl wasn't really as sick as she liked to present to the family, and that the many doctor and hospital visits were merely attempts to gain and keep her family's attention. But this time seemed different. It was the first time the Red Cross had been involved.

In the recent years, Pearl had frequently demanded that Cap be allowed to come home, treating him as if the years of abandonment and neglect had never happened. She had gone from rejecting him time and time again to demanding his constant attention. Her cries had usually been tolerable, merely causing a stir in the family and unrest in Cap's life as he continually answered her demands with explanations and pleas for patience. The turnaround in Pearl's treatment of Cap had occurred during the year following the Christmas they had all spent together at White Mountain Lodge. Each year since then, the demands seemed to grow more strident and more frequent.

Lara couldn't help but view this latest turn of events with a jaundiced eye and a degree of mistrust. She was willing to accept the seriousness of the matter, but only because the Red Cross was involved. Carefully packing her bag, Lara tried to shrug away her doubts. Whatever the situation in Idaho, at least Cap was coming home.

* * *

Three Days Later
New York City

"Cap, I can't believe this traffic! I've never seen anything like it!" Lara exclaimed.

Cap's face was grim as he was swept along with the flow of traffic. The trip so far had been pleasant. The family had been joyfully reunited the previous afternoon, and the first few minutes had been emotion filled, with Cap, Lara, and the girls clinging to each other. After Cap had completed the final paperwork before his leave became official, they had all piled into the car and headed west.

Cap had been exhausted from the long flight, and they had only driven until early evening. Cap had wanted to continue on, but had reached a point when he physically could go no farther. They had found an inexpensive motel in Connecticut, located just over the state line from New York. Cap had fallen into bed and dropped off to sleep immediately. The girls had fallen asleep quickly also, but Lara had lain awake for several hours, finding joy simply in having Cap beside her. When he had stirred awake in the wee hours of the morning, Lara was still awake.

She saw his eyes open in the dim gloom of the motel room. He smiled at her when he realized that she, too, was awake, and she had willingly gone into his arms to lovingly welcome him home. Later, Lara had finally drifted off to sleep, lulled by the beating of Cap's heart and gentle snores.

They had arisen early, eaten a simple breakfast, and hit the road, knowing that they had a long trip ahead of them. With Cap rested, they planned on driving straight through, taking turns driving, napping, and bedding the girls down in the back of the station wagon.

"Honey, I think I missed our exit." Frustrated, Cap ran a hand through his hair. "Traffic is moving so fast, I can't seem to keep track of the exit signs. I can't even read the darn things before we're past them."

"Do you need to look at the map? I'm afraid I've not been much help reading the silly thing for you."

"You've done fine, Bell. You told me what exit we needed. I just haven't been able to find it. And now the numbers are too high, so I think we've missed it. We're going to have to try to figure out how to get turned around and back on the right track."

"What are you going to do?"

Looking in the rearview mirror and seeing a small space, Cap turned on his signal light and began pulling over to the right side of the road. He had to cross three lanes of traffic to get to the side, but he finally made it.

"I think I'll just pull over here on the side of the road and take a look at the map."

"Do you think we should stop right here? Shouldn't we try to get off the freeway?"

"I don't know, hon. I'm almost afraid to take one of these exits. For one, we don't know where they'll take us. And two, we may never find our way back to this freeway. And at least we know that for now, this is the one we're supposed to be on."

As he was talking, Cap continued to slow down and ease the car onto the shoulder of the road, pulling as far over as the concrete and curbing would allow. On the right, the shoulder of the road inclined to meet a chain-link fence at the top of a grassy knoll. To the left were eight lanes of high-speed, congested traffic.

Cap took the map from Lara just as she was reaching to engage the emergency flasher. Before she could do so, however, they were hit from behind. Rachel and Lisa screamed as they were flung forward from the impact. The screech of crumpled metal filled the interior of the car as Lara and Cap both hurtled forward in their seats. The car, still moving from the impetus of the collision, careened up the grassy knoll as if it might roll.

The steering wheel took most of his impact as Cap was thrown forward in his seat. His chest smacked into the steering column, its hard plastic and metal unforgiving, knocking the breath from his lungs and bruising his rib cage.

"Lara! Girls!" Quickly turning his head, grimacing at the twinge of pain in his neck, Cap was relieved to see that Lara and the girls were all conscious. They all had dazed looks on their faces, and Lara had a small trickle of blood oozing from a bump on her forehead.

"Honey?" Cap reached over and gently wiped at the small stream of blood on Lara's face.

"I . . . I'm okay." Lara tried to shake the dazed look from her face as she turned in her seat, suddenly realizing what had just happened. "Girls? Lisa? Rachel?"

The girls answered in small voices, "We're okay." Then they burst into tears.

Relieved that they appeared uninjured, Cap got out of the car. He stood by the crumpled back fender and surveyed the damage. The entire rear end of the station wagon was smashed in, mangled and twisted. Lara stopped beside him as he said, "It looks like the whole undercarriage is shot."

Lara's face paled as she viewed the traffic passing in a blur. "Cap, I don't understand. Where is the car that hit us?" Her voice was soft and choked with confusion.

Before Cap could answer, a patrol car from the New York State Police approached, its lights flashing red and blue in spite of the bright glare of the morning sun. As it pulled in behind them, the front doors opened and two young officers exited, their faces expressing their concern as they walked over to Lara and Cap.

"Are you folks okay? Is anyone injured?"

"I think we're okay, Officer. We can all move and talk, anyway."

"My name is Joe Martinez, and this is Len Perkins. What happened here?" asked the officer as his partner began examining the accident site.

Cap began explaining about getting lost and how they had pulled over to check the map. "My wife was just getting ready to turn on the emergency flashers when we were hit."

As the officer wrote down Cap's statement, Cap continued, "I know I probably shouldn't have stopped, but I pulled far enough over I thought we'd be okay. And I felt like I had to stop for a minute to get my bearings." Cap's voice trailed off hoarsely as the officer stopped writing and looked at him, a serious but kind look in his eyes.

"I understand, sir. New York City can be pretty intimidating, and it's easy to get lost. Where are you folks from?"

"I'm in the navy, and we're stationed in Rhode Island. We're on our way to Idaho. My mom is very ill, and I'm on two weeks' emergency leave." Cap grimaced as he continued, "And now this has to happen. I don't know what we're going to do."

Lara reached over and took Cap by the hand as the officer said reassuringly, "Don't worry, sir, we'll help you get things worked out here. We've called for a tow truck. Are you sure you or your wife and daughters don't need to see a doctor?" The officer smiled at the two pale faces watching him through the space of the cracked side window.

"No, we're fine, thank you."

Just then the other officer returned. "This is a hit-and-run, Joe," he said, addressing his partner. "The jerk stopped about 150 yards down the road. I think his car quit on him or he'd be long gone. His car's a mess, though." Shaking his head, he continued, "Hit-and-run because he didn't stop right away, and it's a clear case of drunken driving. The guy smells like a brewery."

The two officers completed their investigation, and when the tow trucks arrived, they helped Lara and the girls into the cab of one of the rescue trucks. Joe told Cap that their car looked totaled but that he could call the auto body shop for confirmation. He gave Cap the insurance information from the hit-and-run driver and before leaving said, "I hope everything works out for you and your family, sir. I'm sorry this had to happen to you. And I hope your mother is okay."

"Thank you, Officer Martinez. We appreciate your kindness." As Cap climbed into the cab of the tow truck and pulled Rachel onto his lap, he watched as Officer Perkins handcuffed the drunken driver and ushered him into the back of their patrol car.

The tow truck took them to an auto body repair shop, where they were able to call a cab. The mechanic at the shop said that from his initial inspection, it looked as if the car was indeed totaled. He then gave Cap a business card for the insurance company and waved them off.

The taxi driver was gruff, and the interior of the cab smelled like stale smoke and unwashed bodies. Cap asked to be taken to a nearby motel, and a few minutes later they pulled into the parking lot of a large, well-known chain that advertised hospitality. Cap helped the cabby unload their luggage, paid the man, and shepherded his tired family into the lobby. A well-dressed woman stood at the registration desk. She was silent as Cap approached her.

Lara took the girls to sit on an overstuffed couch in the lobby. They all looked bedraggled and tired, and the pile of luggage sitting on the floor next to them looked shabby in the elegant lobby. Cap smiled at the receptionist and asked for a double room.

The young woman looked at Cap for a minute, taking in his disheveled appearance before turning her gaze toward the tired and grubby family. Her features cool and unfriendly, she answered Cap in an icy voice, "I'm sorry, sir, but we have no vacancies."

The woman, whose name tag read *Sharla Jones,* turned away from Cap and began writing in a ledger. Cap stood there for a moment, a look of disbelief on his face. Finally he said, "Excuse me, miss?" As she turned her cool gaze back on him, Cap looked her in the eye and said, "Your vacancy sign was on out front. That's why we stopped here."

"Oh, I'm sure you must be mistaken." Sharla Jones's voice reflected her disdain for Cap and his family, and she once again turned her attention to her ledgers.

"Miss Jones, my family and I have just been involved in a very bad traffic accident. We're stranded here in your city for a few days, and we need a room."

"Then I would suggest you look elsewhere. I'm sure there is another motel that will meet your needs—and your budget—better than this facility."

"I'd like to speak to the manager." Cap's voice was low, his temper brewing beneath a thin facade of calm.

Miss Jones looked at Cap, her upper lip curled into a sneer. "I am the manager. And as I said, we have no vacancies for your family."

Cap stared at her, unwilling to give her the satisfaction of looking away first. "Would you please call a taxi for us?"

Miss Jones maintained eye contact with Cap, her stare unfriendly. Cap thought she was going to refuse his request, but she nodded her head. She reached for the phone, and Cap heard her place the request for the taxi.

"You and your family may wait outside. There are benches under the portal. The cab should be here in approximately ten minutes."

"If it's all the same to you, I think we'll wait inside. Those sofas look much more comfortable than the benches." Cap turned and walked away from the reception desk, seething.

"Cap?" Lara turned as he approached.

Looking into the weary faces of his wife and daughters, Cap grimaced as he controlled his ire and said apologetically, "I'm sorry, girls. I couldn't get us a room here. The manager has called a cab for us. We'll have to find another place to stay the night."

A few minutes later, a yellow cab pulled under the portal of the hotel. A well-dressed man and woman exited the taxi and entered the lobby. The driver followed them, carrying a set of expensive-looking luggage, which he set on the floor a few feet away from the registration desk. As the couple approached the manager, the cab driver walked over to Cap. "You the folks who called for a taxi?"

"Yes, we are, thank you." As the driver and Cap began to gather up the pile of suitcases, Cap heard the well-dressed man ask the manager for a room.

"I'm sorry we don't have a reservation, but we have been unexpectedly delayed. We hadn't planned staying the night in the city." His voice was cultured, his drawl reflecting the genteel South.

Miss Jones, her smile suddenly warm and her voice welcoming, said, "That's no problem, sir. We have plenty of vacancies."

Her voice carried clearly across the otherwise silent lobby, and Cap shook his head. He felt sorry for Miss Sharla Jones. Without a backward glance, he followed his family outside, and together they climbed into the taxicab. A few minutes later, their driver dropped them off at a small but clean motel. The manager of the motel was friendly and very sympathetic to their circumstances. He assured them that they would have access to the phone in their room so that they could make travel arrangements.

Cap and Lara decided that he would fly out the next morning on his own and continue on to Idaho. Lara and the girls would fly back home to Rhode Island. By the time Cap and Lara crawled into bed, it was late and they were both exhausted. It had been a crazy, stressful day, yet they both recognized how lucky they were to have escaped serious injury from the accident. Lara had pointed out that it would have been so easy for their car to have gone the other direction, out into the multiple lanes of fast-moving traffic, when they were rear-ended. They whispered prayers of thanksgiving that they had been protected. Their plans for the trip to Idaho had changed, but at least they were all safe.

Early the next morning they rose, breakfasted, and prepared to leave. They took a taxi to the airport, happy to have someone else do the driving. The traffic was congested and, if anything, seemed faster and more out of control than the previous day. The cab arrived in good time at the airport, first dropping Cap at the terminal for American Airlines.

Lara and the girls hugged and kissed him good-bye, then returned to the taxi, subdued and saddened at being separated yet again. The girls were disappointed that they weren't able to accompany him to Idaho. Lara tried to reassure them that their father would be home again in a few days.

"But we wanted to see Grandma and Grandpa!"

"I know, Lisa, but we'll just have to wait. We just don't have enough money for all of us to fly all the way to Idaho."

"You can have my money," Rachel offered as she held her small purse out toward Lara.

Lara smiled gently at Rachel. "Thank you, honey, but it wouldn't be nearly enough. Besides, you've saved that money for so long, you need to spend it on something special for yourself."

Rachel's eyes brightened. "Maybe I can find a souvenir here at the airport!"

"I'm sure you can, kiddo."

Rachel smiled. She had been saving her allowance for months in a small jar that was almost filled to the top with quarters, nickels, and dimes. It seemed like a fortune to her, and she'd had plans to buy something from every state they drove through on their trip to Idaho. She had almost fourteen dollars and had been looking forward to all the treasures she hoped to find as they traveled cross-country.

"Maybe I'll get me a Statue of Liberty!"

"That would be great, honey."

"Lisa, would you like a souvenir too? I mean, I'll get you one if you want." Rachel looked hopefully at her sister.

Lisa smiled gratefully and said, "Sure, if you want. I'd like that." Even though Lisa received an allowance as well, she hadn't brought any of her money with her. She was saving it for a bike and had decided to go without souvenirs.

The cab driver listened to their chatter with a small smile on his weather-beaten face. The two sisters were cute, and he glanced admiringly at the calm face of their mother. She was a pretty woman, and even though she was pale and there were lines of stress around her eyes, he appreciated the quiet beauty of her face and the obvious love she had for her girls. He had listened and gathered some of the family's story as Lara and Cap talked on their way to the airport. In his heart he wished them well, and as they pulled up to the terminal for Eastern Airlines, he smiled and said, "Here we are, girls!"

As the cab driver pulled up to the curb, Rachel set her purse aside so that she could straighten and button her cardigan sweater. When the cabby opened the door for them, Lisa and Rachel jumped out of the cab and ran to join Lara on the sidewalk, overwhelmed at the busy bustle of the large airport. The cabby helped them find a porter, who then ushered them into the terminal.

Lara paid the cabby and waved good-bye as she and the girls made their way inside. The number of people milling around the ticket desks and the crowds rushing through the airport caused Lara to catch her breath and turn to the girls. Sharply, she instructed them to stay close to her as they followed the porter through the crowds and made their way to a long line at the ticket window.

They had been standing in line for just a few minutes when suddenly Rachel let out a wail. "Mom!"

Concerned, Lara looked at her and said, "What, Rachel?"

"I lost my purse!"

"Are you sure? Maybe it's stacked up with the suitcases." They all began to look through the jumbled pile of shabby suitcases and bags.

"Oh, Mom, it's not here."

Rachel's large blue eyes shimmered with tears as she valiantly fought to control her emotions. Lara said, "Honey, I'm so sorry. I don't know what to tell you."

"Did you drop it, Rachee?" asked Lisa.

"I don't know," whispered Rachel, her lower lip quivering.

Lara put her arm around Rachel's shoulders, "I'm sorry, honey, but it's gone. I'll see if I can find you girls a little something from the gift shops after we pick up our tickets."

Rachel sniffled, trying to quell her disappointment, when they heard a loud whistle. Looking over her shoulder and wiping her eyes with the back of her hand, Rachel looked up, wide-eyed, her mouth open in surprise as she recognized their friendly cab driver running towards them.

"Hey there, girlie! Look what you left behind." He held out Rachel's purse, which looked ludicrously small clutched in his work-roughened hands. His smile broadened as he saw the joy in Rachel's eyes light her face. "You really didn't need to leave me a tip. Your mama took care of that already."

Rachel reached for her purse, and surprising herself as well as the kindly man, she stepped forward and threw her arms around him, squeezing him tight in a grateful hug. "Oh, thank you so much!"

The cabby patted her on the back as he smiled at Lara, whose eyes were bright as she mouthed, "Thank you!"

"Oh, it was no problem. Part of the service. You girls have a good flight, and try to remember New York City with a little fondness."

His Brooklyn accent made the girls smile, and Lara answered, "We'll certainly remember our kind cab driver with fondness!"

As he turned and left, waving over his shoulder, Lisa hugged Rachel, and the two girls giggled as they opened Rachel's purse and shook the little jar, making the coins jingle merrily.

Later, boarded and seated on the jetliner, Lara smiled at Rachel as the girl sat fingering the small replica of the Statue of Liberty she had recently purchased at the airport gift shop. It was made of cheap plastic, but Lara knew that Rachel would treasure her memento. Their trip through New York City had been disastrous and fraught with tension, but the memory of the kind cabby and the special effort he had made to find Rachel and return her lost purse left Lara with a softened feeling of gratitude for the kindness of a stranger.

While the large plane quickly covered the miles taking her and the girls home, Lara closed her eyes as her mind drifted. She pictured Cap on another plane and prayed that he would find comfort throughout his journey, that his visit to Idaho would be peaceful. Her heart yearned to be with him, and she felt the spirit of the love they shared binding them together even as they were carried miles apart by the two planes traveling in opposite directions.

CHAPTER 31

June 1968
Hailey, Idaho

Cap pulled up in front of the small hospital that served the town of Hailey, a town nestled in the rolling foothills only miles from the grand Sawtooth Mountain Range of central Idaho. He had rented a car after flying into the capital city of Boise, a little over ninety miles southwest of Hailey. He had called Lara from a pay phone, grateful that she and the girls had arrived home safely. He had tried again to call Sandy and William, but no one answered the phone at Pearl's house.

The drive to Hailey had been fraught with anxiety as he imagined the worst. His mom couldn't die without him having the opportunity to say good-bye, to tell her that he loved her. It was only in the last few years that they had established any kind of a relationship, one based on communication and acceptance. He had been able to push aside the many years of rejection and loneliness, thrilled to finally have the chance he had searched his whole life for, the chance to get to know his mother. It didn't matter to him that her love was selfish and self-serving. It had at least afforded him the opportunity to be a part of her life.

It was early evening, and the town was quiet when Cap pulled in. The hospital parking lot was almost empty, with only two or three other cars parked. Cap made his way through the front door and took a moment to get his bearings. Following the signs, he made his way to the wing of the hospital assigned to patients' rooms. He approached the brightly lit nurses station and quietly asked the uniformed nurse sitting behind the desk for Pearl Aldrich's room number.

"Pearl Aldrich. She was discharged yesterday morning, sir."

"Discharged? I don't understand."

"Well," the young nurse said, patient and consoling, "there wasn't anything more we could do for her. So she went home."

Cap's face paled, thinking the worst. "What do you mean you couldn't do anything more for her?"

Nurse Myers looked into the face of the worried man standing in front of her. "Well, she was stabilized, and there really wasn't anything wrong with her, so we sent her home."

Cap felt his face flush as he understood what Nurse Myers was saying. "She's not sick?"

"Well, sir, not really."

Cap murmured a quiet thank-you as he turned and left. She wasn't ill. She wasn't dying. Cap felt frustration and annoyance warring with true anger. "How in the world did she pull this off?" he said quietly to himself.

Cap got in the car, deep in thought as he drove to Pearl and William's house. If they were home, why hadn't they answered the phone when he had called from Boise? "I just don't understand," Cap murmured as he pulled into the driveway of his mother's house.

William answered the door immediately, his weathered face drawn and tense. "Cap, come on in."

"William, what's going on? I just came from the hospital. They said Mom was discharged. They said she's not sick."

"Come in and sit down, Cap. I'll try to explain."

Before Cap could sit, he heard a cry from the back of the house. "Cap!"

With a resigned look, William nodded his head, gesturing down the hall. "Go to her, son. We'll talk in a little while."

Cap strode down the narrow hallway, guided by the sound of his mother's voice, which was shrill and excited. "Cap! My son, Cap! You're home!"

Walking into her bedroom, Cap saw Pearl propped up in bed, her face flushed, her eyes unnaturally bright. She held her frail hands out to him, her smile pasted on, not quite reaching her eyes. Cap wondered if she ever allowed happiness to penetrate deeply enough so that it could be reflected in her eyes.

"Cap, you came. I knew you would."

Cap sat down on the edge of the bed and took Pearl's hands in his. Her fingers were cold but strong as they gripped him in a tight hold. "Mom, what's going on? They told me at the hospital that you're not sick."

Pearl's face flushed a deep crimson, and her eyes glittered darkly. "Those stupid doctors don't know anything! I could die right here in my bed, and it would serve them right. I could prove them wrong, and then you could sue them for malpractice and the wrongful death of your poor mother."

She's serious! Cap thought to himself. He could feel the strength in her hands, saw the life burning in her eyes, and yet he felt death surrounding her. She wanted to die. He felt it as surely as he felt the cold, dry skin of her hands against the warmth of his own firm grasp. She wanted to die if for no other reason than to prove the doctors wrong, to make everyone feel sorry for her.

"Mom, you're not going to die. You may be feeling ill, but you're not going to die."

Cap's words angered Pearl, but she was so proficient at masking her feelings and hiding the truth from her family that she had no problem projecting an aura of relief as she loosened her talonlike grip on his hands.

"Of course I'm not going to die, son. I have too much to live for. You came home. That's reason enough to live."

Cap couldn't help but reflect on the years of rejection, the years of abandonment, the times that she had left him behind. He was silent as he tried to dampen down the hurt of years past. He so wanted to believe her words.

"You're home, son. That's all I need right now."

"Mom, I'm home because somehow you convinced the Red Cross that you were deathly ill."

"I was ill!" Pearl spat back at him. "I can't help it that just knowing you're home and safe helped me get better." With a moan and a melodramatic gesture, Pearl pushed her graying hair away from her face, the gesture weak and frail. "I was so sick the doctors couldn't help me. You just ask William. He'll tell you how sick I was."

Cap looked over his shoulder at the tall man standing silently at the foot of the bed. His eyes were sorrowful as he looked at his wife. "Yes, Cap, she was ill. She's been ill for a very long time now."

Pearl's smile reflected her satisfaction at William's answer. And although her smile didn't reach her eyes, it brought a measure of comfort to the loving heart of the gentle man who had stood by her side for so many years. Sandy had once asked William how he could stand to remain with her. She was cold and self-centered, yet he stayed. His answer had been, "I know what she is, Sandy. But it doesn't matter. I love her."

And it was as simple as that. He loved her. He always had and he always would, no matter what she had or would put him through, no matter what she might put her children through. William loved her and he would not leave her.

Cap looked deeply into the weary eyes of his stepfather and nodded his acceptance of William's support for his mother's lie. He turned back to face his mother. "I'm glad you're better now, Mom. It means the world to me to know that you're going to be okay."

Pearl reached out a hand and touched her son's face. That was all she needed to hear. The years of absence meant nothing to her. After all, she had not needed her children when they were younger. All they had offered her were memories and remembrances of the man who had destroyed her dreams and shattered her heart.

Now that they were grown, she found that she needed them to validate her purpose in life, a purpose that was unclear, but centered in the belief that her children would do anything for her, despite the unhappy past and neglectful childhood she had inflicted on them.

And she was right. They would do anything they could for her. Sandy lived close by and was at Pearl's beck and call. Nightly phone calls, panicked and tearful, were the norm. Weekly visits to the emergency room were part of the routine. Sandy spent hours, often neglecting her own home and children, to be at Pearl's side, cleaning, cooking, and chauffeuring on demand. John lived farther away, but frequent visits to Hailey were part of his family's life also.

And now that she had Cap at her bedside, she was assured that the United States Navy was no longer an obstacle. They couldn't take her son away from her when she needed him.

"Son, I'm so glad you're home. I must find the strength to get out of this bed. We have things we need to do and talk about. I'll be up and around soon, and then we'll have all the time we need."

"Mom, I'm home now. But I do have to go back."

Pearl's eyes flashed a dark warning. "No, you can't go back."

"Not right away, but in a few days' time."

"I'll get you back. They can't keep you away from me!"

"Mom, you must have misunderstood. I'm only on leave. I have to go back."

"To Rhode Island?"

"To Rhode Island, and then to Vietnam."

"No!" Pearl's voice was shrill and angry.

"Yes, Mom, I have to go back. I don't want to. You must know that."

"Then why?"

"Because it's my duty."

"What about your duty to me?"

Pearl's selfishness finally struck a raw note in Cap. He suppressed the rising urge to shout at her. "Mom, I have never, nor *will* I ever neglect my duty to you. But you are not my only responsibility! I have Lara and the girls to think about. And I have a responsibility to my employer, the United States Navy. You know that."

Pearl stared at Cap, her face stony as she refused to accept his answer. "I'm sorry you can't understand, Mom. Please don't be angry. I only have a few days. Let's not spend them being angry and distant with each other."

Pearl turned away from Cap and lay on her side, her thin back a barrier to his words. William walked up behind Cap and laid a hand on his shoulder. "Come on, son, let's go out front and talk."

Cap arose and brushed a tendril of hair gently behind Pearl's ear. He leaned closer and placed his lips against her cheek, the kiss lingering as he waited for a response. When none came, he sighed as he straightened up and followed William out of the room. He dimmed the lights and closed the door, leaving it partially ajar.

Just after Cap and William had settled themselves in the front room, the door opened and Sandy came in. Cap rose and met her as she crossed the room to him. Without a word, they hugged. Cap saw the deep lines of worry and stress etched around her eyes, and his heart went out to her. He was angry at Pearl's manipulation in getting him home under false pretenses, but he could never be angry with Sandy, no matter what her role may have been in the charade.

"Welcome home, Cap. I'm so sorry it had to be like this."

"I know, sis, it's not your fault."

"It's just so hard, Cap. When Mom gets an idea in her head, there just is no changing her mind. And she can make herself look so sick."

Sandy and Cap sat on the couch and looked at William, whose face looked perpetually sad. The three of them looked at each other, exchanging rueful smiles. William ran a hand through his hair and said, "What can we do?"

He grinned when Sandy and Cap both shook their heads, dumfounded expressions on their faces. The sight of William's smile broke the tension, and Cap leaned back in his chair, his hands behind his head. "Oh, man! I am so tired!"

"Wimp!" Sandy's scornful reply made William guffaw. She started to laugh, and Cap grinned at her.

"I need to call Lara and the girls. They'll be wondering what's going on."

"Just a minute, son. I need to plug the phone in. Your mom insisted on having it unplugged so that the ringing wouldn't disturb her rest." William's words explained why Lara and Cap had been unable to get through to the house when they had tried to call over the last couple of days.

Lara was grateful to hear Cap's reassurances that Pearl was fine, but she shared his frustration and annoyance for the lies that had caused them so much worry. "I'll be home in five days, babe. That'll give us a week together before I have to fly back out."

Lara and Cap exchanged a few tender words before they ended the call. Cap then called out to William, "Hey, Dad, can a hungry sailor get a good meal around this establishment?"

"You may be a sailor, son, but you can find your way around the kitchen!" William led Cap to the kitchen, followed by Sandy. Together they pulled together a meal of soup, homemade bread, and carrot sticks. Soon, the good food and the assurance that Pearl was fine helped them all to relax, their laughter ringing through the house. During a pause in the conversation, they heard a feeble cry from the back of the house.

"What's that?" Cap asked, puzzled. "Is that Mom?"

William looked at Sandy, his expression saddened and resigned. "Do you want to explain while I go to her?"

Sandy nodded and turned to Cap, the smile dying on her lips as William disappeared down the hall. Cap heard the feeble sounds again and recognized William's low tones answering calmly. "This is what she does, Cap. She gets sick, so we take her to the doctor or to the hospital. Then she comes home because there's not a thing wrong with her. She spends the next week in bed demanding constant attention. If we get distracted or she hears us laughing or having fun, she goes berserk!"

"What is she saying?"

"Who knows." Sandy's voice was filled with discouragement. "She just mutters, and she does it loud enough that we can hear but not clearly enough so that we can understand. If we don't jump up right away and go to her, she'll keep going until the muttering turns into crying."

Pausing, Sandy brushed her hair back from her eyes. "One time we decided to ignore her. She started to scream the most hideous, bloodcurdling scream I've ever heard. And she went on and on, even after we went back to her. We couldn't get her to stop, and we ended up calling the ambulance. She went to the hospital and got a shot of Valium. It took hours for her to calm down." Cap stared at Sandy, unable to fully comprehend what she was saying. "Now, we go to her as soon as we hear her. It's not worth ignoring her."

After a few minutes, Cap could tell that William was getting her calmed down, so he and Sandy spent the rest of the evening perched uncomfortably on chairs around her bed. Often they sat in silence, but as long as they were there, Pearl seemed content. To her husband, son, and daughter, her silence was worth the sacrifice of their time and company.

That first evening set the pattern for the next four days. By the time Cap was set to leave, Pearl was able to get out of bed and join them for short periods in the front room. She looked strong and healthy, but she acted feeble and weak. William and Sandy waited on her, catering to her every whim. Cap felt powerless as he watched them. He wanted to ask them why, why they were giving in to her like they did. But he realized that he would probably do the same if he had to live with her day in and day out. Cap felt vastly relieved when the time came for him to leave. He hugged William and thanked him for loving his mother.

He then hugged Sandy and told her to take care of herself. "If you get sick, this whole thing will fall apart. And don't forget your own family. Theo, Jason, and Maggie need you too. I wish I could take some of the burden from you."

Sandy shrugged her shoulders resignedly. "We can't change the way it is, Cap. One of these days you'll retire and come home."

"Then it'll be my turn?" Cap asked with a smile.

"You better believe it's gonna be your turn!"

Cap gave Sandy one last squeeze. She walked him to his car, and he turned to wave at Pearl and William standing at the front room window. His farewell to Pearl had been brief and unemotional. He had kept it that way on purpose. He couldn't stand another performance like the one on the night before he left.

Pearl had railed at him for hours, crying and screaming, alternating her venomous speeches with stony silences, berating him for leaving so soon. She had found out that he had another week's leave before returning to Vietnam, and she was incensed that he wasn't staying in Idaho with her. He had pled with her to understand that he needed to spend some time with his wife and children too. The argument had finally ended when Pearl disappeared behind the icy wall of her frigid silence. Cap had merely walked out after placing a brief kiss on her cheek, unaware of the single, silent tear that froze in the corner of his mother's eye as he left her.

And as he drove away, his heart was heavy with worry. William had shed a few tears, as had Sandy. Pearl, however, stood silent and dry-eyed as Cap drove away.

She had shed her single tear the night before. There would be no more tears for her eldest son.

CHAPTER 32

"Knock, and it shall be opened unto you."

June 1973
Hailey, Idaho

The sweetness of the summer night was tangible. William could feel it on his skin as he sat on the porch, gathering the warmth of the setting sun, letting it soothe his aching bones. The scent of the mountains was clear, unmarred by smoke or exhaust. The dusky haze of the evening sky softly filtered the knife-sharp silhouette of the surrounding mountains, casting a sense of closeness and coziness to the high mountain valley, yet emphasizing the freedom and the space of the skies and the mountains. William took several deep breaths as he tried to quiet the rapid beating of his heart. He needed the healing balm of the night sky. He dreaded going back inside the house.

The woman he had loved so desperately his whole life was gone. In her place was a monstrous caricature, a woman's body racked with the pain and craving for the drug that had helped her live in a cold and emotion-free cocoon for most of her adult life. William grieved for the girl he had loved so completely in his youth. He yearned for the heartbroken, clinging woman whom he had rescued from the terrors of an abusive marriage. He even longed for the woman who had rejected her children and had run from her responsibilities for so many years. That woman, at least, had been real. She had, at times, been soft and responsive to his touch and to his voice.

She had loved him in a way. Her love had lacked depth, but at least it had been love.

The woman ransacking the house behind him was a stranger. A monster. Someone devoid of human warmth and understanding, and he hated her.

He shivered at the depth of his loathing. He had reached a point that his former love could no longer penetrate. Pearl, the woman, had been unable to drive away his love. It had taken her addiction and her inability to rise above that addiction to turn his love cold. And it wasn't really the addiction. It was her inability to rise above it that had hurt him so much. It made him realize that so much of what he knew about Pearl was a facade—a drug-induced, drug-crazed facade. And it had become obvious that she loved the drugs and the mind-numbing forgetfulness they brought more than she had ever loved him or anyone else.

Pearl's decline had seemed to initially set in after she received word of Jake Martin's sudden death. Spiritually, Jake had killed Pearl during the decade of their marriage, but a larger part of Pearl seemed to die the day they buried him. Since then, there had been moments of closeness, times when Pearl enjoyed her children and grandchildren, times that comforted William and made him feel loved. But the insidious demon of hate, selfishness, and addiction had caught up with Pearl, taking control and ruling her life mercilessly.

And William was tired. He was tired of fighting for her love. He was tired of having to constantly prove his love. He was tired of the drugs and the fighting and the screaming. He was tired of loving Pearl.

Yet even as he recognized the absence of love in his heart, even as he recognized the anger and the hatred, he grieved for what used to be. And the softness of his heart ached with the burden of his anger. He prayed for silent strength. He prayed for insight. And he prayed for forgiveness as he turned his back on the healing beauty of the night and entered the darkness of the house.

He had long since avoided calling it home. Home had been a place where he and Pearl, in their own way, had loved each other. That love and that Pearl were gone. In their place was an emptiness. There was no room in that house for love. Pearl's demons and addictions had driven away all but the anger and the hopeless despair that filled William's heart.

The crashing and the screams of the demented woman chilled William to the bone. His head hurt as he reentered the front room. Pearl had wreaked havoc on the house's furnishings. Tables were upturned, their legs splintered and broken. Cabinets had been emptied, their contents shredded and scattered on the floor. Pictures and mirrors had been ripped from the walls and smashed against the floor. Curtains hung in tatters from the windows. As William walked through the wreckage, he felt the rage burning deep in his gut, like acid rising in his throat as he felt his head begin to throb.

Pearl's screams were shrill amidst her cursing. Her hair was in disarray, matted and uncombed. Her arms were bloody and raw from her own jagged fingernails scratching and clawing at her skin as she raved and cursed heaven. Her eyes, once calm, cold, and unfeeling, burned like fiery embers as she searched frantically through the house. As William entered the kitchen, where she was pawing through the cupboards, pulling the canned goods and food staples from the shelves, Pearl turned to him and screamed, "Where is it! I know you're hiding it from me!"

Wearily, William responded with the same answer he had been giving her for days. "Pearl, I'm not hiding anything. There are no more drugs."

"There are!" Pearl's voice was loud and fever pitched. "Why are you being so despicable? I hate you! I'm dying and you don't even care!"

Pearl's accusation pierced William's heart because he knew it to be true. He no longer cared. His own voice rose in frustration as he shouted back at her, "You're right! I don't care! Your drugs are gone, and you just better get used to it. You ain't getting any more!"

"You dirty, rotten—" Pearl's obscenity was lost as she spun around and grabbed a knife from off the counter.

William gasped. He thought that he had hidden everything that might be used as a weapon. Dr. Lawrence had warned him that Pearl could turn violent. He had urged William to hide all knives and sharp-edged utensils. William had gone through the kitchen, their bedroom, and the bathroom with a fine-tooth comb, taking out anything that Pearl could use to harm herself. But somehow he had missed one, and he backed away as Pearl came at him, brandishing the knife and screaming.

He backed into the front room, spinning as he reached the open doorway. He dashed down the hall, turned left into the utility room, and circled back into the kitchen through the room's second door. He moved so quickly that even Pearl in her manic state couldn't keep up with him. He rushed up behind her, silent and surprisingly quick on his aged legs. He wrapped his arms around Pearl from behind and wrenched the knife out of her hands. He tossed it behind him, pushed Pearl through the kitchen door, and with his foot, slammed it shut.

He and Pearl were in the dining room locked in a furious battle. She was kicking and rocking, her slender form maniacal as she fought to get loose. William was determined to hold onto her, and he wrestled her to the floor, half-lying on top of her as he struggled to contain her hands.

Suddenly, Pearl went limp in his arms. William lay across her, panting and gulping for air. He was drenched in sweat, and his face was gray as he held her down. How many times he had held her in his arms, loving her and comforting her. But now as he held her, he felt only pity. She was so slight and so fragile, but she demonstrated a demonic strength as she fought him for her freedom.

"William, get off me." Pearl's voice was soft but icy cold.

William twisted so that he could look into her face. He shrunk away from the venomous look in her eyes. She hadn't given up. She was like an embattled scorpion, backing away and resting a moment, merely seeking a new angle of attack for its intended victim before it killed with its deadly sting.

"Pearl, I can't."

"Get off me." Pearl's words began softly, but soon escalated, into her mad mantra as she once again began to squirm, kick, and scream. "Get off me!"

William felt his heart thud in his chest as he held her down with every ounce of strength. Suddenly she rocked her head back, and as she glared at him, she spat in his face.

William felt himself begin to lose control of his will not to harm her. Spittle dribbled down his cheek, and a furious red haze gathered behind his eyes. He cried out in shock and hurt anger, betrayal and remorse at war with a sudden surge of the tenderness and love he had once felt for Pearl. She collapsed back onto the floor, tears coursing down her face and sobs shaking her slender frame as William cried out her name. William felt the thunder of his heartbeat sounding in his ears, and he felt the vessels in his head swell from the trauma of his raging emotions.

As he cried out her name once more, William collapsed on top of Pearl, his face gray and twisted in death, his body heavy and lifeless as he won the battle to hold her down.

CHAPTER 33

August 1973
Gooding, Idaho

"That's the last of her stuff."

Lara acknowledged Cap's words with a shake of her head as she surveyed the cramped bedroom. They had just finished unloading Cap's pickup, carrying in armloads of belongings for Pearl Aldrich, a woman who would soon be living under their roof.

The past five years had been years of change for Cap and Lara, with one of the biggest changes in their lives being Cap's retirement from the navy in 1971. With twenty years of service under his belt, he and Lara were ready to settle down.

They had left Rhode Island in 1969. They had spent Cap's last tour of duty on a naval base situated on the small, remote island of Adak, Alaska. Cap, Lara, and their girls had been overcome with excitement when Cap received his last set of orders. The base on Adak had been established during World War II and had, in fact, been the site of William's first tour of duty in the military. A United States congressman had heralded the work of William's battalion as a "minor miracle" when their accomplishments were reviewed by Congress. In ten months, they had built airstrips, docks, hospitals, barracks, and much more, turning the once-uninhabited, unfriendly island into a habitable, if not hospitable, military installation.

Cap and his family felt their bond with William Aldrich, the man they loved as father and grandfather, strengthened as they moved to the isolated island that he had once trod upon and helped colonize.

They found it vastly changed from the rugged, primitive accommodations that he had lived with. The base was much more developed now with housing, stores, schools, and churches. What they found unchanged was the rugged beauty of the Aleutian wilderness.

They had loved their stay in Alaska, but had loved even more the opportunity to retire to Idaho, to settle down in a home where they could reestablish their family roots.

Lisa had graduated from high school in the spring of 1973, and had recently left for college. She was attending Brigham Young University in Provo, Utah. Going to BYU had been a longtime dream, one that she had studiously worked for, earning a full-ride scholarship. Cap and Lara were very proud of her and excited for the adventures that awaited her. Lara was going to miss her daughter, but she knew that it was time for her to be on her own. Rachel was a senior in high school and was also working toward college.

Cap and Lara thought often about the two daughters they had lost, and they still grieved for the loss. But Lisa and Rachel had been a blessing to them. They had talked about having more children, but it had never happened. Nonetheless, they were content with their family and had found fulfillment in raising Lisa and Rachel.

It was the advent of the girls growing up and leaving home that made this latest change in their lives so overwhelming. Pearl Aldrich could no longer live alone. Her husband, William, had died two months previously. His passing had thrown them all into a state of shock and grief. Lara missed the gentle giant who had filled their lives with such warmth and loving tenderness. He had been the greatest grandpa to the girls, the only grandfather they had ever known. His passing had left a huge void. Lara knew that Cap missed him too, and it was with a heightened sense of understanding and empathy that Lara agreed to open their home to her mother-in-law.

Pearl was lost without William. Whether she had recognized it or not, he had been her rock and salvation. He had given her the stability that she lacked on her own, and since his passing, her instability had increased dangerously.

During the years since Cap and Lara had moved back to Idaho, they had come to realize just how unsound Pearl was. And this last year had been the worst. Midnight calls were placed to whomever was closest, demands were issued for attention, and medical care was required despite the cost or the sacrifice.

Pearl's physician, Dr. Lawrence, had finally begun refusing to renew her prescriptions for Valium. She had been on the tranquilizer for years, supposedly only using it periodically when she became stressed or experienced sleeplessness. Over time, however, it became apparent that Pearl's use of the drug was too frequent. Dr. Lawrence began investigating, and he found that Pearl not only had the prescription from him, but from other doctors as well. Her use of the drug was out of control.

She was out of control.

The night William died, she had called Cap, hysterical. Through the garbled words, the tears, and the screeching cries, Cap finally had understood that Pearl was home alone with the body of her dead husband.

Later, after an inquest, the coroner's report indicated that William had suffered a massive stroke. Pearl, her speech incoherent, had not been able to give a clear explanation of the events of that night. Yet through her babbling and cries, one message became clear—she and William had fought.

The authorities and the family could only surmise how intense and upsetting that final battle between Pearl and William must have been. The family grieved over the loss of the gentle man who had loved Pearl his whole life despite the ugliness, weakness, and selfishness of her illness. He had recognized years earlier that she was ill, emotionally and mentally, if not physically. Yet he had loved her and stood by her despite the illness. And he died because of her.

The aftermath of William's death wreaked havoc in the lives of his family. Pearl continued to be lost in the crazed world of withdrawal from her addiction. She was hospitalized for a period of time, but when the time came for her to be discharged, they knew she couldn't live alone.

Cap and Lara agreed to have her come live with them. Lisa was leaving home for college. They would have the room. And Cap swore that he would not reject or desert his mother during her time of need. He remembered too poignantly the pain of rejection and desertion. It didn't matter to him that he had learned those lessons at the hands of the woman that he now refused to turn his back on.

Lara loved him all the more for his generosity and devotion to his mother. It was with a renewed sense of dedication to Cap that Lara set about making her mother-in-law comfortable in their home. She and Rachel attempted to make the room cozy and comfortable for her, making sure they set out her pictures and knickknacks from home. Pearl was quiet and subdued as she watched them unpack.

"Grandma, do you want these pictures set here?" Rachel asked, pausing in her work to include Pearl in the efforts to make her room seem familiar. When Pearl ignored her question, Rachel shrugged her shoulders and said, "That's okay, Grandma. I think they'll look just fine here. You'll be able to look at them every day."

Rachel turned back to her task of setting out several framed photographs of Pearl's family. Her face reflected her sadness as she picked up the last picture. It was a candid shot of William, taken while he worked outside. His smiling face shone in the late afternoon sunshine, reflecting his pleasure for the company of the person taking the photo.

Pearl was aware of the sacrifice being made on her behalf, but a lifetime of self-centeredness had hardened her. As she watched Lara and Rachel work, the only thing she felt was a blend of resentment and self-pity. Her body and mind were still racked with the incredible pain and the all-consuming desire for the drugs that she could no longer have. The desire was like a fire that ate away at her nerve endings, burning out of control one moment, then smoldering like hot coals another. There were even moments when the coals turned to ash, but the desire still smothered her with its coldness, turning her world gray and hazy with need.

"Pearl, I think we've got you all unpacked," Lara intoned, turning to the silent woman who sat in her easy chair from her home. They had placed it near the window in her bedroom, allotting her a place of sanctuary. An overstuffed, chintz-covered armchair was in the living room so that she had a place amongst the family also.

Pearl merely nodded as she turned away from her daughter-in-law and granddaughter, mirroring her lifetime habit of turning her back on the people who only wanted to love her.

Lara quietly ushered Rachel out the door, whispering quiet words of reassurance to the young girl who was worried about her grandmother.

"Grandma will be okay. She's still in shock. She's missing Grandpa. And I'm sure she misses her home too. And she's still not feeling well, honey. We're going to have to be very patient with her."

Rachel accepted her mother's advice, and they joined Cap in the front room to sit down to the supper of stew and homemade bread that Lara had prepared earlier in the day. Pearl had disregarded Lara's invitation to join them for dinner, and as the gray shadows of evening descended, she sat alone in her room, beyond the glowing light of her family's love.

CHAPTER 34

October 1973
Gooding, Idaho

Cap and Lara's home in Gooding was a large, double-wide manufactured home set on a foundation. They had it on ten acres of land outside the city limits of Gooding. Their nearest neighbor was a mile down the road, and they loved the sense of isolation enhanced by the openness of the Idaho prairie. The stand of poplar and elm trees that protectively encircled their home provided them with shade and privacy, and Cap used the few outbuildings as a shop and storage sheds for his many ventures. They kept a few animals, which was typical of Cap. In the past he had always tried to provide for his family's needs by raising a calf and one or two pigs in order to put meat in the freezer. Some of the places they had been stationed hadn't allowed Cap to indulge in his love for raising animals, but now that they were retired, he could have as many animals as he desired.

He raised the animals for food and kept their freezer stocked with homegrown beef, pork, and chicken. They also had a garden and several fruit trees that kept Lara's pantry shelves filled with home-canned fruits and vegetables.

Since Pearl's move into their home, Cap, Lara, and Rachel had frequently been grateful for the isolation that surrounded their humble abode. At times it seemed as if their lives had turned into a long, dark nightmare, one from which there was no awakening. Lara had expressed to Cap that it was a good thing they had all their own food on hand, as it seemed as if they were prisoners in their own home, kept there by the constant need to supervise Pearl.

One night, Cap and Rachel were out in the barn doing their evening chores when suddenly a piercing cry rent the quiet autumn night.

"Oh, Dad. Not again." Rachel's plea tore at Cap's heart even as he echoed her sentiment.

Cap rubbed a weary hand across his eyes as he quickly turned and handed Rachel the bucket of feed he was carrying. "Here, sis. You finish up. I'll go help Mom."

"Hurry, Dad."

Cap ran from the barn, his sense of urgency increasing as the volume of cries rose. He broke through the front door, sweating and panting with anxious anticipation, knowing that his family was in for yet another horrendous night.

"Get out of here! I hate you!"

There was another crash, and then Lara's voice, soothing and quiet, yet with undertones of annoyance, answered, "Pearl, calm down. You know I can't give you any more."

"You hate me . . . all of you . . . well, I hate you . . . I hate this house . . . I hate this room . . . I hate my life." Pearl's words were screeches in the night, her voice piercing Cap's heart as he raced down the hall. The brief silences between her phrases were filled with the sound of breaking glass and splintering wood.

As he entered Pearl's room, he quickly took stock of that night's carnage. She had broken a wooden stand that had held her bedside lamp. The lamp now lay on the floor, surrounded by the shattered shards of pottery that used to be an attractive ceramic lamp base. Pearl was on the floor, huddled in the corner, screaming, her eyes wild and her hair a tangled mass of gray. It had been a rough day, and they had been unable to get her to bathe that morning. The room stank of her sweat and excrement.

Lara looked at Cap as Pearl's screeches died to moans and she rocked back on her haunches, her arms wrapped around her legs. She sat there moaning and crying, rocking back and forth, her head resting on her knees.

"Cap, I can't take it anymore." Lara's face was white with shock and fatigue. Her blue eyes blazed with buried emotions as she continued, her voice tight and hoarse as she whispered fiercely, "I can't take it anymore. She's out of control."

"She's been out of control, babe."

"I know that, Cap! And she's not getting any better!"

"Please don't yell at me, Lara." Cap's request was made in a low, terse voice.

"Well, then, who can I yell at? I can't yell at her, now can I?" Lara's question was resentful as she pointed a trembling finger at the pitiful figure crouched on the floor. "I can't yell at her! I can't tell her to go jump in a lake! I can't do a dang thing and I'm sick and tired of it, Cap!" Lara's last sentence had lost the vehemence of her anger. Her voice was soulful in its distress, and as she slumped against him in weariness, Cap gathered her close.

"I know, babe. There isn't a cotton-pickin' thing any of us can do about it. All we can do is follow the doctor's orders."

"We've been following his orders, Cap. And she isn't getting any better. Sometimes I think . . ."

"You think what, Lara?"

Lara pulled away from Cap and turned to look at Pearl. Lara's face was set as she watched the wretched figure. Her voice was quiet and remote as she answered, "Sometimes I think she's faking it."

Cap sighed and closed his eyes.

Lara continued, "Please don't be angry. She just keeps going on and on. The doctor said that the drugs should be out of her system by now. He doesn't know why she's continuing to act like this."

"I know, honey. I've wondered that too. She's either faking it, or . . ." It was Cap's turn to pause as if he were afraid to utter the next thought.

"Or what, Cap?"

Swallowing hard, his Adam's apple bobbing, Cap whispered, "Or she's just plain crazy."

Lara turned back to Cap and put her hand on his arm, her touch comforting and commiserating. Before she could utter a word, though, the scrawny, disheveled figure crouching in the shadows of the room leapt to her feet and screamed, "I ain't faking it! And I ain't crazy, either!"

Shocked, Cap and Lara broke away from each other, unconsciously taking a step away from the approaching woman, her gray head shaking, and her brown eyes wild as she ran toward them. "I ain't crazy, you stupid boy . . . I'm sick . . . can't you tell a sick body when you see it? . . . I think you're the crazy one . . . do you hear me . . . you're crazy . . . you and that stupid wife of yours . . . you're both crazy!"

With a sense of alarm, Cap pushed Lara behind him, blocking her from the fingers and arms that were clawing at him. With a grimace of distaste, Cap captured the thin wrists in his hands, surprised at the strength with which Pearl continued to attack.

"Stop it, Ma! Stop it, do you hear me? If you aren't crazy, then stop acting like it!" Cap's words were shouted, harsh, penetrating as he struggled to hold Pearl at arm's length.

"I ain't crazy . . . your pa, he was crazy . . . and you're just like him . . . crazy and mean . . . you and that woman treat me like a dog . . . I'm sick of it . . . I'm sick of you . . . I hate you . . ."

Cap reeled from the hurt of her words. He had always tried so hard to live his life opposite from the example set by Jake Martin. To hear the demented old woman accuse him of being just like Jake hurt him to the very core. Suddenly, all of the emotions of a lifetime welled up and spilled over, causing Cap to respond on an emotional level that he had so carefully avoided. Dropping her hands, Cap grasped Pearl by the upper arms and began to shake her.

"I'm not like him . . . I'm not him . . . why can't you see that . . . why can't you see that I'm not him . . . I'm your son . . ." Suddenly letting go, Cap buried his face in his hands, his voice muffled. "I'm your son . . . for heaven's sake, Ma. I'm your son."

When Cap released her, Pearl collapsed to the floor, her thin nightgown spreading out around her, sheathing her in a wrinkled, stained cloak. Her cries died in her throat as she stared, horrified, up at her son. Her hands were trembling as she slowly reached up to him, her eyes wide and frightened. Her mouth hung open, silent and toothless, spittle dribbling down her chin. Cap didn't see her outstretched hand, nor did he hear her whispered acknowledgment, "My son."

Lara was in shock, standing behind Cap, her arms wrapped around his waist and her face buried in his back. Cap's head was bowed, his shoulders hunched as he hid behind his clenched fists. Neither of them saw the only sincere attempt Pearl had ever made to reach out to her eldest son. Nor did they hear the spoken words, for the first time in her life coming from her heart, as Pearl's voice called for the child she had abandoned so many years earlier.

The momentary softening of her heart, the fleeting entreaty spoken with sincerity was lost in the shadows of the room as hurt, betrayal, and despair crowded into the heart of the man who was her son. Pearl dropped her hand into her lap, her head drooping forward, her shoulders hunched as the moment was lost.

Cap, gathering his emotions, made an obvious effort to regain his composure. He ran a hand over his cheeks, grabbed his hankie out of his jeans' pocket, and wiped his face. As he blew his nose, he took a deep breath and stepped out of Lara's embrace. Lara dried her tears with a trembling hand as she watched Cap approach the frail figure sitting so calmly and quietly on the floor in front of them. Cap crouched down, gently took Pearl's hands, and lifted her to her feet.

Not a word was spoken as he led her to the bed and gently lifted her onto the mattress. With great tenderness, Cap pulled the covers up, tucking them around Pearl's shoulders. "Try to sleep, Ma."

Pearl nodded and soundlessly turned onto her side, pulling the blankets and quilts around her in a gesture of self-protection. Cap and Lara slowly exited the room, turning the lights off as they went, leaving the now-silent woman in a cocoon of deep, dark isolation.

CHAPTER 35

Thanksgiving night 1973
Gooding, Idaho

The happy voices and laughter faded as car doors were shut and engines started. Cap, Lara, Pearl, Rachel, and Lisa all stood on the porch steps and waved until the last of their family drove out of view. It was Thanksgiving night, and as the day drew to a close, Cap ushered the women surrounding him back into the warmth of their home.

As he closed the door against the cold, dark night, Cap put his arm around Lara's shoulders and gave her a squeeze of gratitude. "Thanks for making today so perfect, babe."

"You're welcome, hon. It wasn't just me, though. Everyone worked so hard."

"I know. Ma," Cap turned to Pearl, "thank you for today."

The thin, gray-haired woman turned to her son with a smile softening the drawn features of her face. "You're welcome, son. It was a good day, wasn't it?"

Cap smiled his agreement. "Yeah. It was a good day."

Pearl walked over to Cap and Lara and reached up, placing a soft kiss on Cap's cheek. She then turned to Lara and kissed her. "Good night, you two."

"Good night." Cap's and Lara's voices joined in harmony as they watched Pearl slowly walk down the hall toward her bedroom. They saw her pause at Lisa's and Rachel's doors and heard her bid her granddaughters good night. She then continued on to her room and disappeared inside, closing her door behind her.

Lara sighed gratefully as silence and calm filled the house. She then started to chuckle as relief washed over her, filling her with giddiness. Cap understood her feelings without having to be told. The last few weeks had been so fraught with tension, fear, and uncertainty. Since the confrontation in Pearl's room nearly six weeks earlier, the old woman had made a slow but steady move toward improvement.

That night six weeks before had been the last for the screaming hysterics. Yet Pearl was still frequently lost in a world of silence and depression, unwilling to talk to anyone or join the family for meals. She lost more weight, and often still refused to bathe or get dressed, but overall Cap and Lara could discern gradual changes. Slowly she began to emerge from the depths of her personal torment, and slight improvements began to manifest themselves.

Those manifestations began with brief, quiet talks with Rachel. Pearl seemed to feel safe with Rachel. Soon the talks turned into conversations and hugs. Then came the night when Rachel emerged from her grandmother's room, with Pearl hanging on to her arm. That night Pearl had joined the family at the dinner table.

Her improvement since that dinner had continued. She had joined Lara in making preparations for their Thanksgiving feast, and she had been the one to place calls to John and Sandy, inviting them to come for dinner. She had encouraged Lara to include her brothers in the family day. Through all the activity, Pearl had still remained calm and quiet, speaking, but not often. Her silence, though, was not that of one sunken in deep depression. Rather it seemed as if she was soaking up the cheerful atmosphere, trying to garner the joy and make it her own.

Lara's brothers and their families had accepted the invitation to join them for dinner, so Cap and Lara's home was filled to overflowing with their extended family. It had been a busy time, one of renewal for them all. Lara loved her brothers and was grateful to have them close by. Her older brother Tom and his wife had joined the Church a few months earlier, and Lara felt a special connection with them and was grateful for their spiritual strength. She had been pleasantly surprised by the positive changes it had brought to her relationship with Tom. When they were kids, he had bullied Lara, and as adults, their relationship had often been strained and difficult. Paul and his family were doing well, and Matthew had recently married a lovely girl named Sandra. Lara loved Sandra, and the two women had forged an immediate bond of friendship.

Lara was worried about her brother Luke, however. He had never married and suffered from frequent bouts of depression, having never recovered from the trauma of finding their father the morning Sam Straddler had died. Lara knew that Luke was troubled and unhappy, but she didn't know how to help him. So she merely tried to love him as much as he would allow. She was grateful that he had at least been willing to join them for their family celebration. He had seemed to enjoy himself and had actually come out of his shell a bit. He had spent most of the day conversing with Sandy's husband, Theo. The two men were much alike—quiet and gentle. Theo, however, lacked the deeply embedded sense of unhappiness that made Luke so quiet and withdrawn. Whatever connection drew the men together, Lara was grateful that Luke seemed to enjoy the day.

Sandy and Theo, as well as John and Karen, all seemed happy and content, though Lara knew their lives still weren't easy. John and Sandy both still carried with them the memories and the emotions of those long-ago days when they had been so badly abused. They both had battled with the demon of alcohol addiction, and both had suffered the guilt that accompanied bouts of intense anger and physical violence, a side effect of the alcohol consumption. Their marriages and families had suffered at their hands, both falling into the ugly patterns set during their childhood. But the years had brought them both to a point of self-awareness accompanied by the desire to change.

Sandy's moment of truth had begun during the Christmas spent at White Mountain Lodge. With the help and the encouragement of her husband, Theo, she had sought counseling for both herself and her children. The road to recovery hadn't been easy. There had been many rocky spots, but slowly, they were making it.

John's turnaround had taken a little longer. He loathed what he had become when he saw the fear of his youth mirrored in the eyes of his wife and children. It had taken him years to get a handle on his anger and the pent-up emotions, both burdens from his childhood. But he was going to make it. Karen loved him and had found an inner source of strength that made her start to stand up to John when he showed signs of becoming abusive. She began to protect herself and her children, and her strength gave John what he needed to begin making the changes in his life that would bring his family safety and security.

Even though John and Sandy had both been baptized years earlier, neither one had fully embraced the gospel. Cap and Lara continued to pray for the day that they would finally recognize where true healing lay. They knew that one day the gospel's light and the truth about their Father in Heaven's love would soften their hearts. Cap, especially, yearned for John and Sandy to come to know what the Atonement of Jesus Christ could do for them. It was Cap's own journey through life's trials and heartaches that had taught him to turn over the pain and the burden of grief and sin to the One who had already borne those burdens away. He longed for John and Sandy to know the peace of forgiveness and the joy of hope. One day, he knew they would. They were drawing closer to that awareness with each passing year.

To Cap, this Thanksgiving, with the family together, symbolized the gains they had each made in their personal lives. The effects were noticeable in the dynamics of the gathering. And it left them all with a renewed sense of hope for the future.

Cap and Lara knew the source of that hope, and they did what they could to share their understanding with their loved ones. They were proud of their family and grateful that they had all been able to gather together to celebrate the holidays. Plans had been made for Christmas gatherings, and as Lara and Cap began to settle down for the night, they felt their hope renewed and reinforced by the love they had shared with their family that day.

"Cap, what do you think of your mom's request to move back home?" Lara's question arose from a conversation earlier that day.

Someone had mentioned Pearl's house in Hailey, and she had stunned everyone when she asked when she would be able to move back home. Pearl had always been so dependent on others to take care of her, and they had thought moving back to the empty house in Hailey would be the last thing she would want to do.

The resulting discussion had led to an agreement that Pearl remain with Cap and Lara until spring. If she continued to regain her health, to grow physically and emotionally stronger, and if her doctor thought it possible, then she could move home in March or April.

"I think it shows just how much she's improved."

"I think so too. I think she needs the next few months, though, here with us."

Cap sighed and said, "Yeah. I think we all agree on that. I think even Ma recognizes that. The winters in Hailey can be pretty severe, and physically she's just not up to handling a hard winter. And I don't think the isolation would be very good for her either."

Cap wiped his hands on a dish towel hanging from the kitchen rack. He had just finished wiping down the counters while Lara washed up the last of the dirty dishes. Stretching his arms over his head, Cap groaned tiredly. "C'mon, babe. Let's go to bed. I'm pooped!"

As Cap and Lara headed for their room, Cap put his arm around Lara's waist. "You know what, Lara Bell?"

"Huh?"

"I think we may have seen the worst of all this."

"You think?"

"Yeah, I do. Mom seemed really stable today. Almost at peace."

"I noticed that too. And you know what else?"

"What?"

"I think the rest of our family is doing okay too. I mean, my brothers haven't had nearly the trials that you and John and Sandy have had. Their lives have been challenging, but not so filled with hurt. You know, the kind of hurt inflicted by those who you are supposed to be able to trust."

"I know what you mean, hon."

Lara lapsed into a contemplative silence. "You know, our lives have been touched by so much tragedy. I know other families experience heartache, but do you think they have this much to deal with?"

Cap grinned ruefully at Lara's question. "You know, Bell, I'll bet we're more typical than not. Sad, ain't it?"

Lara smiled. "But you know, the gospel teaches us that through our weaknesses we'll be made strong. And we know that we came to earth to learn from our struggles and trials."

"Yeah. How much more do you think we need to grow?" Cap grinned as he continued, "Sometimes I think I'm big enough already. Do you think God agrees?"

Lara smiled ruefully as she answered, "Probably not. I don't see us getting 'caught up to heaven' anytime too soon. I know that I still make too many mistakes."

Groaning with fatigue, Cap's smile faded. "I was just being facetious, babe. I know that I have a long ways to go myself." Cap didn't speak the remainder of his thought out loud. He almost trembled at the idea that he still had additional trials and challenges ahead of him. Sometimes he just felt so weak and tired.

But he knew that whatever the future held, he wouldn't have to walk it alone. He had his wife and his daughters, who had always been there for him, and he had his faith in God. He, more than most, knew the fragility of life and that one day he might lose Lara and the girls. Yet he drew strength from the knowledge that their separation would be for just a brief time. He also knew that any time he was required to walk this earth without his loved ones, he would never be truly alone. God was only a prayer away.

Cap and Lara finished undressing for bed in silence. Both were deep in thought, remembering not only the horrifying violation of innocence that they and their loved ones had experienced, but also remembering the losses. So many of their nights together had ended on their knees, their hearts and spirits joined as they offered thanks to their Father above, beseeching Him for comfort and guidance. And as Thanksgiving Day 1973 drew to a close, they again opened their hearts to Him and allowed their thanksgiving to be carried to heaven.

CHAPTER 36

March 1975
Hailey, Idaho

Pearl Aldrich woke with a lighthearted feeling, something she hadn't experienced in years. It was such an unusual sensation that she lay in bed for a few extra minutes, wondering about the unfamiliar sense of peace. Although the last year and a half had passed quietly for Pearl, it had not necessarily been peaceful. Pearl harbored too much of the past in her heart for peace to find room. She had spent the holiday season of 1973 with Cap and Lara, and had enjoyed the comfort of their home through the long winter of 1974.

Now it was almost a year to the day that she had moved back home to Hailey. She had faced the move into the solitary house with an outward calm that hid the turmoil never very far from the surface. She had spent her life hiding behind the anger, the hurt, and withdrawal that had been her safeguard. The withdrawal had allowed her to survive the final years of her marriage to Jake Martin while the anger and hurt had fueled the rejection of her children for so many years. During the years she had spent with William, she had found a place of safety, a plateau of indifference and distance that allowed her to continue coping even as she reestablished ties with her children.

Sandy and John had come back into her life more quickly and easily than Cap had. Their ties to Jake were somehow more tenuous and therefore easier to bear. If Pearl were honest with herself, she would recognize William's gentle hand behind the reestablishment of her relationship with Cap. Over the years she had come to rely on

William's sturdy and faithful service. He was like a rock in her life, and only recently had she come to recognize how unfair she had been to him all of his life. But her pride had prevented her from admitting her mistakes.

As for Cap, though she welcomed him warmly into her home, she still kept him at an emotional distance. Nevertheless, Cap had come to cherish whatever love she seemed willing to share. The months Pearl had spent in his home had given her an appreciation for their family life. She could see the differences in their lifestyles, Cap's gentle and loving manner of discipline, his open and honest love for his wife and daughters. She respected Lara for her hard work and generosity. And she loved her granddaughters.

Even though she had appeared to soften towards Cap and his family, there was still a hidden part of her heart that their love and acceptance couldn't reach. It was the part that had been deeply injured by Jake. She welcomed her family into her life, but not into her heart. Even then, it was a selfish welcome. Her intent always centered on herself and what they could do for her, what she felt they owed her. She forgot about the years of abandonment and rejection. She forgot that Cap had always been the one to reach for her, bringing his wife and daughters with him. In Pearl's mind, she had always been a loving and selfless mother and grandmother. The playacting allowed her to accept herself, to find something to like about herself.

Pearl quickly pushed aside the lingering questions as she prepared to get out of bed, intent on calling Cap. She needed his help. She wanted him to turn the soil in her yard preparatory to the seeding and the planting of a new lawn and garden. She knew that he probably had other plans for the weekend, but she also knew that he would be willing to delay his plans in order to help her. Pearl used Cap's long-embedded yearnings in order to get him to do her bidding.

As she swung her legs over the edge of the bed and stood, Pearl felt suddenly weak and light-headed. With a gasp, she clutched her chest as pain exploded through her body. She fell back on the bed, pale and trembling, waiting for the pain to subside, but it increased. She felt herself fading into a dark void as she reached with a trembling hand for the bedside phone.

Her shaking fingers closed over the receiver, weakly bringing it to her ear. Fighting to stay conscious long enough, Pearl used her other hand to grasp the rumpled bedclothes, and she pulled herself across the bed, every movement causing unspeakable, numbing pain to shatter through her body. Finally, pale and dripping sweat, her lips blue, Pearl reached for the phone, her fingers finding the zero.

When the operator answered, she heard only silence. She was about to hang up, convinced some kid was playing games, when she heard a faint noise. She responded tentatively, "This is the operator. Would you please repeat your request?"

Again, silence greeted her query. "Hello, this is the operator. What is your request?" The young female operator turned pale as she finally heard the gasped words, the voice weak and faraway.

"Help me."

CHAPTER 37

Cap and Lara Martin hurried down the sterile, white hall, dodging various medical personnel bustling about their business of caring for the sick. Cap pulled Lara to a stop beside him at the door leading into the Intensive Care Unit. A phone on the wall instructed visitors to call before entering, so Cap picked up the phone and exchanged a few words with a nurse.

"Come on, honey. We can go in."

Wordlessly, Lara followed Cap into the suddenly quiet environment of the most seriously ill patrons of the small hospital. They had been summoned to this same hospital so many times in the past that Lara's first response to the call to come again had been irritation. But now that they were here, there was something so final about the situation that Lara found herself suddenly afraid.

The nurse behind the circular desk rose and beckoned them to follow her to the nearest cubicle. They approached and saw the body of a small, aged woman hooked up to a myriad of machines and tubes. Lara gasped as she recognized her mother-in-law. Never had she seen Pearl look so small, helpless, and ill. She grasped Cap by the hand, knowing instinctively how distressed he must be by his mother's appearance.

Cap's face was white with shock as he gazed down at the near-lifeless face of his mother. Lara released his hand when he reached for Pearl. She put her hand through the crook of his elbow and leaned against him, suddenly feeling faint as she realized that they were gazing into the face of death.

This was a new experience for them. All of the losses they had endured in the past had been unexpected, their loved ones gone before they had a chance to look into their faces one last time. Pearl was near death, but she was still alive. Tears threatened to overwhelm Cap as he reached out and stroked the wrinkled cheek of his mother. It was with great effort that he controlled the urge to cry. Pearl looked ancient. The years of hardness had melted in the face of her illness, leaving her skin softly parched and crackled with age.

"Oh, Ma. I'm so sorry." Cap didn't know what he was sorry for, but the overwhelming sadness in his breast demanded expression. "I'm sorry Sandy and John aren't here. They're on their way, though."

But as Cap and Lara stood by her bedside, Cap knew they would never make it. He was surprised that he and Lara had made it in time. As he whispered a silent prayer of gratitude that he had made it to his mother's bedside in time, Pearl opened her eyes.

"Hi, Mom." Cap's voice was hoarse with emotion as he took Pearl's hand in his. "We're here, Mom. We love you."

Pearl's eyes were blank as she stared up at the ceiling, oblivious to her surroundings. Lara looked at Cap as he watched Pearl, his eyes sad and his face grave. Pearl continued to stare at the ceiling, her pale, drawn lips moving silently as if she were trying to speak.

"Mom, what can I do for you? Are you thirsty?" Cap reached for the cup of ice sitting on the bedside table. With a gentle hand, he held a sliver of ice to the parched lips, which quickly sucked at the moisture. Her eyes closed briefly as a drop of icy water trickled between her lips and moistened her dry tongue.

She opened her eyes again, and this time she turned and looked right at Cap. Lara gasped at the sudden fires burning in the depths of the clouded brown eyes. It was as if black smoke rolled from the depths of Pearl's soul, clouding her eyes, yet at the same time making them vibrant with emotion. Her frail jaw worked as she opened and closed her lips, never taking her burning gaze off of Cap's face.

Suddenly, venom-filled words shattered the silence. "How I hate you."

Cap's features blanched from the force of his mother's pronouncement, and he choked on grief as her eyes closed and she drew her last breath. Cap dropped her hand and turned away from the bed, his body shaking as the shock and the enormity of his mother's deathbed farewell hit him like an avalanche.

Lara was crying, tears of anger and hurt and confusion forcing her to gulp for air as she ran to Cap and threw her arms around his middle. Cap struggled to maintain his composure. His years in the military had reinforced the teaching of his childhood—that he was to hide his emotions at all costs. But for one brief moment, he gave in to the shattering pain. Cap buried his face in his hands, and sobs shook his shoulders. He cried the tears of a lifetime as his mother's last words of rejection tore his heart to shreds, leaving the tender shards of his love bleeding and wounded.

CHAPTER 38

May 1976
Salt Lake City, Utah

Cap Martin sat in the chapel of the temple, listening to the soft strains of the organ playing the sacred hymns he had come to love so much. Cap had a tremendous appreciation for music, and when given the chance, would sing his heart out in praise. It didn't matter to him that he was tone deaf. It didn't matter that he rarely hit a correct note, nor did it faze him that he often drew impatient glances from others in the congregation. He didn't care that his voice was off-key and upsetting to the discerning ears of those sitting around him. He knew that an ear more discerning than any of humankind's accepted his offering. He knew that even though the physical manifestation of his praise was out of sync, the spiritual offering of his heart was beautiful to those who listened on high.

And as he sat in the temple, the sacred strains soothed his soul and allowed him to drink in the holy aura of the house of the Lord.

He smiled at Lara as she joined him. He took her hand as she sat down beside him, and he gazed into the serene features of the woman who was his wife, his confidante, and his best friend. Her eyes were as clear and as blue as the day they had met. Grooves followed the curve of her cheek and the tilt of her smile, and soft lines fanned the skin around her eyes, engraved there from a lifetime of experiences. *She is so beautiful!*

Cap felt his eyes well with tears of gratitude as they were summoned to rise. Cap gave Lara's fingers one final squeeze as they separated to follow the temple workers into the ordinance room. He would see her at the end of the session in the celestial room.

They were there to do the temple work for his parents, as well as for William Aldrich. It was a moment of healing for Cap, although his heart still hurt when he thought about his mother's dying words. Pearl Martin Aldrich had died inflicting a final wound that cut deep.

As he settled himself into his chair, Cap glanced across the narrow aisle, and a smile of surprised pleasure creased his face. Lara was sitting in the chair directly opposite him. He reached across the expanse and felt for her fingers. As his hand grasped hers and their eyes met, he heard the words she had spoken to him on the day of Pearl's funeral. His heart swelled with acceptance and understanding as the truth of what she had told him again brought him a modicum of peace.

"Cap, your mother loved you. In her own way, you know she did." Lara had paused, her throat working as she fought the conflict of emotions that strangled the words of healing she knew Cap needed to hear. Lara was still angry with her mother-in-law, and she hated the impact those destructive, parting words had had on her husband. But she knew in her heart that Cap needed to be reassured, and beneath the anger, Lara believed the things she was saying.

"She was so hurt by your father, and she never learned to forgive him." Lara had then put her arms around Cap. "And, honey, that's something you were able to do. You forgave Jake. And you forgave your mother. You forgave her a long time ago. And you're going to be able to forgive her for this too." Tears were running down Lara's cheeks as she reached up and caressed the strong line of Cap's jaw. "Because you love her."

Cap had nodded at Lara's words, unable to answer her. During the months that followed the funeral, they had immersed themselves in the preparations for attending the temple, for doing the proxy work for Pearl, Jake, and William. The temple had been a beacon for Cap, offering him a safe harbor, a place to put to rest the hurt and the anguish of his past.

Cap knew that his struggles would probably continue. He had experienced so much pain at the hands of his parents that it could take him a lifetime before he was able to completely let go of the hurt. He also knew that he might never know the motivation behind his mother's dying words, and he still struggled with the impact of that hateful statement. It still had the power to cause his heart to constrict with pain.

But he knew that one day he would understand. And he had forgiven Pearl. That forgiveness had brought him to this place, the temple of the Lord. Cap knew that in these hallowed rooms, he would find ultimate peace.

CHAPTER 39

June 1985
Boise, Idaho

"I hope Daddy's okay," Rachel whispered as she stood in the cafeteria line with Lisa and their aunt, Sandra Straddler. Each young woman held a tray that bore a light snack. The Boise hospital cafeteria was sparsely populated and the woman at the checkout counter was quickly processing them through the line.

"I'm sure he's fine, kiddo." Sandra looked into the pale, worried faces of her nieces. Lisa and Rachel were more like kid sisters to her. She was only six years older than they were, and she felt a kinship with them as they mourned the imminent loss of their mother. They had left Lara's hospital room ten minutes earlier, Sandra insisting they come with her to get something to eat. They had tried to talk Cap into coming with them, but he had felt compelled to stay at the bedside of his dying wife.

It had been ten years since the death of his own mother, and the intervening decade had been difficult for Cap. He had never fully recovered from the devastating words spoken to him by Pearl. Lara had been his mainstay during the following days and weeks as he had finally come to the sad acceptance of his mother's final rejection. The time spent in the temple, performing the sacred ordinances for his parents, had allowed Cap to lay to rest some of the anguish. He was human, though, and there were times when he wondered if he would ever be able to understand the hate that had been the driving force in Pearl's life. He would also never fully understand the pain and the anger that had kept her from loving him. Over time, he had finally found a measure of acceptance, and it was Lara's unfailing love that had given him the courage to move forward.

Lisa and Rachel had never known of their grandmother's deathbed confession to her eldest son. They had mourned her loss, but had moved on with their lives. Lisa had married and started a family after completing college. She and her husband, Brent, and their two-year-old daughter, Cammy, lived in Boise. Rachel had also graduated from college, served a mission for the Church, started a successful career, and now also resided in Boise. Both girls had stayed close to their parents.

Lara's illness had taken them by surprise. The girls had rushed home to Gooding earlier that week after Cap's frantic call informing them that Lara was desperately ill. The day after they arrived, Lara had been transferred to Boise, where she could receive state-of-the-art treatment for her illness. The prognosis, however, was grim. Lara's liver and other internal organs were filled with cancer, metastasized from a breast tumor that had been removed years earlier.

Cap and his daughters had been inseparable for the past three days, with Lisa and Rachel insisting on staying with Cap by Lara's bedside. The nurses had brought them food from the cafeteria, and family and friends had also been by, bringing food and flowers. Cap and Lara's bishop and home teachers had visited, anointing and blessing Lara and bringing a measure of comfort to the family.

Their prayers of faith had been answered as a spirit of peace descended on the room and Lara slipped into a coma. The family sensed that the Lord was calling her home.

Cap and the girls took turns napping on the couch located in Lara's room. They were nearing the end of their strength, but somehow they continued to find the courage and the determination to stay at Lara's side. It was where they belonged.

Sandra's insistence that the girls accompany her to the cafeteria was their first foray from the third floor of the large medical center in days. Sandra didn't know why she felt so compelled to take the girls with her, but as they left Cap alone in the room with his dying wife, she had looked back over her shoulder. The room was dimly lit, but there seemed to be a glow surrounding the hospital bed. Sandra ached for

Cap as he gazed down at Lara with a look of such love and devotion. As she ushered the girls out of the room and gently closed the door behind them, Sandra felt as if she had just shut the door on a piece of heaven.

Cap was unaware of the door closing. His entire focus was on the woman lying so still and so quiet in the bed. His entire energy was centered on loving her. He held her hand gently as her lips moved, and he realized that she was once again hallucinating. The pain medication she was receiving frequently caused this, and she often talked to herself or others.

Cap listened to her one-sided conversations until he realized that Lara was talking to her mother, Lily Straddler. It made Cap wonder if she truly was seeing someone, talking to them. It brought Cap a sense of comfort to think that Lara was close in spirit to her parents, that Lily was there waiting to escort and welcome Lara into the portion of their family who resided on the other side of the veil.

Cap felt the thinness of that veil, realized how closely heaven and earth were linked, and he momentarily panicked. As Lara's lips moved silently, Cap felt a sudden sense of anger and denial surge through him. He kicked his chair back and jumped to his feet. She couldn't die. She couldn't leave him alone. The girls needed her. He needed her.

He loved her so much. He felt a genuine, physical pain in his chest at the thought of losing the love of his life. He quickly lowered the steel rail of the hospital bed, put his arms under Lara, and gently scooted her across the mattress. His bed at home was so empty without her. And it would remain empty. Never again would he hold her in his arms, kiss her lips, love her as only a man and his wife could love. Their marriage had been fraught with trials and loss and heartache, but it had also been filled with love and happiness and completeness.

Cap didn't care what the nurses thought. He lay down beside Lara and put his arms around her, knowing that this would be the last time he would hold her. He gently kissed her eyelids, her cheeks, her lips. His tears bathed her face as he buried his face in her hair. He whispered words of love into her ear as the spirit of his adoration encircled them in a halo of warmth and unity. Cap felt his heart race and then still as a sudden light entered his mind and overflowed into his soul. His tears of sorrow and grief continued, but they were tempered with the spirit of comfort and peace that his testimony of eternity brought to him. He felt the tears dry on his cheeks as the spirit of healing touched the hurting places of his heart.

Suddenly, Cap felt Lara's hand move at her side. He sensed the movement of her head, and he raised his eyes to her face. Once again, he was gazing into the vivid blue eyes of the woman he loved more than life itself. Through all the pain and the loss and the rejection that had overshadowed his life's path, it was her love that had been a constant in his life. Cap smiled, his lips curving gently as he stroked her cheek and whispered, "Hello."

Lara's eyes shone with the clarity of her love, and she shared words of love and promises for the future. Lara was not afraid to die, and she didn't want Cap to fear living. She comforted him with her words and with her touch. And as she closed her eyes for the last time, her last words touched him to the very center of his soul. "How I love you."

Her utterance was a healing echo to the painful words spoken over a decade ago. He held the still, silent body of his wife, and even though her spirit had departed, the strength of her love continued to enfold him with warmth and healing. He lay there, his mind rapidly replaying their life together. It was odd how he was able to condense a lifetime of experiences into a few seconds of thought. Finally, his mind centered on the silent scene that had just passed.

He saw Lara lying in the bed, her chest rising and falling gently as her lips moved in quiet conversation with the unseen specter of her mother. A vivid picture flashed through Cap's mind. He was suddenly transported to another hospital room where another woman was lying, still and lifeless, in a sterile, impersonal hospital bed. He saw those blank brown eyes staring at his face; he heard the devastating words her mouth had uttered. And suddenly he understood.

His entire life Cap had carried with him a curse. He had been born a curse, the image of the man who had fathered him. As a little boy, he had resembled his father. Growing up, his face had matured into the chiseled features of the man Pearl Martin Aldrich hated with every ounce of her being. He had been cursed to look like his father—the father he had eventually learned to forgive, the father he had even found the courage to love.

But Pearl had experienced no such transition from hate to love. She had lived hating Jake Martin, and she had died staring into the face of her son whose face mirrored the features of the man she could never forgive or forget.

Cap once again began to sob, holding Lara in his arms. Lara's death had given him the greatest gift possible—a release from the ten-year pain of knowing that his mother had died expressing her hatred for him. Lara had echoed her words, substituting her great love for the devastating hatred. Lara had died just as she had lived—loving him.

And Pearl had died just as she had lived, hating Cap's father and seeing in her son the hateful, unforgettable features of the man she had never been able to forget, the man she had loved so passionately, the man who had hurt her so deeply, the man whose memory had haunted her for the remainder of her life, whose face and cruelty had crushed the very spirit of her love.

Finally, Cap found himself able to lay to rest the hurtful past and the devastation of Pearl's deathbed farewell. Through Lara's love, a love that would lift and carry and sustain him into eternity, he had found healing and peace. After years of abandonment and years of searching, Cap's search had reached an end. His seeking spirit had found a place of rest, a place of knowledge, and a place of understanding. His love for his mother was finally validated, and as Lara returned to her heavenly home, Cap vowed that he would move forward, living his life to the fullest until the doors of heaven were opened for him and he and Lara could be reunited in celestial realms.

With healing tears dampening his cheeks, Cap arose from Lara's side, tucked the blankets around her still form, and whispered, "Good-bye for now, Lara Bell. I love you." As his quiet words faded into peaceful silence, Cap turned his eyes toward heaven and smiled through his tears. His searching heart had found its way home.

ABOUT THE AUTHOR

Lorraine drew upon many of her life experiences, as well as those of her parents, to feed her imagination for the novel *Last Words*. Her father was a Seabee in the United States Navy, and the family had the privilege of living in many different states. Growing up a navy brat instilled in her a love for travel and seeing new places. Lorraine currently lives in Caldwell, Idaho where she shares a home with her sister, Ava. She has never had the privilege of marrying or having children, but has been blessed with many opportunities to mother children. She has eleven nieces and nephews, scores of Primary children she has taught over the years, and students who have filled her life with laughter and love. Lorraine has a tender spot in her heart for children and adults with developmental disabilities. She worked for sixteen years at the Idaho State School and Hospital, where she devoted herself to her friends who call the facility home. She left ISSH last summer to pursue her dream of becoming an author. She currently is employed part-time, providing occupational therapy services to elementary students in the Caldwell public school system. Lorraine served a full-time mission in the California Ventura Mission, and she has served two stake missions. She is currently serving as a ward missionary in Caldwell.